CALGARY PUBLIC LIBRARY

FICTION
Ihimaera, Witi.
Dear Miss Mansfield

✓

Dear Miss Mansfield

VIKING

Dear Miss Mansfield

A tribute to
Kathleen Mansfield Beauchamp

Witi Ihimaera

VIKING

VIKING

Penguin Books (NZ) Ltd, 182–190 Wairau Road, Auckland 10, New Zealand
Penguin Books Ltd, 27 Wrights Lane, London W8 5TZ, England
Viking Penguin Inc., 40 West 23rd Street, New York, New York 10010, USA
Penguin Books Australia Ltd, 487 Maroondah Highway, Ringwood, Australia 3134
Penguin Books Canada Ltd, 2801 John Street, Markham, Ontario, Canada L3R 1B4

Penguin Books Ltd, Registered Offices: Harmondsworth, Middlesex, England

First published in 1989
Copyright © Witi Ihimaera, 1989

1   3   5   7   9   10   8   6   4   2

All rights reserved. Without limiting the rights under copyright reserved
above, no part of this publication may be reproduced, stored in or introduced
into a retrieval system, or transmitted, in any form or by any means
(electronic, mechanical, photocopying, recording or otherwise), without the
prior written permission of both the copyright owner and the above publisher
of this book.

Designed by Richard King
Typeset in Compugraphic Berkeley
by Typocrafters Ltd, Auckland
Printed in Hong Kong

Library of Congress Catalog Card No.: 89-50432

ISBN 0 670 82624 3

Back jacket photograph by Robert Cross

CONTENTS

This book is dedicated to Katherine Mansfield
(1888–1928), the greatest short-story writer among us all.

Acknowledgements are also due to Maata Mahupuku, and
to P. A. Lawlor, author of *The Mystery of Maata*, published
in 1946.

*Risk! Risk anything! Care no more for the opinions of others,
for those voices. Do the hardest thing on earth for you.
Act for yourself. Face the truth . . .*

— Katherine Mansfield's Journal, October 1922

A LETTER

Dear Miss Mansfield

Dear Katherine Mansfield,

On the occasion of the hundredth anniversary of your birth, may I offer you this small *homage* as a personal tribute to your life and your art. Throughout the past year many, many people from all over the world have wished to say 'thank you' for illuminating our lives and our literature. Mine is but a single token of aroha and respect.

Miss Mansfield, we in New Zealand have laid proud claim to you because you were born and brought up a New Zealander. Although you spent most of your adult years in England and the Continent, you always looked back to these southern antipodean islands as the main source for your stories. On our part, we have long since acknowledged that New Zealand could not fulfil your expectations of Life, Art, Literature and Experience. The world was waiting in England, Germany, Switzerland, Italy and France. And out of all those restless voyages of the intellect, mind, heart and soul, out of that singular life, came the stories. Better people than I have praised their fine art, their subtle craft and their focus on inner truth. They are stories spun sometimes from gossamer, at other times from strong sinew, sometimes kept afloat by a strength of voice, at other times by a mere thread of breath. Near the end, they were stories grabbed from out of the air at great cost. They have kept you in our memory over all the years since you have gone.

It is the modern way, Miss Mansfield, for us to have become as much fascinated with your life as with your stories. I myself have always wished to write about your Maori friend Maata and why, if she had indeed possessed a novel you had written, she may have chosen not to part with it. The novella 'Maata' is my attempt to provide a Maori response to this question. But the main part of this collection, Miss Mansfield, comprises an equally Maori response, not to the life but to the stories.

Like most New Zealanders, Miss Mansfield, I came to know the stories during my school years. My first acquaintance was as a young Maori student, struggling with English, at Te Karaka District High School. This was in 1957 and the story was 'The Fly'. At the time I resisted anything compulsory and I did not really grow to love and appreciate your art until I had left school behind. I can remember, one sunlit afternoon in Wellington, reading 'At The Bay' again, surely, for the fourteenth time. What had simply been words suddenly sprang to life and *there* it all was, happening before me — the sleepy sea sounding Ah-Aah!, the flock of sheep rounding the corner of Coronet Bay, and then Stanley Burnell racing for dear life over the big porous stones, over the cold, wet pebbles, on to the hard sand to go Splish-Splosh! Splish-Splosh! into the sea. It was all such a revelation to me and I leapt up and down as if I had suddenly discovered a pearl of inestimable value. Does it happen like this for others?

Dear Miss Mansfield, my overwhelming inspiration and purpose comes from my Maori forebears — they are my source as surely as New Zealand was yours. The art of the short story, however, has taken its bearings from your voice also. I do hope that the variations on your stories find some favour with you. They are stories in themselves, some Maori and some with European themes, recognising the common experiences of mankind. But they found their inner compulsion in my wish to respond to your work.

Ah, New Zealand, New Zealand. One hundred years on, Miss Mansfield, and it has changed beyond your recognition. Life, Art, Society — all can be had here now. There is not as much need to make those forays, as you did, to seek it elsewhere. And when we do, it is merely to satisfy our island urgings to go plundering and raiding the world's riches and retreating with them to our island fortress. In the process of exploration within and without, the literary legacy of the New Zealand short story has been greatly enriched. These are the years of fulfilment — of Janet Frame, Patricia Grace, and Keri Hulme among others.

Please accept, Miss Mansfield, my highest regard and gratitude for having been among us and above us all.

Witi Ihimaera
New York, July 1988

This novella owes its provenance to the late P. A. Lawlor's *The Mystery Of Maata*, published by The Beltane Book Bureau, Wellington, in 1946. I first read Pat's research in the early 1960s. I have been fascinated and moved by Katherine Mansfield's relationship with Maata Mahupuku, and the possibility that Katherine Mansfield had written a novel about Maata, ever since. The novella draws extensively on Pat's research and reprints extracts from it, including his account of his meeting with Maata in 1941.

Only 250 signed copies of Pat Lawlor's book were released. My thanks are due to Chris Newman, Pat's grandson, who obtained the copy of the text for me in 1988 which enabled me to write 'Maata', to Pat himself for his friendship, Mrs Lawlor, and Ruth, Naomi Margaret and Peter (living in New Mexico).

I should note that I have quoted Pat's sources, particularly Ruth Mantz's *Life of Katherine Mansfield*. Other sources helpful to me have been Vincent O'Sullivan and Margaret Scott's *The Collected Letters of Katherine Mansfield*, vol. 1 1903–1917, (Oxford 1984), and Claire Tomalin's *Katherine Mansfield: A Secret Life*, (Viking, London, 1987). I have acknowledged these in the text but there may be occasions where research, rather than quotes, appears without acknowledgement. If so, I fully acknowledge Mansfield researchers, past and present.

'Maata' is a work of fiction. Nevertheless, the fiction encompasses recent history including Maata Mahupuku, who died in 1952. I do hope that her family will forgive me if I have trespassed unwittingly. I wrote 'Maata' as a token of love and in homage to a luminous friendship between two of New Zealand's most fascinating daughters. While the existence of the 'Maata' novel can be questioned, that friendship cannot.

PART ONE

1

So much has been written about Katherine Mansfield, her life, her work and her books, that I marvel that no one has been moved to inquire about or to speculate on the MS of her novel 'Maata'

— P. A. Lawlor, *The Mystery of Maata, a Katherine Mansfield Novel*, The Beltane Book Bureau, Wellington, New Zealand, 1946, p.7.

1953 . . . CORONATION YEAR . . . NORDMEYER MAKES BID TO REPLACE WALTER NASH AS LEADER OF THE OPPOSITION . . . GOVERNMENT PASSES MAORI AFFAIRS ACT . . . EISENHOWER BECOMES NEW U.S. PRESIDENT . . . EDMUND HILLARY AND SHERPA TENSING CONQUER MOUNT EVEREST . . . ARMISTICE ENDS WAR IN KOREA . . . NEW QUEEN VISITS N.Z. . . . . PEOPLE DIE ON CHRISTMAS EVE — NORTHBOUND AUCKLAND EXPRESS SWEPT OFF THE WHANGAEHU RIVER BRIDGE NEAR TANGIWAI . . .

The moment, when it happened, during that hot summer of 1953, was one that Mahaki would never forget. He had been eleven years old, the son of the shearer, Te Rangi. The shearing contract at the Gemmells' shed had that very day been completed. Most of the gang had gone on to the next shed but Mahaki's father had stayed behind to finalise the shearing contract for the next year with Mr Gemmell.

'Why don't you go down to the river,' his mother, Wai, said. 'Go and have a swim.' She was sitting in the back of the old Dodge, holding the baby. 'I'll sound the horn when your father gets back.' The car was already packed — with double mattress tied to the front fender, the cot for his sister roped to the roof and all the pots and pans packed in the boot — and there was nothing more that Mahaki had to do. 'Take your book with you — you know your father — he'll be gassing with old man Gemmell for hours.' His mother jerked her head up at Mr Gemmell's gracious homestead and, sure enough, a burst of laughter and clink of glasses drifted down. Mahaki grinned at his mother and she winked at him with that special '*Your father . . .*' wink that she always gave when she talked about Te Rangi. 'Go,' she said

13

again. She began to breast-feed Mahaki's sister, Teina, turning away from him.

The river was a deep dark green. It moved slowly through the bush and overhanging ferns like an eel slithering along a seam of earth. The bush was alive with the presence of the river — its deep-throated gurgle, somnolent swish and surprised *boom* as it woke up, just in time, to fall as a glistening arc into the downriver chasm. Mahaki headed for the swimming hole — the place used by the men to soap up and clean themselves after each day's work. There it was — still, and glittering with sun-stars. With eagerness, Mahaki shucked off all his clothes and, with a whoop and a holler and a Tarzan yodel, jumped off the stone buttress into the water. He splashed around with adolescent joy, laughing whenever he felt an eel nibbling at his toes or his *ure*. Then, after a final dive he waded out into the sun. For a while he sat there by the river trying to see all of him in the surface mirror — the only real mirror he ever saw was the one his father shaved with. He was always disappointed in what he saw but, today, he felt compensated by the obvious physical evidence of his burgeoning manhood. Indeed, on other evenings at the river the shearers would joss and kid him and — with sly allusions to the women bathing further upstream — tell him to keep himself fully clothed because he was becoming too much competition.

Mahaki lay in the sun. He reached for the book, a biography which had been given to him as a prize at his last school. The others in the gang had often asked him, 'What the heck do you read about in those books!' He used to try to hide that he loved reading but would, eventually, answer, 'Oh, I read about life, I suppose.' Then the men would laugh and say, proudly, 'Life is for living, not for reading about.' And they would wink and say, 'You keep reading about *it*, boy. Give us old fellas a chance while we still have it!' But behind their joking he sensed their respect — or hoped, anyway, that they respected him. At that time he craved nothing more than the respect of his parents and the gang.

Mahaki stayed down at the river for a long time — how long, he did not know. But the sun was just leaving the pool when he laid the book to one side. He found, to his embarrassment, that his cheeks were wet with tears. *At about 10 o'clock she said she was tired and began to go to her room. As she slowly climbed the big staircase to the first floor, where her room was, she was seized by a fit of coughing. I took her arm and helped her into her room. No sooner were we inside than the cough became a paroxysm. Suddenly a great gush of blood poured from her mouth. It seemed to be suffocating her. She gasped out, 'I believe . . . I'm going to die.' I put her on the couch and rushed out from the room calling for a doctor. Two came almost immediately. Wisely, I suppose, they thrust me out of the room though her eyes were imploring me. In a few moments she was dead.* It was then that the moment occurred. All of a sudden Mahaki saw something glistening, like two jewels, on the stone buttress. He sensed something strange, like a veil on the river. Curious, he stood up and walked toward the twinkling apparition. As he got closer he could see that the two jewels were a pair of red shoes, placed side by side, in the sun. The shoes had red bows and low heels. Incredulous, Mahaki went to touch them — and recoiled because they were so hot. He looked around, suddenly aware of his nakedness, but there was nobody to be seen. Perhaps they fell out of a plane, he thought. Whatever, they were incredibly beautiful and with their femininity — the way they curved to the heel — extremely erotic. The sun made them brilliant like bejewelled blood — and Mahaki went to touch them again, his fingers desiring to feel them and —

From afar the car horn sounded. Mahaki looked up at the sound and, when he looked back at the shoes, they were gone. He laughed with surprise. From that moment onward, in that pure magical epiphany of wonder, Mahaki always associated Katherine Mansfield with the red shoes.

2

There undoubtedly was an original Maata. Katherine spoke to me about her on several occasions . . . It is also true that, at some time or other, Katherine contemplated writing a novel with the title 'Maata'. I have a notebook of hers which contains the first chapter of such a novel. I imagine this was written somewhere about 1912 or 1913. But it breaks off, and was obviously never taken any further at that time. . . . I have a vague recollection that the real Maata married a N.Z. lawyer. But the recollection is vague.

— extract, letter, J. Middleton Murry to P. A. Lawlor,
25 January 1944, in *The Mystery of Maata*, p.24.

1957 . . . KEITH HOLYOAKE BECOMES PRIME MINISTER . . . AUTHOR JANET FRAME WINS PRAISE FOR 'OWLS DO CRY' . . . PRESIDENT ORDERS U.S. FEDERAL TROOPS TO LITTLE ROCK, ARKANSAS . . . WALTER JAMES BOLTON HANGS IN N.Z. . . . BRUCE MASON'S 'THE POHUTUKAWA TREE' SUPERLATIVE DRAMA . . .

Mahaki never visited the river on the Gemmell Station again but he did, almost, become a shearer like his father. 'There's nothing wrong with shearing,' he told his mother. 'No,' she agreed, 'but there are plenty of other, better jobs.' Over the next four years Mahaki tried desperately, almost viciously at times, to persuade his mother to let him leave school at fifteen. In many respects he was afraid of leaving the gang or of becoming so different that they would scorn him — his mother did not seem to understand that he simply wanted to be like everybody else. Nor could he understand why his mother equated 'better' with working in a Pakeha job. 'You already have some brains,' she yelled at him one day. 'Now *use* them!' He argued back, saying, 'What for, e ma? So I can work for the council like Rawiri? Or teach in the Pakeha school like Arapeta? So the gang can laugh at me? The collar and tie is the Pakeha ball and chain. Maoris are shearers, that's what we do.' His mother replied, 'Forget about the gang, son. Be your *own* man.' Then he smiled and said, 'You mean, don't you, be a *Pakeha*, ay.' She hit him hard and, when he was down, she said, 'Never say that again. Never.'

The next day Mahaki's mother was strangely quiet. She got dressed in a grey suit and put her gloves and hat on. 'I want you to come with me,' she said. 'Put on your good coat and comb your hair.' When Mahaki was ready, his mother drove him to a huge two-storey home in the Pakeha part of town. 'No,' she said when they got out, 'we don't go in the front way. You and me go round the back.' He followed her and she rang the bell. A Maori woman, in apron and smock, opened the door and said, 'Kia ora, Wai. Haramai. Haramai.' The woman kissed his mother and ushered her into the kitchen. 'Long time no see,' the woman said. 'And is this your son? You never told me he was so *big*. Mrs Crosbie will be so surprised.' At the mention of the name, Mahaki saw his mother's eyes begin to dull. She was changing in front of him, seeming to lose shape and strength. And when a voice called from the sitting-room, 'Judith? Has Mary arrived? Show her in, Judith, tell her to come in,' the transformation was so total that his mother was no longer recognisable as the person he knew.

'Why, Mary!' the woman said. She was patrician. Pakeha. 'Good afternoon, madam,' his mother said. Her eyes were downcast and her demeanour subservient. 'And is this your son, Mary?' the woman asked. 'Yes, madam,' his mother answered. 'And what is his name, Mary?' the woman asked again. 'Mahaki, madam.' And Mahaki saw that his mother's eyes were brimmed with tears — not from emotion but out of humiliation that her son should see her like this, so servile in this splendid drawing-room. As the afternoon tea was served on its silver tray with its china setting, Mahaki felt such a rage building within him — How dare this woman call his mother by that name, *Mary?* Who gave her the right? His mother saw this and, through her hot tears, sent him a quivering glance, *Oh, my son. Support me, support me,* his mother who had always appeared so proud, so utterly proud. And so he sat with her, close to her, listening to her quiet 'Yes madam' and 'No madam', and when Mrs Crosbie gave his mother a purse for his education he grieved with her as she said, 'Thank you, madam.'

Mahaki had not known that his mother had once been a servant. This had been a secret she had kept to herself all these years — and he felt ashamed that she had now had to reveal it — all because she had needed to show him that 'better' meant being equal. On the way home that night he saw her face, so desolate, so lost. 'You know, e ma,' he said, 'I've always liked books, ay.' She smiled and replied, 'You and your books . . .' The silence grew. Then, 'I think I might like to be a journalist when I finish school,' Mahaki said.

1959 . . . 'NO MAORIS NO TOUR' . . . MORMONS RAISE NEW TEMPLE AT TUHIKARAMEA . . . EISENHOWER AND KHRUSHCHEV MEET AT CAMP DAVID SUMMIT . . . DAME MARGOT FONTEYN VISITS N.Z. WITH THE ROYAL BALLET . . . NOEL HILLIARD PREVIEWS 'MAORI GIRL' IN THE AUCKLAND 'FREE LANCE' . . .

Mahaki stayed at school another two years. He managed to get his School Certificate and just scraped through his University Entrance. At seventeen he applied for a job on the *New Zealand Herald* in Auckland — and got it. His father wanted him to stay for the shearing, but his mother said 'Go!' There were tears in her eyes as she virtually threw him out the door.

Auckland held Mahaki spellbound. The teeming metropolis seemed to provide everything he had desired. He worked hard at the *Herald* office and played hard at the dances and parties. He made friends with an older journalist, Melvin, and one day, without really knowing why, was compelled to tell him about the red shoes. Melvin, who could be very sarcastic, simply cocked an eye and asked, 'And did you put them on, click your heels three times and think of Kansas?' Mahaki laughed and threw a paper dart at him. 'No,' he answered — and because he saw more sarcasm beginning to form on Melvin's lips said, 'And I didn't dance to my death like Moira Shearer either.' Melvin subsided, obviously disappointed. Then, because he was a clever so-and-so he asked, cunningly, 'They weren't *glass* slippers, perchance?' Mahaki laughed again. 'Anyway,' he explained to

Melvin, 'ever since then I've read everything that Katherine Mansfield ever wrote. Everything.'

'Rather you than me, young son,' Melvin said. 'We had to swot "The Fly" at school, in my day, and the wondrous Katherine has ever since been, for me, an ink blot.' Melvin tried to tap a few words on the typewriter and, giving up, took out his pipe and lit it. 'Well, let me know when you read the divine lady's novel,' he said, *and a flash of red danced and dazzled in Mahaki's mind.* 'Novel?' Mahaki asked. 'What novel? I thought she only wrote short stories?' Melvin rolled his eyes to the ceiling and, 'Don't we all?' he murmured, referring to the other reporters in the office, all aspiring to be the next Hemingway. Then he said, 'Actually the novel would really interest you.' He puffed reflectively on his pipe — honestly, Melvin could be so maddening — and continued, 'It's supposed to be about her friend. If the novel exists, that is. Didn't you know? The great Katherine was singularly without good sense or upbringing. She had a *Maori* friend. Maata was her name, I recollect.' Melvin started typing again. 'There's bound to be lots on KM,' he said, 'down in the morgue' — referring to the paper's clippings-files. 'Perhaps there will be something on Maata.' Then his face went red and his stomach began to jiggle. In between his coughing spasms he choked out, 'Ah, ah, Mahaki . . . about your shoe fetish . . . listen, I have these fantastic black high heel pumps at home . . . What say you — ' His guffaws echoed throughout the room.

That afternoon, Mahaki visited the newspaper's morgue. Katherine Mansfield had been the first, and perhaps the last, of the great New Zealand short story writers. Forty years after her death in 1923 at Le Prieuré, Fontainebleau, France, her work and life had made her the omnipotent and charismatic presence in New Zealand letters. It was therefore only natural that the newspaper should have such a daunting amount of information about her. The card index was simply the beginning of what would be a long quest.

MANSFIELD, Katherine: Born Kathleen Mansfield Beauchamp, Wellington, 14 October 1888, at 11 Tinakori Road, Wellington. Third daughter of Annie Burnell Dyer and Harold Beauchamp, banker (cross index: Beauchamp, Sir Harold). Other siblings: sisters Vera, Charlotte and Jeanne; brother, Leslie, d. France 1915. Attended Karori Village School, 1895–8, Wellington Girls' High School, 1898–9, and Miss Swainson's private school, 1899–1902. Parents took children to England where KM went to Queen's College, Harley Street, London (at 14 years of age) 1903–1906. First published stories in The Native Companion (Melbourne) in issues of October–December 1907. For subsequent career see NZ LIT: NZ Writers:

Maata

Short Stories: Mansfield: Also LIT: UK: Letters of K. Mansfield: Murry.

Nevertheless, as his quest deepened and widened, Mahaki became thoroughly absorbed. Nor could he help but think that seeking as he was 'through the last rubbish can left in the Western world', which was what Melvin called the morgue, only made Katherine Mansfield more real. Every yellowing article, every musty news report reduced the mythical proportion of the person — transformed the goddess into a woman, the icon into a creature of flesh and blood.

And here and there, scattered in the files were photographs of the writer who had formed such a major intersection, historical and theoretical, for New Zealand life and letters. Here, Katherine Mansfield with a capricious glimmer on her lips. Here again, the detested 1913 photograph. Such a modern, *challenging* face! Dark eyes under dark eyebrows, saying 'This is me, like it or lump it, you who stare at me so rudely!' A mouth impatient to open and hair that looked as if it were accustomed to the impetuous toss of the head. A private, knowing face, all the more provocative for that. A face that would be locked away, suffering, into French soil ten years later like a locket in a jewelled box, there to await resurrection and everlasting life at the hand of her husband.

MURRY, John Middleton: Born 6 August 1889, Peckham, London. Impressed by Katherine Mansfield's stories in New Age and by her first book 'In A German Pension', published 1911. Met Mansfield in 1912 — the love affair, eventual marriage on 3 May 1918, and continuing relationship until Mansfield's death in 1923, when she was 34, is one of the most famous in literary history. After marriage, Mansfield published her second short story collection, 'Bliss' (1920) and 'The Garden Party' (1922). Murry published two more collections following her death by tuberculosis, as well as her 'Letters' and her 'Journal'. [See NZ LIT: Short Stories: Mansfield, Katherine]

But the achievement? Murry may have had a hand in it, but one only had to look at the *face*. Ah, yes, the face would indeed have remonstrated '*I* did it. *I* did it all. Myself. Me. Katherine. *Kathleen*. Kass. Kezia. Me. *Mansfield*.'

Later that afternoon, as he was finishing, Mahaki came across the paragraph, the resolute sigh, like a credo, which made sense out of that glorious, remote face. 'Here, then, is a little summary of what I need — power, wealth and freedom. It is the hopelessly insipid doctrine that love is the only thing in the world . . . which hampers us so cruelly. We must get rid of that bogey — and then, then comes the opportunity of happiness and freedom.'

Mahaki made further visits to the morgue. Nowhere, however, could he find any references to Maata.

3

The novel of Maata is still a mystery. Nobody, except perhaps Mr Middleton Murry, has seen the first chapters. We have no idea whether so far as it went it satisfied Katherine's searching criticism. The first mention of it in her Journal [January 1st, 1915] suggested that it was well under way, fully planned and partly written. In the circumstances, it is highly improbable, I think, that this story of Maata would be of her best.

— Guy H. Scholefield, Introduction to *The Mystery of Maata*, p.5.

1963 . . . PRESIDENT KENNEDY ASSASSINATED . . . KIRI TE KANAWA HAS FEATURE ROLE IN JOHN O'SHEA'S FILM 'RUNAWAY' . . . REVEREND MARTIN LUTHER KING, JR. LEADS CIVIL RIGHTS MARCH ON WASHINGTON . . . 23 PEOPLE KILLED IN DC-3 AIRCRAFT CRASH IN THE KAIMAI RANGES . . . ARNOLD NORDMEYER SUCCEEDS NASH AS LEADER OF THE OPPOSITION . . . TENSIONS MOUNTING IN VIETNAM . . .

Three years later, when Mahaki was twenty, his sister Teina telephoned him — he was subbing a story on the Cuban missile crisis when the call came — to tell him that his mother, Wai, had passd away. 'She never told anybody here,' Teina said, 'that she had cancer. It was in her left breast. And when the doctor advised that she should have the breast removed — well, you know what Maoris are like.' Mahaki was bewildered by the news. 'But she must have been in terrible pain,' he said. 'Yes,' Teina said. 'Didn't Te Rangi know?' Mahaki asked. 'Well, he says everything falls into place now that he knows Mum had cancer. But you have to remember, Mahaki, that in all their days as husband and wife, Dad never ever saw Mum fully undressed. That's just like Mum and her Mormon upbringing. Then, in the last few months, he's been going down South with the gang — so Mum was able to hide it. When the pains got too bad she told Aunt Iris and went to stay with her in Hastings. Aunt said Mum made her swear on the Bible not to tell Te Rangi. Mum died in Hastings last night. She's being brought back to Gisborne tomorrow.'

The next day Mahaki took the morning flight from Auckland to Gisborne. His father was waiting at the airport to take him to the Mormon chapel in Mangapapa. 'Your mother was always like this,' Te Rangi said. 'I could never figure her out. She never told me anything.' Mahaki, bitter, replied, 'Perhaps that's because you never asked.' Te Rangi turned on him, and said, 'And did you? Ay? Don't come that one with *me*.' Together, they drove in silence to the chapel where they met up with Teina. Te Rangi said, pointedly, 'Well, at least she's with her Mormon people now. I hope she's happy. She ran to her sister when she was sick and, if that's the way she wanted it. . . . She never seemed to be happy with me anyway.' And Mahaki thought — You don't understand at all, do you, Te Rangi? She didn't run away. She made a choice. She chose not to be a burden on any of us. She did it this way out of love and because this is the way that all animals do it. When they're sick they just go off and find somewhere to die. That's right, ay, Mum —

The service the next day was sweet and tender. In keeping with Mormon practice, the rites of the tangi were not observed to their full extent. The shearing gang was there to mourn Mahaki's mother, coming out of their respect and allegiance to Te Rangi. After the service Mahaki sought them out, individually, to talk with them. 'Your mother knew what she was doing,' they agreed when they saw how well Mahaki was. Then they added fondly, 'You and your books — ' Mahaki embraced them all. 'You know,' he said, 'I always wanted to be a shearer like you all.' The gang was astounded, saying, 'You? Be like us? Nah, son, you're better off where you are, your mother understood that' — but Mahaki knew that they felt proud, really *proud*, that he had wanted to be like *them*.

Later, there was an argument between Te Rangi and Aunt Iris over where his mother was going to be buried — in Hastings where she came from or in Gisborne — and Aunt Iris won. Te Rangi refused to have anything to do with the decision, so Mahaki and Teina took their mother to the graveyard just outside Bridge Pa and, there, laid her to rest. When this occurred it seemed to Mahaki that one part of his life had come to a close. 'What will you do now?' Aunt Iris asked. 'You know, Aunt,' he said to her, 'Te Rangi will be okay, and he has his shearing gang. Once upon a time I wanted nothing more than to be part of the gang. But our mother set our faces, Teina's and mine, in another direction. I guess I'll keep on walking that way.' Aunt Iris nodded and, then, said, 'You must forgive your father, Mahaki. There are things that happen between a man and a woman, a husband and a wife. Your mother only had good words for Te Rangi. If there was any blame she took it on herself.' Mahaki was puzzled. 'What was wrong between them?' he asked. Aunt Iris paused and then, said, 'You know, Mahaki, if your mother had wanted you to know she would have told you. She wanted to keep it to herself. And you and I must accept that. Don't force it, tama — ever.' His aunt kissed him then and wished him well. 'Come back and see me soon,' she said.

1966 . . . KING KOROKI DIES: PRINCESS PIKI IS SUCCESSOR . . . NO. 14 SQUADRON RETURNS FROM SINGAPORE . . . NEW FERRY 'WAHINE' ENTERS STRAIT SERVICE . . . NORMAN KIRK NAMED LEADER OF THE OPPOSITION . . . PRESIDENT JOHNSON AUTHORISES THE FIRST COMBAT OPERATIONS ON THE GROUND IN VIETNAM . . . PRINCE CHARLES VISITS N.Z. ON WAY TO THE EMPIRE GAMES . . .

Mahaki continued to consolidate his career as a journalist in Auckland. Then when he was twenty-four, he successfully applied for a position as deputy editor in Wellington and moved there the following year. It was in that year that he met Susan and took up again his quest for Maata.

It was Melvin who began it all again by breezing in on a cold Wellington morning in that year of 1969. 'Hullo, cock,' he said as he perched himself on Mahaki's desk. 'I thought you must be missing me so I decided to visit your fair city for the day.' Melvin then whispered conspiratorially, 'Actually, I understand that a new bird is on my perch so I decided she needed commiseration.' Melvin then produced, from behind his back, a huge bouquet of red roses. 'For Susan?' Mahaki asked. ' Why, yes,' Melvin said — and then kissed Mahaki on the lips, in full view of the office, 'but that will keep everyone guessing, won't it!' Mahaki gave a sick smile and waved his little finger at the other reporters.

Melvin took Mahaki to luncheon at a new restaurant in Kelburn. Unfortunately the cuisine did not meet Melvin's expectations — he declared the soup analgesic and, after the main course, said he could quite understand why the chef would want to numb the palate beforehand. 'Are you really going back today?' Mahaki asked. 'Why don't you stay overnight and meet Susan. I've told her so much about you.' Melvin's eyes gleamed hopefully, 'All lecherous lies, I trust,' he said. Then he looked at his watch and said, 'But speaking of women in your life, there's another whom we should visit. Come on.' He sped Mahaki away in a taxi.

Half an hour later, Mahaki asked, 'How on earth did you know about this?' They were walking, with a small group of elderly men and women, in a small park near the American Embassy. The roar and *boom* of motorway traffic was a reminder of the real world, just there beyond the trees. 'Dear heart,' Melvin reproved, 'not only do I write newspapers. I also read them.' The gravel pathway, bordered by brilliant green lawns, led to a small paved area. On one side was a reflecting pool, filled with fallen leaves. On the other was a wooden pergola. People were standing in gentle circles beneath the pergola, drawn to the memorial below it. As Mahaki approached and joined them, a shower of red leaves drifted downward like a breathed-out sigh.

Looking between the people in front of him, Mahaki could see that the memorial was like an open book, propped on a six-inch podium. The smaller, left-hand page had words which read:

> The Plaque on the right came from the Memorial once standing at
> the end of this avenue removed in motorway construction 1968.
> Opened by His Worship the Mayor Sir Francis Kitts at a ceremony
> arranged by the N. Z. Women Writers' Society and the Wellington
> City Council 5th June 1969.

'We're a little late,' Melvin whispered, for the plaque had already been unveiled, the cloth cover lying like a discarded dress on the paving stones. Behind, in the pergola, the Mayor was returning to his seat. There was a polite round of clapping like soft rain and, then, a woman stepped forward to read an address. She spoke calmly but firmly about the motorway construction and how it had necessitated the removal of a plaque which had been in its original setting since the 1930s. She told how the rush of civilisation had destroyed much of Wellington's history — the old houses and locations. As she did so, Mahaki overheard a gentleman in a dark suit call out, 'They wouldn't do this in France,' to which there were murmurs of 'Hear, hear. Hear, hear.' The woman bit her lip and seemed near to tears. She turned to one of her colleagues and asked her to step forward. As the woman was doing so, and in that mood of reverent devotion, Mahaki saw the words on the plaque.

This Memorial was erected
by Sir Harold Beauchamp
in loving memory of his daughter

KATHERINE MANSFIELD

who during her short life achieved
great distinction as an authoress

Dear Miss Mansfield

Born in Wellington, NZ, 14th October 1888
Died at Fontainebleau, France, 9th January 1923
Before leaving for England in 1906
Katherine Mansfield lived at No.47
Fitzherbert Terrace

And, when the woman said, in a clear voice, 'I should like to read from our dear Katherine's "Prelude", he looked up at the grey clouds and he wanted to chant in Maori to express his grief, and assuage the feelings locked in his heart. The clouds seemed to be the sides of a well, and he felt as if he was falling, falling, falling into the well, falling within a huge teardrop without ever reaching the bottom.

Later, at the airport, Mahaki thanked Melvin for coming to Wellingon. 'No trouble, my possum,' Melvin said. 'And thank you,' Mahaki continued, 'for taking me to the unveiling.' Melvin smiled and, then, said, 'Did you know that you were the only Maori there? I think that is why, perhaps, that gentleman was taking such an interest in you.' Mahaki asked, puzzled, 'Which man?' Melvin responded, 'Didn't you notice? The one in the dark suit. The one who called out about France.'

The boarding call was made. Mahaki embraced his friend. 'You should find somebody to fill your life,' Mahaki said. 'Like your Susan?' Melvin asked. 'My dear chap, my dear, dear foolish Mahaki — ' Suddenly Melvin turned away. 'Almost forgot!' he said. He handed Mahaki a large envelope. 'Speaking of Maoris — ' he began. Then he was gone, turning away and through the doors.

Mahaki opened the envelope. Inside was a reproduction of a school photograph — forty-three girls of various ages. Melvin had written below the group: 'Miss Swainson's School, class of 1901.' A rather plain face, in the fourth row was ringed in red. 'The Divine KM', Melvin had written. Another face, in the front row, was also circled with red ink. The face belonged to a young girl who looked as if she was already a woman. She wore a long dark dress, high at the neck, which fell to her ankles. The girl was sitting on the ground facing the photographer, resting her weight on her right arm. Her left arm was draped over her legs. The pose was prim and innocently schoolgirlish. But there was a suggestion in it of feminine awareness and provocation. As for the face, there was no doubt of its beauty. Framed in a mass of heavy hair the face would have been distinctive in any company. It was Italianate more than Maori with dark brooding eyes, full lips and a perfect oval chin. It was a face that provoked an emotional response because of its beauty. At the same time there was also something slightly secretive about that beauty, something sad, which

24

reminded Mahaki of his mother. Beneath that face Melvin had under-lined the name: *Maata*.

4

A week later, although Mahaki was due at Susan's at 7.30 that evening, he went to the Alexander Turnbull Library. He wanted to see whether or not he could advance his quest for the 'Maata' novel and obtain information on Maata herself. He was awed by the excellence of the institution and the kind and patient assistance given him by the librarians, in particular, a gentle lady whose name was Janet. She had greeted him in Maori, indicating that she knew more about Maori custom than her appearance might have suggested. Janet had then assisted him to begin his research — bringing him a number of refer-ence books on Katherine Mansfield. 'There are more,' she smiled, 'and then there's the microfiche material, but this will be enough to begin with.' Mahaki looked at her gratefully, saying 'Thank you.' She patted his hand and grinned. 'This is a whare taonga for all peoples of Aotearoa,' she said. 'It is a library of treasures for all of us. We don't get many Maori in here — yet. But they will come when they under-stand that this is their house as well as ours.'

Although it soon became clear that references to Maata and the novel were fairly scarce — footnotes as it were to the blinding brilliance of Katherine Mansfield's actual life and achievements — Mahaki was able to piece together, from the fragments, the beginnings of a whakapapa about Maata. He was ludicrously excited when he found her name the very first time, vicariously thrilled that a Maori woman had been a friend of Katherine Mansfield's. At the same time, he was puzzled that the friendship should be so glossed over — as if biographers didn't know quite what to make of it or how to make it fit. He began to set down details in his notebook, making notes in the margins for himself: *Maata (or Martha Grace) Mahupuku (check spelling) Tena Koe, Maata. Born 1886 or 1890? — Confusion here. Check — 10 April? See KM's birthday telegram, 10 April 1907, to Maata 'Birthday greetings to my sweetest Carlotta, K'. Descended from 'an important wealthy Maori family in the Wairarapa, across the Rimutaka Range north of Wellington' (Ngati Kahungunu? Too far east for Raukawa? Check.) Of Pakeha and Maori descent. Mother — a Miss Sexton of Glad-stone North. Father (name?) was the brother of a tribal chief, Tamahau Mahupuku — a 'colourful Mormon (!!!!) reputed to have had six wives'. Because TM had no offspring, Maata's father inherited the tribal lands and mana. When he died, it all came to Maata (paramount chieftainess then? The way described sounds romantic — beware Pakeha fantasies and check). Interesting about Miss Sexton — a Pakeha woman marrying a Maori? In those days? She must have been most unusual — but on death of husband (how?) Maata's mother married Nathaniel Grace, hence Martha Grace (Find out more about Nathaniel Grace).*

Maata went to school in Wellington. (How come? Did mother and new father move to Wellington?) KM first met Maata when Beauchamp sent girls from Wellington Girls' High School to 'Miss Swainson's School' in June 1899 (founded as a boarding school with Anglican affiliations — several Jewish pupils). KM must have been 11 and Maata 9 or 13, in 1901 photograph looks much older than KM, surely! Both girls became firm friends during period at School 1899 to 1902. Indeed, see KM's first journal entry, in her prayer book: 'I am going to be a Mauri missionary' (missp.) Description of Maata: as having 'none of the English in her hot glowing eyes. They were wide set in their dark fiery beauty . . . The Maoris would have said she possessed mana — "personal magnetism".' Quote: 'It is said that their kindred and individual spirits gave no little concern to their teacher, also that Sir Harold and Lady Beauchamp did not favour the friendship. [Why?] Even so, it was generally agreed that Maata was bewitching in face and form, and her speech was soft, musical and vital.' The two girls sound irrepressible! — Oh my God, here is the 'Maori princess' bit — a wealthy heiress to Maori lands — dark-skinned and exotically beautiful — sometimes called Princess Martha to emphasise just how little she had in common with the 'half-castes' in the squalid houses in Tinakori Road — uncle a friend of P.M. Dick Seddon. Also, 'Maata was not typical either of the Maoris or the blending of Maori and English blood, partly because her social position was unique. Maata was said to be a Maori princess in her own right, as well as heiress to Maori holdings, and very wealthy.' (Check, check, CHECK — who called her Princess Martha!? Surely not her own iwi. Did she regard herself as a princess? Whatever, she was certainly more than an equal to the Wellington establishment — Quotes: 'Her [KM's] intellectual peer in her own country.' — and — 'Martha was constantly at the Beauchamps' home. The girls, who were not allowed much money, were pop-eyed with the amount Maata always had to spend. All the same she was very pretty, bright and generous and nothing of a snob herself. She and Kathleen were particularly friendly' — Burney Trapp to his son Joseph Trapp, unpublished letter). AH, HERE WE HAVE IT! First reference by KM to writing about Maata! KM Notebook: 1906–1908 'I should like to write a life much in the style of Walter Pater's "Child in the House." About a child in Wellington . . . I should call it "Strife" — and the child

I should call — Ah, I have it — I'd make her a half-caste Maori and call her Maata.' Is this THE Novel?

Mahaki was so excited with his progress that he quite forgot about Susan. 'It's closing time,' Janet said gently. 'Don't worry, there's always tomorrow.' By that time it was nine o'clock, and when Mahaki tried to telephone Susan he realised she had taken the phone off the hook. Anxious now, Mahaki jumped on his motorbike and raced up to the flat on The Terrace which Susan shared with her friends Thea, Gill and Margot. The flat was typical university student digs, converted into a top flat and bottom flat out of a large old house which had seen better days. The girls rented the top flat — three bedrooms, large lounge and a bathroom with a hole in the roof just above the loo (you opened an umbrella if you were sitting there when it rained). The bottom flat was currently rented by two ladies of the night whose Japanese fishermen clients were either constantly mistaking the address and trying to get into the top flat — or hopeful. In the daylight the flat looked exactly what it was — scungy — but at night it exhibited a kind of ratty eclectic elegance. Mahaki had met Susan there at a party — both had been on the rebound from other relationships — and they had spent an appalling night together. To make matters worse, just as he had been getting out of bed, Mahaki had spilt his coffee over Susan's precious volumes of *Lord of the Rings*. But, because they were both masochists, refusing to believe the evidence of their obvious mismatching, they had stuck it out.

Mahaki parked his motorcycle in the lane outside the flat. Thank God, the light was still on in Susan's second floor bedroom. He shimmied up the drainpipe but, when he tried the window, it was locked. 'Susan?' he whispered. She was sitting up in bed, reading glasses and granny-style nightdress on, concentrating grimly on *Pride and Prejudice*. Her cat, Gertrude, lay curled up beside her, also pretending not to hear this intrusion on its comfortable domesticity. 'Susan!' Mahaki rattled on the window, which was a hard thing to do when hanging from a drainpipe. He could see Susan muttering to herself but, eventually, she threw aside the bedcovers and padded over to the window. 'What do you want?' she hissed through the glass. Her hot breath misted the pane and she rubbed it away so that she could see him. 'It's cold out here,' Mahaki replied. 'Well go home then!' she said. 'But I want to see you,' Mahaki answered. He saw Gertrude extend herself in a complacent yawn, *Oh fall off and kill yourself, mate*. Luckily, however, Susan must have been in a sympathetic mood because the window squeaked open. Gertrude sniffed at the affront.

27

Susan padded back to the bed and hopped in. As Mahaki climbed over the ledge he saw her take a quick look in the mirror, remove her glasses, and pull a brush through her hair — but when he came to sit beside her she had put back her appearance of disapproval. 'Well?' she asked. She had just taken a bath and looked so endearing with those freckles of hers. 'I've been working late and — ' Mahaki began. He saw the disdainful look in Gertrude's eyes, *Yeah, we've heard it all before, brother.* 'You were supposed to be here two hours ago,' Susan said. Mahaki tried to embrace her, saying, 'Truly, Susan, I was — ' Susan edged away from him and Gertrude, claws gleaming, licked her hand, *Yeah, you tell him, baby.* 'Mahaki,' Susan began, 'we really must do something about this. About us.' And Mahaki felt his heart sink — she was really giving him the boot this time. 'You are unreliable,' Susan continued. 'You take me for granted, you're just impossible and —' and Gertrude purred, *You tell him, sister* — 'Oh, Mahaki, the drain-pipe is so ruined now, can't you use the door?' She burst out giggling and punched him in the chest. She and Mahaki wrestled each other, laughing and letting off steam. Then he kissed her, saying, 'But I wouldn't feel like Zorro.' The mood changed. 'Watch out for Gertrude,' Susan whispered as she moved over in the bed to let Mahaki in.

Later, after their healthy sexuality had been satisfied and Susan was getting ready to be taken out for midnight dinner at the Green Parrot, she turned to Mahaki and asked, 'What was it you were working on?' Mahaki told her about Katherine Mansfield and Maata, knowing that she would approve the literary nature of the assignment. 'Oh yes, I think I've read something about that,' Susan said. 'Why didn't you tell me!' Mahaki said. Susan pursed her lips. 'You didn't ask and, anyway, I have learnt not to tell you *everything*.' Before she and Mahaki had really got serious, and were trying to fool each other about this, they had told each other about their past experiences — and Mahaki had laughed when she'd mentioned the French film director who had unsuccessfully tried to do unmentionable things to her on the band rotunda at Oriental Bay.

'Right-o,' Susan said. 'Ready? Thank goodness I can sleep in tomorrow. I don't teach until the afternoon. The little dears go to swimming in the morning, praise Neptune.' Susan grabbed Mahaki's hand and gave it a squeeze. 'Thank you for telling me about Katherine Mansfield,' she said. 'If I must be stood up for another woman I'm glad it's her. I'll see if I can find out more for you through my library friends.' Then, just before they left the flat, Susan knelt down beside Gertrude and stroked her till she purred. 'What's up with Gertrude?' Mahaki asked, wondering why Gertrude hadn't batted at him once.

'She's pregnant again,' Susan sighed. 'I *must* get her done.' Mahaki joined Susan in tickling Gertrude. 'Look at the size of her! Is Claudius the father?' Susan glared like a protective elder sister. 'We think,' she said, referring to two other local and notorious tomcats, 'that it was Rosencrantz *and* Guildenstern.'

Two days later, Gertrude gave birth to a litter of seven kittens and began, almost at once, to kill them. Susan rang Mahaki at the office, saying, 'Please come, Mahaki. Gertrude has gone mad.' When he arrived the first sound he heard was Gertrude's extraordinary low yowling. Susan had separated Gertrude from the kittens and locked her in the bedroom. As soon as Mahaki saw the kittens he knew why Gertrude had killed two of them. 'They're diseased,' he said, kindly, to the tearful Susan. 'Can't you see?' The kittens were terribly deformed, their eyes small vacant pits, and three of them were having constant seizures, spitting and sneezing and kicking themselves into macabre shapes. Within the patches of fur, Mahaki could see that they were riddled with parasites. 'You should have let Gertrude finish the job,' Mahaki said.

Susan quietened down. She looked at him pleadingly. 'Okay,' he nodded. He got a bucket, took it into the bathroom, and filled it with water. He put the kittens in a sack, locked the door behind him, and pushed the sack into the bucket below the waterline. The kittens' squeals were submerged. The sack was filled with frantic movement. Then, soon, there was no movement at all. For some reason, despite his farmboy upbringing, Mahaki was affected by the drowning. He sat on the toilet, his head in his hands. Suddenly he heard a scrabbling on the roof and, when he looked up through the hole in the ceiling he saw Gertrude, a feline Medea, looking down at him. Somehow she'd got out of the locked room. Her eyes were black and wide with ferocity. Spittle and blood had congealed at her jaws. She stared intently at the bucket, her ears pricking up. Then she looked at Mahaki, *So it's done then?* — and her face disappeared.

That night Mahaki and Susan took Gertrude to the vet. When they returned they went to bed early and made love. Afterward, Susan asked him if he had known that Katherine Mansfield's name for Maata had been Carlotta. When he said 'Yes', Susan then asked him if he knew why. He said 'No' — and that is when Susan told him it was because Maata had always worn red shoes.

1969/1970 . . . N.Z. CELEBRATES COOK BI-CENTENARY . . . MY LAI MASSACRE TRIAL . . . THE EAGLE HAS LANDED — NEIL ARMSTRONG WALKS ON MOON . . . MARY BEARD, TASMANIAN HITCHHIKER,

MURDERED . . . U.S. TROOPS ENTER CAMBODIA . . . JAMES McNEISH
PUBLISHES 'MACKENZIE' . . . N.Z. FORCES JOIN AMERICANS IN
VIETNAM . . .

PART TWO

1

> '*I met her only once, . . . and that was some time in 1906 when
> I was present at a dance given by the Beauchamps at their
> house in Fitzherbert Terrace. I have a vivid memory of Maata
> at that dance, and she was a beautiful half-caste girl. There
> is no doubt that she was a great friend of Katherine's, but
> more so, I thought, of Chaddie's (Katherine's elder sister).*
>
> — E.K.B. in an interview with P. A. Lawlor, recounted in
> *The Mystery of Maata*, p.31.

1972 . . . LABOUR SWEEPS INTO OFFICE UNDER N.Z.'S OWN KENNEDY,
NORMAN KIRK . . . 'BROADSHEET' BEGINS PUBLICATION . . . THE
EQUAL PAY ACT PASSES . . . LANDSLIDE 60.7% — NIXON U.S.
PRESIDENT FOR SECOND TERM . . . JAMES K. BAXTER DIES . . . WOOL
PRICES DOUBLE ON THE PREVIOUS SEASON . . . THE LAST U.S.
COMBAT TROOPS LEAVE VIETNAM . . .

In 1972, at the grand old age of thirty, Mahaki told Susan that it was
about time they legitimised their long-term relationship. The earlier,
headier, days had mellowed and ripened, though not without some
forced growing on Mahaki's part. Susan had said 'Yes' and, to save
bother to her parents, they had their marriage solemnised in the
Wellington Central Registry Office. Mahaki's sister Teina and Aunt
Iris were overjoyed and relieved.

The next year Mahaki and Susan decided that they should go
overseas to Britain and the Continent for a few years and then return
to start a family. Susan went down to Dunedin to say goodbye to her
parents and Mahaki drove to Hastings to see his Aunt Iris. Together
they went out to the cemetery where Mahaki's mother was buried.
'She would have been proud of you,' Aunt Iris said, 'and I know that
she would want me to tell you this on her behalf. You have become
equal with the Pakeha but' — she chided him — 'don't forget your
Maori background and your iwi. Wherever you go we are here to
support you. Come back to us when you are ready. Above all, never
forget the teachings of the Church.'

Later, when they were reminiscing in the kitchen about the old days, Mahaki told his aunt about the time he had been at the river and seen the red shoes. 'I thought I had it all figured out,' he laughed. 'I thought it all had to do with Katherine Mansfield. But when, a few years ago now, Susan told me about Maata Mahupuku — at the name, a flicker of light flashed in Aunt Iris's eyes — 'I realised that, whatever it is about, Maata and not Katherine Mansfield is at the centre of it.'

Aunt Iris was silent for a while. Then, 'What was that name?' she asked. 'Mahupuku,' Mahaki said, 'Maata Mahupuku.' And his aunt said, 'He Moromona ia?' Astonished, Mahaki asked, 'How did you know!' but Aunt Iris refused to be drawn. 'I should have known you'd be like my mother,' Mahaki said.

At Aunt Iris's bidding, Mahaki travelled on to Gisborne to see his sister and to try to end the long estrangement which had occurred between himself and Te Rangi. His sister, also, entreated Mahaki to be kind and, when he saw his father, his heart melted and he wished with all his might for reconciliation. Mahaki had known that leadership of the gang had gone to his cousin. He had hoped that although his father would have found standing down difficult to accept, time would have brought some inner resolution enabling him to enjoy his retirement. The semblance of a peaceful old man was upon Te Rangi but, when Mahaki touched his father, making the old man look up, he saw instead — blackness. Then from out of the blackness he saw a bull elephant charging, one which had been driven away by younger males of the herd, a battle-scarred veteran with vengeance and blood lust burning away all reason. He saw a once-leader who had now become a rogue elephant, following after the herd and skirmishing with them, his mind intent on regaining the power that was once his but would never be again. And he saw that the bull elephant was now turning on him.

'Tena koe, Te Rangi,' Mahaki had said. His father was staying in a house which the gang had bought him. He was living with the current woman among the succession of women he had had since Mahaki's mother had died. Mahaki bore Te Rangi no grudge on this issue — he had known his father to be a virile man with strong and sensual appetites. Nor was he concerned at the extreme youth of his father's woman — he was only too pleased that his father was able to find companionship of any kind in his old age. He remembered that his father had bruised his romantic notions of love by telling him — when he was twelve and scrubcutting with Te Rangi — that if he had not met Wai he would have married someone else. At the time Mahaki had considered that to be a negation of his entire existence and he had hated his father for some months.

So it was only to be expected that Te Rangi would find a woman for his bed — he was that kind of man — and the kind of women he attracted were those who needed to be needed in his way. But what Mahaki was not prepared for, when he touched Te Rangi's shoulder, was the implacable and territorial rage of the bull elephant — for his father, not seeing a son (or perhaps seeing the male who had taken the love of Wai from him), simply, irrationally, *charged*.

Shaken, Mahaki later talked it over with the cousin who had taken control of the gang. 'Don't worry about it,' his cousin laughed, 'there's nothing wrong with the old man. And if there was, you know that we look after our own.' Then his cousin eyed him curiously. 'Maybe you just don't know him like we do, cuz.' They talked a while longer and it came to Mahaki that his cousin, the male ascendant, appeared to be engaging him, also, tusk to tusk. He smiled to himself at the notion. Such was the way of things when the new order replaced the old. The iwi were regrouping under a new, proven leader. A rogue, like his father, or a loner, like himself, were not appropriate members, rampaging as they did according to their own dictates. *Like father like son.* 'Pakeha missus, ay? Good on you.' His cousin wished him well and Mahaki knew that the welfare of the gang would be safe in his hands, the dynamic imperative of the iwi forever protected, the dynastic succession assured. He promised to send tracksuits back from England for his nephews and nieces. The next month he and Susan flew to London.

2

The London that was waiting for Mahaki and Susan had been the capital of a colonial empire and was now the mother to the Commonwealth. It was Britannia and, under an earlier Queen, had sent out English settlers to a land far to the south — New Zealand. There, in uneasy alliance with the natives, and perhaps because of the natives, the colonists had established a *new* England. But life, legislation, traditions and culture were still determined from the place of satanic mills. It was to be expected that at least once in their lives most New Zealanders should visit the Home Country and, if possible, attend the new Elizabeth at the Court of St James.

Mahaki and Susan therefore thronged with other young visitors from all those countries identified on the globe in red — from Trinidad, South Africa, Canada, Rhodesia, Australia, and India — and, as far as their purse allowed, indulged themselves in the wonders of the new Elizabethan age. They thronged with their colonial counterparts to Earls Court and were lucky enough to find a ground-floor bedsitting room at No. 67 Harcourt Terrace, just off the Old Brompton Road. The excitement of being in London was such that they lived in a state of intoxication — to be *there*, walking down streets and seeing historic buildings that had been such an integral part of their education, left them wide-eyed with delight. They quickly made friends and often found themselves in the company of intelligent as well as enjoyable people, staying up till all hours of the night discussing England and the EEC, the future of Rhodesia, Watergate and Wimbledon. Surely, London was the hub of civilisation and the home of liberal wisdom.

From that small bedsitter, Mahaki and Susan made frequent excursions throughout London and lightning strikes to Cornwall in the west, Scotland to the north and the Fen country to the east. They thought nothing of going to Paris for the weekend (didn't *everybody* do that?) and to Rome for five days. While in France they had visited Fontainebleau and, with a shiver of sadness, Mahaki had thought, *This is the place where Katherine Mansfield died. Somewhere near here she went to see Gurdjieff and coughed out blood from her mouth. E Katerina, haere, haere, haere.* Whenever they returned to London, Susan would find a bunch of fresh flowers at her doorstep, delivered by the barrowman down at the corner. And, of course, they would exchange stories with their friends — like when an aged prostitute in Montmartre had thought Susan had poached an 'Algerian' Mahaki from her territory and, upon swearing and attacking Susan in French, fell back in alarm at Susan's own very expert and delightfully filthy vituperation.

1974 . . . NORMAN KIRK DIES . . . MAORI RIGHTS ARE PROTESTED AT WAITANGI . . . THE INDUSTRIAL RELATIONS ACT IS PASSED . . . PATRICIA HEARST FOUND . . . ASH ERUPTIONS OCCUR ON MT NGARUAHOE . . . WALLACE ROWLING TAKES UP LEADERSHIP OF THE LABOUR PARTY . . . NIXON RESIGNS . . .

It was during the winter of 1974, while he was hunting for some papers in an old suitcase, that Mahaki came across the notes he had written in his notebook in 1969 on Maata — *So it was you, Maata, who was with me down at the river. He aha to pirangi mo ahau?* And following the note were further jottings he had made about the whakapapa on Katherine Mansfield and Maata — and the novel.

What was New Zealand like in 1902 when KM and Maata were young? More to the point what was it like for two girls, on the verge of puberty, living in a cage gilded by the very best Society, Education, Literature, Liberal Thought, Music and the Emancipation of Women, could give in colonial New Zealand? Certainly Miss Swainson's School which encouraged Higher Education for Women must have been an inadvertently appropriate hot-house context for two daring girls, one 'imaginative to the point of untruth'. (Note Oscar Wilde and fin de siècle influences on KM.) Then on 29 January 1903, the Beauchamp family sailed on the S.S. Niwaru for London. There KM and her sisters entered Queen's College, in Harley Street, the first institution to be created in England for the higher education of women. Katherine Mansfield's literary, intellectual, emotional, feminist and cultural sensibilities developed there until the Beauchamps returned to New Zealand on the S.S. Corinthic, arriving 6 December 1906, when KM had just turned 19. ('For the generation to which Katherine belonged, the decadents were the gateway to the imaginative life' — John Middleton Murry, 1933.) And Maata? Conjecture only, but she probably stayed at Miss Swainson's a few more years before being sent to a FINISHING SCHOOL IN PARIS (!) under the guardianship of a Miss Turton. Next record is that Maata met KM in London (possibly also in Paris?) in 1906 — she was a finished little 17-year-old Parisienne in dress and manner — 'She kept her feet as exquisitely as her hands' (Mrs Grace). Maata must have been quite a flamboyant character already: 'She took with her an introduction to a Madame Louise who made the Beauchamps' clothes . . . Maata was mad on dress and went in donkey deep with Louise and left England without squaring up. Madame claimed the amount from the Beauchamps and if you knew Uncle Harold you could imagine the commotion. I think the upshot was that the friendship was compulsorily cut short.' (Burney Trapp to his son Joseph Trapp, unpublished letter, 4 March 1947.) But this aside the meeting of the two young women was 'rapturous and romantic'. Two years later when they were both keeping diaries (and Katherine preserved Maata's all her life, expecting to make some use of it) she looked back longingly to that time together in London: . . . 'We (KM and Maata) were floating down Regent Street in a hansom — on either side of us the blossoms of golden light — and ahead a little half hoop of a moon.' (Ruth Mantz, The Life of Katherine Mansfield, Constable, London 1933.)

Maata must have returned to Wellington around the same time as KM because E.K.B. recalls the vivacious Maata at a dance given in 1906 (must have been December) by the Beauchamps at their house in Fitzherbert Terrace. She came back polished with a vengeance. She had poise, beauty, and a lovely voice for singing and speaking. She could talk French like a Parisienne, and she dressed like one. KM resumed the friendship and there is no doubt that Maata enjoyed the great bond between them, their *kindred and individual spirits. At the same time, Maata had marriage plans and Katherine Mansfield had —*

The door opened behind Mahaki. Susan came in and draped her arms over Mahaki's shoulder, nuzzling his neck. 'What are you doing?' she asked. 'Reading the notes,' Mahaki said, 'I took on Katherine Mansfield and Maata a few years ago.' Then, after pausing, he asked Susan, 'Would you ever have considered Katherine Mansfield a very sexual person?' And he read: '*Maata, 10 April 1907: I am 17 today. It is extraordinary how young I am in years and how old in body — ugh! I am miserable and oh! so bored. . . . I had a letter from . . . K this morning. . . . dearest K writes "ducky" letters. I like this bit. "What did you mean by being so superlatively beautiful just as you went away? You witch; you are beauty incarnate."* ' Susan looked at Mahaki, wonderingly. 'The things you come up with,' she said. 'Well?' Mahaki continued. 'She *was* married,' Susan said, 'and there were a number of others in her life — like the *rest* of us,' she added. 'What about her *friendships*,' Mahaki persisted. '*Katherine Mansfield, Notebook 39, 1907: Do other people of my own age feel as I do I wonder — so absolutely powerfully* licentious, *so almost physically ill . . . . I want Maata — I want her as have had her — terribly. This is unclean I know but true. What an extraordinary thing — I feel savagely crude — and almost powerfully enamoured of the child.*' 'Oh,' Susan said, 'I suppose you're talking about the most well-known secret in the New Zealand literary world.' Mahaki nodded. 'There's no doubt in my mind that Maata was her first love,' he said. Susan eyed him curiously. 'Do you find that objectionable?' she asked. 'No,' Mahaki said. 'Good,' Susan said as she kissed him. 'After all, a person's integrity and not her sexuality is what counts. What happened to Maata?' Mahaki smiled at her. 'Maata? It appears that when Katherine Mansfield decided that she should return to England in July 1908 — oh yes, there had been a trip to the Ureweras just before that — her passion and fascination for Maata declined. It was still *there*, up until 1915, because Katherine Mansfield was still known to be thinking of writing a novel about Maata but then — ' Mahaki held his hands apart in a gesture of conjecture. 'And Maata?' Susan asked again. 'She married, apparently. Lost a lot of her wealth by foolish investments including a flutter on the Melbourne Cup. She lived for a while in Greytown where she had a beautiful house in Kurutawhiti Street — the house had imposing brick walls surrounding a spacious garden where she grew many varieties of English trees. Then she moved to Palmerston North. She died in 1952. She was sixty-two, I think.'

'And the novel?' Susan asked. Ah, yes, the novel —

Not the projected short story called 'Strife' at all but something much more ambitious. Started inconclusively 1913? (Mantz.) If not, then definitely in 1915 — '25th Jan 1915. Wrote opening chapters of Maata a "book" never completed' (Mantz) — or KM to John Middleton Murry, 25 March, 1915 'I fell into the open arms of my first novel. I have finished a huge chunk, but I shall have to copy it on thin paper for you. I expect you will think I am dotty when you read it . . . it's queer stuff.' — or Murry himself in The Scrapbook of Katherine Mansfield, *1939, quoted from* Maata: *'They did not fall like leaves — they fell like feathers — fluttering and floating from the trees that lined the road — '*

'The novel?' Mahaki repeated. Outside the dusk was falling like a shroud. 'It was begun. In 1915. Then Katherine Mansfield's brother died. The war came. Life intervened — passion, the Bloomsbury set, writing it all down. The novel — who knows? The general consensus is that it was never finished.' The dusk falling, falling. 'She never came back to New Zealand,' Mahaki said. 'She lived another fifteen years, till 1923, and then she died of tuberculosis. She was thirty-four. You know, she once said to her friend Ida Baker, '*I am a secretive creature to my last bone*', so who knows — ' Outside, the lamps in the street were coming on like tiny pinpricks in the velvet night.

3

1976 . . . THE BEGINNING OF THE MULDOON YEARS . . . DAWN POLICE RAIDS MADE ON POLYNESIANS IN AUCKLAND AND WELLINGTON . . . U.S. CLOSES LAST BASES IN VIETNAM . . . ROGER HALL'S 'GLIDE TIME' PREMIERES IN WELLINGTON . . . U.S. CELEBRATES TWO HUNDREDTH BIRTHDAY — HAPPY BIRTHDAY UNCLE SAM . . . NEW ZEALAND DAY RENAMED WAITANGI DAY. . .

Mahaki and Susan decided to extend their stay in England. Mahaki got a job on Fleet Street and Susan was lucky enough to secure a teaching position in Hounslow. Susan put their names into a lottery run by the New Zealand High Commission — and they were among the select few that year who received invitations to go to the Queen's annual garden party. Mahaki could have given it a miss but Susan insisted that it would be fun. She bought a pretty floral outfit, a large pink picture hat and pink shoes and handbag to match — she looked a royal herself. Mahaki hired a morning suit.

The party turned out to be a huge affair with people parading as if it were Sunday in the park — very reverent, very proud, and showing their wealth or rank either in the size of the pearls or the handmade shoes from Church's. Rolls Royces were in abundant evidence and helped to set off to perfection Mahaki's dirty blue Mini-van in the car park. Halfway through the proceedings it began to shower and Mahaki and Susan dashed into the nearest marquee where they found themselves in the company of the Sheriff of Nottingham. 'Typical Queen's weather,' the Sheriff sniffed. Whenever further showers threatened, Mahaki would repeat the observation to all and sundry, 'Typical, typical, typical *of* the Queen's garden parties, just like last year — you *were* here, last year, weren't you? Yes, typical, what?' Then the Queen appeared, and Mahaki and Susan raced across to get a glimpse of the Royal Presence. After that, they promenaded some more and ended up looking at some of the palace rooms. There, Mahaki whispered to Susan, 'See over there? In the corner? I'm sure those two women are Maori.' The two women were looking at Mahaki, also, so everybody edged closer together — and that is how Mahaki met Miria Simpson. From that time onwards both Mahaki and Miria liked to say, 'Oh, where did we meet? At Buckingham Palace of course!' Nobody ever believed them.

Just after the garden party, Mahaki and Susan flew on vacation to Greece. The interlude was idyllic, the white marble shining against the deep blue of sea and sky. They stayed in Athens for two weeks, dreaming their way through the ancient landscape and dancing every evening in the Plaka. Then they spent three weeks in the Greek Islands, staying in a small taverna on Mykonos. Just prior to returning to London, Susan wanted them to consult the oracle at Delphi. They went by bus — a three-hour journey — and felt that they were travelling into the past. When they arrived at Delphi the mood was mystical — and when Mahaki asked for a sign of his future there was a rain of red blossoms. 'And you?' Mahaki asked Susan. 'Well, I saw the number twelve,' she said. 'Oh my God,' Mahaki responded, 'we'd better get started *quick.*' He knew that Susan was referring to children.

Mahaki and Susan returned to London on a dull grey afternoon. A letter was awaiting Mahaki from Melvin —

My dear Mahaki,

Hail, o sybaritic one. The pleasures and delights of Albion still have you in their thrall, otherwise you would have returned to our fair shores before now. Be that as it may, things are going well I trust. I do not intend to write at length in this missal but suffice to say that you are fondly remembered. Apropos of which you may recall a memorable afternoon we spent together in Wellington at the Katherine Mansfield memorial. Should you not — and it does not matter — I spent an interesting evening with an elderly gentleman who was there and remembers you with some clarity. His name is Mr P. A. Lawlor and, as it happens, he has written a short book on the Maata novel. He told me that he actually met Maata in 1941 — I have been able to locate a copy of this meeting for you and enclose it with this letter.

Incidentally Mr Lawlor doubts the novel's existence though he is interested in the journals and letters KM and Maata exchanged. Apparently the journals are virtually *indistinguishable*. For tutor both girls had read Marie Bashkirtseff, dead of consumption at 24, *vide* KM. The Russian aristocrat and painter left behind her the journals in which she reflected with endless fascination over her own development, as did KM and Maata, obviously, a generation later. All this adds credence, I must say, to Maata's avowal, back then in 1941, that KM sent her a manuscript which she, Maata, was to complete. What a pity that the manuscript was not passed to Mr Lawlor! His own comments on this are pertinent, I think.

With affection,
Your fellow Antipodean,
Melvin.

Later that evening Mahaki read the enclosure Melvin had sent.

4

P. A. Lawlor: My Interview With Maata: Extracted from *The Mystery of Maata*, published by the Beltane Book Bureau, Wellington, New Zealand, 1946 (Limited Edition of 250 signed copies) pp.16–20.

Some time in December 1940, I was discussing books with a Maori friend. I chanced to speak of Katherine Mansfield. Immediately my friend was very interested. He said that a lady friend of his, a Maori, went to school with Katherine Mansfield.

What was her name? I asked. In turn I became more than interested when he said her name was Maata, that she had a huge bundle of letters written to her by Katherine Mansfield, also the MS of an unpublished novel.

My friend avowed that when Katherine was in London, and in need of money, Maata sent her £50.

At my request, my Maori informant promised to produce Maata on her next visit to Wellington.

Meanwhile I called on Miss Mabel Tustin, who had attended school with Katherine Mansfield. I did not mention the Maata incident. I was anxious to secure some other information about Katherine. In the course of our conversation, Miss Tustin said that Mr Eric Waters, another friend of the Beauchamp family, had unintentionally destroyed interesting photographs and papers of Katherine Mansfield interest, possibly also a beautiful miniature of her grandparents. Let us hope that the Maata MS was not included in the burning!

It was not until May the following year that my Maori friend introduced me to Maata. As the meeting took place in my office, I had ample opportunity of studying her. She was of medium height, dark skinned; anything but the fat, round-faced, thick-lipped Maori women with whom we are familiar in this country. Maata was attractive and interesting, but her eyes were hard and keen. She was also very serious. She was neatly dressed — not overdressed as Maori women are wont to be.

I asked her if she had read the Ruth Mantz biography. She said she had and added briefly that she thought it was by no means complete. There were many important aspects of Katherine Mansfield's life not included.

I then asked her did she not think that after reading the book one might presume that Maata was dead? The Maori lady who claimed to be Maata said she did not think so. Would it not be inferred that Miss Mantz was indicating, merely, that this was 'the end of a chapter'?

I was impressed with the intelligence behind this answer. Maata's voice was low pitched and a trifle metallic, but she spoke well.

Maata said she had no recollection of meeting Ruth Mantz when she visited New Zealand. She added in characteristic Maori fashion: 'If I am not interested or dislike a person, I never remember.' There was a faint suggestion of a smile on her face.

Maata then told me some unpublished incidents about Katherine's life. I shall not mention all of the things that she spoke of, for it would not be wise to do so at this stage. She did say, however, that Katherine Mansfield left New Zealand because of a flirtation. Earlier in this little love affair, said Maata, Sir Harold Beauchamp locked his daughter in her room as punishment. To console her friend, Maata climbed up to her room and it was then that Katherine told her the whole story.

Maata went on to refer to other rather sensational aspects of her alleged knowledge of Katherine Mansfield, and concluded with the brief statement that she last met her in London early in the century and had corresponded with her until she died.

I now introduced the all-important matter of the MS.

Without any hesitation, Maata said that she had the MS in her possession. It was an unfinished novel entitled 'Maata.'

I asked her the approximate length. She replied 'About 60,000 words,' adding that the arrangement was that she (Maata) was to complete the story.

'Is there any possibility of my seeing the manuscript?' I asked.

Maata remained silent for a space of about thirty seconds.

'I cannot give you an answer just now,' she said in a modulated yet very emphatic voice.

I turned aside from this, the main question I was concerned with, and encouraged her to speak about her early days with Katherine.

Her recollections were many and varied. The most interesting was that while they were at school, Katherine and Maata produced a hand-written magazine. The former did most of the composing while she was in the playground. Maata said that as her writing was more legible, she transcribed Katherine's notes into an exercise book. Maata also mentioned that Katherine called her Carlotta because of her red shoes.

Sure enough I found Maata referred to as Carlotta on page 219 of the Mantz biography, but there is no reference to the red shoes.

At this stage, Maata appeared to be tiring of my questions and rose to leave.

Before she left, she turned to me with a Mona Lisa smile, and said: 'No, I don't think I'll let you see "Maata" — possibly though, the letters and an inscription Katherine wrote for me in a book of poems.'

She then left with her escort. I noted that she carried herself well and that she still 'kept her feet as exquisitely as she did her hands.'

I was left wondering, but impressed. I noted in my diary a skeleton of what I have outlined above.

A fortnight went by before I met them again. They took their seats in my office with solemnity. Maata was spokeswoman. She said she had decided to produce the MS if she was satisfied as to what I had in mind about its disposal.

I then outlined my scheme which was that after reading the MS, I would make proposals about its publication. I added that I did not wish to participate in the profits. I would be well repaid by having played a small part in giving to the world what might be a most important book.

Once more Maata debated silently with herself, tapping her neat foot on the floor the while. Then looking at me very seriously, she said she would decide that day.

The next morning Maata's friend called and asked me had the MS reached me. It had not. The reply was that it should have reached me by post that day.

Four days later (there was no sign of the MS in the meantime) Maata called — this time alone. Without any hesitation she made certain proposals about the MS.

'Have you it with you?' I asked.

She shook her head.

I then replied very firmly that I could do nothing further until she produced the MS.

Maata then left, quite friendly, but obviously disappointed.

As for myself, I was left wondering more than ever.

And that was the last time Maata called at my office. Her friend has been to see me several times and is emphatic that the MS is in Maata's possession, also many letters. He said he had seen them.

I asked him why it was that Maata would not let me see them.

His explanation was that the Maori had a complex regarding such matters. The inevitable question of the sacredness of such personal objects intruded and they just went on postponing the ultimate decision.

Undoubtedly the Maori mentality is a curious thing. Some of them have long memories. They cannot forget that their land was taken from them less than a hundred years ago, and may consider that in their dealings with the Pakeha to-day an attitude of suspicion is justifiable.

This, of course, is merely supposition. One of our most noted Maori students, Elsdon Best, spent many years living among the Maoris, and one of his comments about the Maori mind was as follows:

'The mentality of the Maori is of an intensely mystical nature . . . We hear of many singular theories about the Maori beliefs and Maori thought, but the truth is that we do not understand either, and what is more, we never shall. We shall never know the inwardness of the native mind.'

Commenting on this observation, Professor I. L. G. Sutherland, M.A., another eminent authority, states:

'But what this really means is not that there is an intrinsic difference between Maori and European mentality (as Levy-Bruhl quotes it to mean) but that through the profound difference of social tradition the varied contents of the two minds forms patterns or configurations which are very diverse. It may be, of course, as Elsdon Best says, that we shall never know fully the inwardness of the mind of the Maori, but in exactly the same sense we shall never know fully the mind of a man of the Middle Ages, with its different contents and patterning of emotion and thought.'

Translating these opinions in terms of Maata, there is evidently some strange mental reaction on her part as against my inquiries of her, causing her to retain possession of the MS.

5

The mentality of the Maori is of an intensely mystical nature. A week later Mahaki worked late at the newspaper. He telephoned Susan and told her to meet him at a small coffee shop in Regent Street. By the time he got there the evening had fallen completely. The lamps were like blossoms of gold light. The street was crowded with traffic — double decker buses, the ubiquitous London taxis, and dark shining cars. The pavements were crowded with pedestrians. Ahead lay a little half of a moon.

Later Mahaki wondered whether Melvin's letter had caused the incident. All of a sudden he sensed something strange, like a veil over the street. He swayed and put his hand on a lamp post to steady himself — and recoiled because it was so *hot*. Then behind him he heard the clip clop of a horse's hooves and a peal of girlish laughter like silver filigree. He turned and saw a hansom cab — and a young woman wearing a rich velvet cape was looking beyond him and waving to someone further up the street. 'Katerina! Katerina! Regardez! Regardez! Je suis ici!' The woman was waving so vigorously with her gloved hand that her domino loosened from her head and revealed a face of rapturous entrancing beauty.

From up the street another young woman came running, passing Mahaki, toward the hansom. And the girl in the hansom said, 'Oh, stop, cabbie!' and, laughing, helped her friend in. 'Katerina! Haramai! Oh ma cherie, ma cherie, je suis arrivée de Paris! Mon coeur, mon amour, haramai! Dites-moi qu'est-ce qui s'est passé? Embrasse-moi.' The cabbie set the hansom in motion. Mahaki saw the two women clasp each other and talk and giggle secretively in a schoolgirlish fashion. And he caught a glimpse, beneath the long gown of the girl in the cape, of shoes that were blood-red.

A double-decker bus went past and a voice called, 'Wotcher, mate!' But all Mahaki could think of was, *Why are you still with me, Maata? Why?* It was not until he and Susan returned to New Zealand that he found the answer.

PART THREE

1

*Maata married twice. She had two daughters of the second
marriage, and spent her fortune lavishly until it was gone: she
had 'plenty of charm, a clever talker and in her adult years
a distinct disinclination to sleep by herself. Quite irresponsible
about money . . . . On a small scale she was a kind of Amber.
I think that is the best way to describe her. I have lost count
of how many times she was married!*

> — from Claire Tomalin's *Katherine Mansfield: A Secret Life*, Viking,
> London, 1987. The quote is from an unpublished letter from Burney
> Trapp to his son Joseph Trapp, 4 March 1947. Amber was the heroine of
> a bestselling novel, *Forever Amber*.

1978 . . . MAORI PROTESTS, SPURRED BY THE LAND MARCH OF 1975,
CONTINUE AT BASTION POINT AND RAGLAN . . . MULDOON IS IN
POWER . . . THE ADVISORY COMMITTEE ON WOMEN'S AFFAIRS IS
ESTABLISHED . . . GANGS RIOT AT MOEREWA . . . 'PLUMB' BY MAURICE
GEE IS PUBLISHED . . . U.S. AND CHINA ESTABLISH DIPLOMATIC
RELATIONS . . .

Mahaki and Susan returned to New Zealand in 1978. They did so just
as news of the malfunction of the atomic nuclear reactor at Three Mile
Island near Harrisburg, Philadelphia, hit the news-stands. That event
at the nuclear hub of civilisation only reinforced their relief about
returning to the non-nuclear diamond that was New Zealand. The
return, however, was not entirely happy — New Zealand had changed,
the society lurching from one extreme to another under oppressive
government. 'Not a good time, old chap,' Melvin observed, when he
met Mahaki and Susan during their stopover at Auckland airport, 'to
be coming back.' Mahaki was surprised to see how Melvin had aged
— 'Haven't we all?' Melvin responded, referring to Mahaki's receding
hairline — and saddened at his friend's continued solitary status.
'Hope springs eternal,' Melvin said. Just before re-boarding the flight
to Wellington, Mahaki asked Melvin for the address of Pat Lawlor.
'Didn't I tell you?' Melvin asked. 'That grand man of letters passed
away; sometime last year it was.'

Wellington was quite a change after London. Both Mahaki and
Susan had difficulties finding employment and, with a great sense of

shock, Mahaki found himself contemplating registering as unemployed. Right at the last minute, however, he secured a position as features editor for the morning daily and, not long after that, Susan obtained a relief teaching position at Newtown Primary. Assessing the situation later, Mahaki felt that his and Susan's experience was symptomatic of the stress in New Zealand society. People seemed embattled — Maori divided against Pakeha, young separated from the old, wealthy from the unemployed, the powerful from the powerless. Radical movements — pro-Maori activists, feminists, unionists and dissidents — flourished. When the National Government allowed the 1981 South African rugby tour to take place in New Zealand, that act simply provided the climax to a long period of internal civil war — uniting the movements against Government and setting the stage for a long Labour reign.

Against this background it was somewhat heartwarming for Mahaki to find, on an assignment to Gisborne, that the shearing gang remained remarkably unchanged. His cousin had survived the various charges made by Te Rangi, and the whanau structure of the gang continued to be as strong as ever. 'That doesn't mean it's the *same*,' his cousin laughed. 'Nothing is ever the same. But we get by. And our kids are the shearers now.' And Mahaki saw that, yes, another generation had arrived and it would not be too long before a new leader, replacing his cousin, would be anointed.

As for Te Rangi, time had not mellowed him. 'Your father was always a strong man,' Aunt Iris agreed. 'He would never give in, even when he was wrong. That is an asset as well as a — a — *curse*.' She shivered at the word. Mahaki had told his aunt that on this occasion he had had a strained conversation with Te Rangi. Whenever he had tried to engage his father on an emotional level Te Rangi would retreat. Near the end his father had looked at him, saying, 'You and your mother, you both left me. Your sister too. But I have forgiven your mother now.' A shadow had crossed Aunt Iris's face. Then she had sighed, saying, 'My sister would have been pleased. After all these years. To be, finally, forgiven, *for having looked into him and seen what he was.*' And Mahaki realised again that there was some mystery about his mother and her years as wife to Te Rangi. Then, Aunt Iris surprised Mahaki by referring to their conversation, those many years ago, about the red shoes and Maata. Mahaki told her he had reached a cul-de-sac. 'Maata was the only one who could have told me,' he said. 'But she died in 1952. Perhaps her secret is better kept by her.' His aunt laid her hands in her lap. She was like the sphinx. She nodded in agreement.

2

Two years later, in 1980, Mahaki's and Susan's son Edward was born. In that same year, Mahaki ran across his old friend, Janet, from the Alexander Turnbull Library, and what she told him appeared to be an appropriate conclusion to the enigma of the 'Maata' novel — a plan and two fragmentary chapters had been found. 'Why has it taken so long?' Mahaki asked. Janet laughed and said, 'Writers are such untidy creatures and, of course, people who inherit their work are sometimes possessive of it or unaware of its importance. It takes a good scholar to hunt it all out — and one clue leads to another and, if you're lucky — ' Her eyes twinkled. 'But you must beware,' she cautioned melodramatically, 'because sometimes when one becomes the possessor of the knowledge one has responsibility for it. And then?' She shrugged her shoulders, offering no answer to her own question. She gave Mahaki a copy of the article, written by Margaret Scott, about the novel.

Mahaki read that 'Maata' had been inspired by Katherine Mansfield's reading of D. H. Lawrence's powerful novel *Sons and Lovers*. She and Murry knew Lawrence and Frieda, and Lawrence had given them the novel when they were all on holiday at Broadstairs on the Kentish coast in 1913. Within days of reading the novel, on 2 August, Katherine Mansfield completed a thirty-five-chapter plan for 'Maata' and began work on it. The autobiographical nature of the projected novel was obvious but — at this point Mahaki began to feel puzzled — the article suggested that the heroine was based on Katherine Mansfield *herself*, although she gave her persona *Maata's* name.

The eight-page synopsis which Katherine Mansfield sketched out and two fragmentary chapters she wrote later in the year bore little structural and artistic resemblance to the masterly Lawrence novel which had been the spark — or even to Katherine Mansfield's own high standards. At the same time, Mahaki discerned some incipient inspiration from the style of the Russian aristocrat Marie Bashkirtseff, whose journals had earlier so influenced Katherine Mansfield and Maata.

The heroine, Maata/Katherine, living in London's Bohemia/Bloomsbury, is an ambitious woman, Beauty Incarnate, using her physical attributes and obvious charisma to advance her career as a singer, she craves luxury — 'I need these things. They help me, I can't sing if I'm draggled and poor' — and inhabits the realm of melodrama and heightened senses, of Sardou perhaps or Puccini. When she undresses her skin 'flames like yellow roses'. When she is magnificent or manipulative she is so with a capital M. Within the hot-house atmosphere of intrigue, passion, deceit and cruel love, Maata/Katherine is all-powerful, all-Goddess. She is a fatal beauty into whose fascinating web are drawn a number of cipher characters including 'Rhoda Bendall' who was modelled — so the article suggested — on Katherine Mansfield's devoted friend Ida Baker. But Mahaki conjectured that because the 'Maata' figure was so similar to the *real* Maata could not Rhoda be Katherine Mansfield herself? A Katherine — the lover who loves excessively — who was, possibly, as hopelessly bound to Maata as Ida was to Katherine?

Whatever the case, Mahaki found himself alternating between excitement and puzzlement. The excitement came from the news that the projected 'Maata' novel was now firmly established as a fact — and although the synopsis was cardboard there were enough fragments to suggest that the writing might have lent credibility to the character of Maata/Katherine. But as Mahaki continued to read the puzzlement increased. First, the synopsis dated from 1913 and Mahaki had understood that the novel which P. A. Lawlor had referred to was one dated 1915. Secondly, the synopsis appeared to be so unlike the MS described by the Maata whom P. A. Lawlor had met in 1941: *Without any hesitation, Maata said that she had the MS in her possession. It was an unfinished novel entitled 'Maata'. I asked her the approximate length. She replied 'about 60,000 words,' adding that the arrangement was that she (Maata) was to complete the story.*

As the days went by Mahaki became more and more convinced, though without any evidence to support his conviction, that there may well have been another, later, attempt by Katherine Mansfield to write a novel. If there had been, it may have looked back before the London meeting of two New Zealand women to the very beginnings of their friendship — a memoir of childhood, of two young girls Katherine/Kezia and Maata/Tui — trying to find their destinies in New Zealand. It could have been the companion piece to 'The Aloe', filled with similar enchantment and falling leaves, and a breathless sense of wonder. Certainly, it would have needed to have been a piece which a woman of high literary expectations, living in London, would fairly entrust to her only peer in New Zealand. Something central to their mutual experience.

Later Mahaki read that Katherine Mansfield's Journal of 1915 referred to 'a book' — first on 1 January of that year and then three days later: 'I make a vow to finish a book this month. I'll write all day and at night too and get it finished. I *swear*.' On 24 May of the same year, reference was made again: 'My book *marche bien*. I feel I could write it anywhere, it goes so easily and I know it so well. It will be a funny book.' The book could have been 'The Aloe' itself. But it could also have been 'Maata'. Ah yes, *I am a secretive creature to my last bone.*

3

1981 . . . MAORIS CLASH WITH POLICE AT WAITANGI . . .
DEMONSTRATIONS CONTINUE AGAINST SPRINGBOKS . . . MULDOON
RETURNS TO POWER . . . QUEEN VISITS . . . RONALD REAGAN ELECTED
PRESIDENT . . . BASTION POINT REKINDLED . . . DAVID LANGE IS
DEPUTY LEADER OF THE OPPOSITION . . .

Twenty-eight years after the incident at the river, and immediately following the physical and emotional maelstrom of the protest against
the Springboks at Hamilton, Mahaki received a letter from his Aunt
Iris. The letter was about his mother — and Maata — and when he
opened it *a flash of red danced and dazzled across his mind.* His aunt
wrote:

Dear nephew, tena korua te tama mo to hoa wahine, Huhana.

I pray that you and Susan are both well and that the baby, Edward,
is healthy. As for us up here in Hastings we are okay, although
your uncle got in the way of a policeman at the Springbok protest
last week. I told him he should wear a helmet like I do but he never
listens. The result is that he has ten stitches on his head, serves
him right. Not many people protesting this time, and it hurts to see
your relations going in the gate, but we stand by our principles.

Nephew, this is very hard for me. I have to tell you about a
family matter. It has to do with whakapapa — genealogy. I know
you've never been interested in this but it is something that we try
to keep up as Maoris. It is also part of the Mormon faith. Anyway
your whakapapa through your mother links you to some people
down in the Wairarapa. In particular it links you with a Mormon
chief who had six wives. He himself had no issue but his brother
did. The brother had a daughter from his loins, that woman, Maata
Mahupuku. This is why I knew about her when you were talking
to me a few years back.

Now I know I should have told you all this then but I was
afraid. First of all I got a shock when you told me about those red
shoes and I had to pray hard, really *hard*, nephew. Second, when
you said about that old lady dying in 1952 I thought, ka tika, the
dead to the dead, the living to the living. And third, if I had told
you I would then have needed to go on about my sister, your
mother Wai.

You know, Wai was a wonderful sister to me and I pray that God has found a special place for her in one of his many mansions. She was very staunch in her faith but it was a faith that was put to the test many times. The old people used to say that she was like *a lightning rod*, someone through whom others in our whakapapa could speak. You have to be Maori to know what I am saying. You have to be Mormon, also, to understand that death is not a separation of family. You know what I mean? Even when I was nursing her, as she was dying, others were still trying to talk through her. Trying to sort out old family things. Whakapapa unites us all and death is simply a veil between us.

I pray my sister will forgive me for telling you all this. But perhaps it will help to explain what you saw that day at the river. What puzzles me now is that I am involved — and I don't like it one bit. I have met a lady in the Church, about my age, called Bella and her old mother is a kuia whose name is Maata. It can't be the same one as Maata Mahupuku. But it could be a sister, a friend, or somebody. Anyway, I am coming to Wellington soon — this old kuia lives in the Hutt — so maybe you can be my mate and we can go to see her? Ka pai.

I pray that the Lord will watch over you and keep you and your family safe from all evil and harm.

Arohanui.

'*Amandla! Amandla Soweto!*' A week-and-a-half later Aunt Iris arrived in Wellington to support the protest being made that Saturday against the Wellington-Springbok match. She and Mahaki got prepared with helmets and padding. Susan was not able to join them because of baby Edward. Just before they left the house to join up with Mahaki's friends, Aunt Iris said a prayer. Then, as she picked up her banner she smiled — a radiant smile — and said, 'Isn't it a lovely day for a walk in the sun?' *Remember! Remember Steve Biko!* Five thousand protesters were out that day, linking arms and trying to storm through the police barriers to Rugby Park. Newtown became a war zone, with small attack groups trying to get through and to stop the game. Protesters were batoned in Constable Street and three girls were felled by flying beer bottles. Mahaki was astonished at the aggressive tactics of his aunt — she was always having a go at the police or at rugby supporters, trying to persuade them to join her side. 'Well,' she said, 'if we don't stand up to them we may as well just lie down and die.' The protest did not stop the game but, as Aunt Iris said later, 'We didn't lose. We survived to fight another day.' Her visor was smeared with spittle and blood. As their group broke up, three young men began to sing to the police lines: 'When constabulary duty's to be done, to be done, a policeman's lot is not a happy one . . . Amandla! Down with apartheid.' Aunt Iris grinned at them affectionately.

That evening Aunt Iris excused herself from eating dinner. She wanted to fast and pray again. Then she opened her suitcase and took out a grey suit, gloves and a hat. She said to Mahaki, 'Well, time for you to put on your coat and comb your hair,' and, oh, his breath caught with the memory of his mother and the day she had taken him to meet a woman who had once been her employer. 'Do you know the address?' Mahaki asked. Aunt Iris nodded. Susan saw them to the door, saying, 'Don't you two be late coming home.' She started to say something else, hesitated, and the moment was lost. Mahaki kissed her. Then he and Aunt Iris drove from Wellington City to the Hutt until, 'Well, here we are,' Aunt Iris said.

4

The house was like a giant lizard squatting across the suburban land-scape. It was two-storeyed weatherboard with two large upper windows like eyes looking out and over the Hutt River. It seemed appropriate that a woman born last century should live in this baroque building, so out of time with the flat, quarter-acre, state house sections surrounding it.

'Did my mother know about all this?' Mahaki asked. 'Sometimes I get the feeling that — ' Aunt Iris pursed her lips. 'Yes. Perhaps. Your mother never liked talking about the past. She was secretive that way.'

Mahaki went to say something but, all of a sudden, he noticed that there was a small diamond-shaped opening, like a third eye, between the two upper-storey windows. A woman was there, her face like a basilisk, observing their approach. Then she was gone.

Aunt Iris rang the doorbell and Mahaki had the feeling that someone was already there, on the other side of the door, waiting almost a hundred years, for his coming. The door opened and all the pent-up forces of the ages rushed out like wraiths to surround him.

'Why, hullo!' the woman said. The woman's greeting was too hearty to be spontaneous. She was in her early fifties, tightly corseted but otherwise well preserved. Her makeup was tasteful. 'It's lovely to see you again,' she greeted Aunt Iris. 'And this must be your nephew.' She clapped her hands together, complimenting herself on her clever-ness, and her mouth made a small round red O. 'My name's Bella,' she said, 'but you can call me Aunt Belle. Come in then, come in.' She ushered Mahaki and Aunt Iris into the hallway, her hands describing carefully choreographed movements of welcome. They were beautiful hands and Mahaki noticed throughout the evening that she was always drawing attention to them — as if someone had said to her once, 'Oh Bella, you have such fine hands.'

At the end of the hallway Mahaki glimpsed the face of the woman at the window. 'That's Ilona,' Bella whispered. 'You must excuse my sister, she's a very shy person. We don't get many visitors.' She called to her sister, 'Do we, Ilona?' The sound boomed along the hallway, and Ilona seemed to cower at the authoritarian tone. 'Ilona,' Bella confided, 'has looked after mother all her life. She devoted herself,' she said with dramatic emphasis, 'to caring for mother. I couldn't assist very much,' she continued, 'being married to Mr Forsythe. But when he died four years ago I was able to help out.' Bella laughed gaily. 'So here we are, a household of women, mother and her two daughters, just as we used to be when we were children.' Her lips creased in a command to her sister. 'Ilona? Are we taking tea in the front room? Good.'

Ilona stepped aside as Bella led Aunt Iris and Mahaki into the parlour. Mahaki smiled at her but she looked away. There was something strange about Ilona's appearance but it wasn't until ten minutes later that he realised what it was — although she looked nothing like Bella, Ilona had attempted to dress exactly like her sister and to copy her every movement. But no grace or dignity could ever mould Ilona's hands to Bella's balletic style.

'It's nice to see you again, Bella,' Aunt Iris said. Bella smiled and took a delicate sip of her tea. The small talk was stilted despite her best attempts. She rolled her eyes and addressed Mahaki. 'You could have knocked me down with a feather,' she said, 'when your aunt told me that you wanted to meet Mother. We don't know much about her life. Mother never talked to us about her childhood friends and about the Maoris.' She turned to her sister, 'Did she, Ilona? But we always knew that she loved you Maoris.' Her attitude was patronising as she patted Mahaki on the hand. 'Of course,' she proceeded, 'we always knew that Mother had been brought up in Wellington. We *think* she knew Katherine Mansfield — you know — the writer? But we're not sure. There was another Maori girl at the same school — she was a friend of Mother's also. Mother had a very colourful life, but she put all that behind her when she married Father,' Bella said firmly, closing the subject. 'Didn't she, Ilona?' The aforementioned Ilona took the trouble to nod in assent. She was watching her sister carefully and mimicked the movement of handkerchief applied to the corner of the mouth. However, whereas her sister merely dabbed, Ilona wiped, and smeared her lipstick across her cheeks.

'What a pity,' Bella continued, 'that you didn't come to see mother five years ago. Before she had her stroke. She loved a good conversation, did Mother, oh she was such a one.' 'Yes, she loved a good yack,' Ilona said, surprising them all with her intervention and her language. 'What a pity.' Her hands hovered over some peanut brownies before pouncing on the unfortunate choice.

It took some time for Bella to recover. Mahaki had the feeling that she wasn't used to Ilona being so forward; our Bella liked to keep company to herself. 'Mother used to be so lively. Goodness me, she kept us on our toes. And bright, my word, you couldn't put anything past her. Now she just lies there, just waiting for the day.' She averted her eyes and sighed. The effect was destroyed by Ilona, who copied the sigh but added in an exaggerated lugubrious tone. 'Yes, she'll be deader than a dormouse.' She slurped at her tea as if needing to wash away the thought. 'Ilona dear!' Bella said, 'The things you say!' She leant over to Mahaki and whispered, 'You mustn't mind our Ilona. She's a bit, well, *slow*.' Then she pressed his hand. 'Well,' she said, 'have we finished our tea then? Good. Then let's go up to Mother.' Ilona got up to accompany them. 'Not you, Ilona. Why don't you go into the kitchen.' Poor Ilona, she wilted like an unwanted weed.

Once upon a time the house must have been very gracious. Vestiges of its earlier glory still shone through the faded damask chairs, worn velvet curtains, and the dull crystal of the huge chandelier which was suspended above the spiral staircase. 'It's a bit of a climb,' Bella said as she pulled herself up along the handrail. 'Trust Mother to want to stay on the top floor.' Aunt Iris answered, 'That's okay, Bella, we're fit and young, and you're as slim as ever.' Bella giggled. 'When we were children,' she said, 'we used to call this place Faversham Castle —' 'Oh,' Mahaki said, 'after Miss Faversham in *Great Expectations*?' Bella paused and nodded to Auntie Iris. 'Isn't he clever? I should have known he would take after the family.' *Oh, Bella, flattery will get you everywhere.* 'Father had it specially built. It took four years. We've often tried to persuade Mother to sell, but she loves the monstrosity.' Then they reached the top of the stairs. The upstairs hallway was musty and dark. Mahaki had the feeling that he should tiptoe along the carpet — for an old lady lay in a room here and she was like porcelain which would break at the slightest vibration. 'Here we are,' Bella said. She began to turn the handle of the door. 'Come then,' she motioned as she opened it. 'This old house is full of draughts, and we don't want Mother to catch a cold, do we?'

The room was huge and overlit with strong lighting. It looked just like what it was — a room which had been renovated into a basic hospital unit. It was clinical. Antiseptic. Bare of all furniture except for a very high bed and some stainless steel chairs. No air circulated in the room. On a bedside table a small pink rose like a blood stain struggled to assert itself. Bella hustled Mahaki and Aunt Iris up to the side of the bed. 'Mother?' she shouted. 'Mother?' Her voice was a shock in that room, so large of tone and force. 'We have visitors.' She turned to Mahaki and giggled. 'Don't stand back,' she said. 'There's nothing wrong with Mother. It's just that she's *old*.' She turned to the woman lying in the bed. 'You can't help that, can you, Mother?' She giggled again and explained. 'That's just our little joke. Mother likes jokes.'

If this old woman had ever been beautiful that must have been many years ago. Age had stripped her of all those attributes which attract. There was no glorious hair to catch the light, no eyelashes, no artful curl of lips to give coquettishness to that face, and no lively flirtatious glint in those eyes. Instead, everything had been taken away leaving simply a skull over which skin had been stretched. Two black holes held the orbits of her eyes and her mouth was a slash of red. But in her way she was more than beautiful; she was unearthly because of the sheer alien quality of her appearance, and her skin was extraordinarily translucent. 'I've brought you some visitors,' Bella announced. 'We don't get many of those, do we? But they've come a long way just to see you. This is Iris and her nephew.' She spoke to Aunt Iris saying, 'Say something to Mother. Ask her something.'

'Tena koe, e kui,' Aunt Iris said. Bella was irritated. 'No, not in that lingo,' she said. 'Mother wouldn't understand. In English, say it in English.' So Aunt Iris said, 'Hullo, kui.' Pleased, Bella instructed, 'Now press her hand. Mother knows you're here. I can tell, I can tell.' She watched with prim satisfaction as Aunt Iris held the old woman's hand. 'And now you, boy. Press her hand. Press her hand.'

Aunt Iris stepped aside. She looked near to tears and she smiled at Mahaki reassuringly. Although the woman was lying beneath white blankets, her arms were lying at her side. There seemed very little substance to that body. Mahaki could feel himself recoiling from any physical touch. His hand hovered over hers. Then suddenly her eyes *flickered* up and locked his gaze. And her fingers reached up like a nightmare to interlock with his. Her nails were like claws digging into his. She seemed to be clinging to him with supernatural strength and, yet, her face remained unchanged and remote. Bella clapped her hands with glee. 'Oh,' she cried, 'Mother likes you, she really likes you.' Ah yes, and *Aunt Iris knew what was happening*, but Bella was not aware of Mahaki's struggle — for the old woman's hand was so *hot*, burning into his with excruciating and unbearable pain. He couldn't free himself. Then he began to hear the voice in his head, and it was like the voice of a *madwoman*.

5

Maata was well aware of the interest her association with K.M. aroused, and claimed to have sent her money, although there is no evidence of any contact after Katherine's return to Europe in 1908. A fragment of a diary kept by Maata was acquired by Ruth Mantz and is in Texas, and there was talk of a further manuscript, which she encouraged; even after her death in 1952 her daughter made mysterious reference to it, but nobody has ever produced it and it is almost certainly a piece of pure invention.

— Claire Tomalin, *Katherine Mansfield: A Secret Life*.

'You must be disappointed,' Aunt Iris said. 'I know how much you wanted to meet that old kuia. She wasn't the woman you were looking for was she? She certainly must have seen a lot in her lifetime.' Mahaki and Aunt Iris were driving back into Wellington. Behind them the house appeared again — a huge lizard crouched over its nest of aging women, protecting them against the ravages of time. It was midnight. 'It doesn't matter,' Mahaki said. 'Perhaps it's better this way.' Aunt Iris nodded. 'What a pity we didn't know about her five years ago. Before her stroke. When she was able to talk. I suppose we'll be saying "if only" for the rest of our lives, ay?'

Mahaki shivered. 'I don't think I want to live as long as her,' he said. 'She must be almost a hundred.' Aunt Iris was amused. 'Why not?' she smiled. 'There's nothing much you can do about it. You either do or you don't.' Mahaki shrugged. 'But you would see too much,' he said. 'Too much sorrow, too much pain, too much war. You would know too many secrets. The *burden*.'

Ah yes, the burden. The words tumbling out, spewing out, rushing out like flames from that old woman. *Knock knock who's there? Why it's a little Maori girl Will you be my friend? Such pretty shoes! Such tiny feet and perfect hands* But the voice not the old woman's voice. Instead a young voice like a ventriloquist's marionette *Fee fi fo fum I smell the blood of a Pa man Oh when I grow up I shall be a missionary and go among the Maoris like you are Away from papa Will you come with me? We can stay with Armena and Warbrick can guide us Oo oo I should be happy like I've never been before* Pouring out, flowing out, so many words flooding out of that ancient head with its black sockets and slash of mouth *Oh you are so adorable I could hate you for it   You minx   And you have such a beautiful script   Why, we could be writers together   Oh and have such dreams* The words licking through, flaming through those dried veins and burning through the portals of the heart   *Who comes knocking at my door?   Oh it's you   Oh hold me close hold me hold me   Touch me here and here and here   Oh The Pa man has found me out   Oh kiss me take me enter me and make us one   What a lovely thing night is let me kiss you   Oh your scent is spicy I shall remember just this moment I shall always remember what I like and forget what I don't like   How still and quiet it is   I wonder if there really is a God   You are God!   I shall worship you like this and this and this* So many, many words emptying out so quickly and yet not fast enough. Rippling through that tired body like a torrent from some volcanic furnace until, until —

Enough, Mahaki commanded. And he sent a sweet rain across the flames and began to flood the old woman with compassion. *It is time to forgive yourself.* There was no sign at all in the old woman's face. *I will make it right.* A small star appeared, gleaming at the corner of her eye.

'It *was* Maata, then, wasn't it?' Aunt Iris said. Her voice was fearful and frightened. In the rear-vision mirror, Mahaki caught a last glimpse of the old house. *Oh yes, whare taonga, noble house of treasures, guard and protect your women and your secret till world's end.*

'No,' Mahaki told his Aunt. 'Maata died a long time ago — remember? But this women was a kinswoman to Maata. A woman of great faith. A woman to whom Maata entrusted all her secrets.'

Ah yes, there had indeed been a manuscript — or so Maata had told this kuia — which had been sent to her to complete. Although Maata had been concerned because the manuscript was, in part, about passionate love between women, her vanity was flattered that her friend should still consider her an equal — twinned to her. She began to fulfil her part and, out of love, would have completed the manuscript except for one crucial event — the death of her beloved friend at the Gurdjieff Institute near Fontainebleau, France. *Suddenly a great gush of blood poured from her mouth.* When that happened the manuscript, which *was also* Katherine Mansfield, became a tupapaku — the dead Katherine — too, and all the more *tapu* for that. It was something which, in Maori tradition, would have been returned at the tangi — like a piece of greenstone or feather cloak — to be joined again with that person and taken with her to earth, as an act of honour and aroha.

But the manuscript was also *Maata* herself, who was still living. So she carried the burden of love, the tupapaku of Katherine all her years. At times she was tempted to reveal the manuscript, out of vanity, but her understanding of Maori beliefs and, then, her friendship with her Mormon kinswoman, sustained her in her vow that when *she* died the manuscript which was both Katherine *and* herself should be closed away with her like a jewelled locket. So it was done, and done well by the kinswoman.

'And the red shoes?' Aunt Iris asked. 'I think,' Mahaki said, 'that this old woman wanted someone to know. Someone to understand. Someone to carry the burden of knowledge — and responsibility — as she has done all these years. Although it was probably correct to bury the manuscript with Maata, it could not have been easy, especially in these days of the European. Burying the manuscript would not have been understood as the supreme acknowledgement it was to her friend.' Aunt Iris was silent a while. 'Well, your shoulders are broad enough. You can handle it.' Mahaki nodded, 'I suppose I can. I think though, Aunt, that this must have been like it was for my mother. To be the lightning rod and to bear the responsibility and burden forever. I understand her better now, and Te Rangi.'

Mahaki and Aunt Iris became reflective, the mood deepening between them. And Mahaki looked at his Aunt and it came to him that they were all secretive people — his mother, Te Rangi, Aunt Iris, Katherine Mansfield, Maata, Melvin, Susan and even he — and his very bones were flutes whistling and whispering of secrets like locked up voices whispering, whispering —

And he saw himself and Aunt Iris walking along the passageway of that ancient house, that tuatara sitting on its clutch of eggs. A door was opened and, as they were passing, Bella gave a gasp and began to shut it. 'Oh, that Ilona,' she said crossly. Ilona had been standing there in the dim light. She had put on a long dark Victorian dress and was admiring herself in a pysche mirror. Then she began to do a little curtsy, lifting her dress as she did so, her image bowing, bowing, bowing through a myriad reflections. 'She's always dressing up in Mother's clothes,' Bella said. And Ilona, unhearing, had smiled secretly to her image, lifting her dress a little further, and pointing her toes.

Suddenly an absurd memory had come into Mahaki's head — a cat glaring down at him from a hole in the roof. So it's done then? He gasped, a gasp of surprise. And when he looked back the door to Ilona's room had almost closed.

The following thirteen variations on Katherine Mansfield stories have been chosen from a number which were written during the period Christmas 1987 to the end of February 1988.

Most of the variations have been directly based on short stories as diverse as 'The Woman At The Store', 'Her First Ball', 'The Garden-Party' and 'The Doll's House'. Some have been less directly based on Katherine Mansfield themes — like the *New Age* 'Pension Sketches' — or the themes of 'Prelude' or 'At The Bay'. Then there are those which have taken their course from characters portrayed in such stories as 'Bliss' or the great New Zealand stories.

The variations were begun at Naragansett, Rhode Island, developed at East Hampton, Long Island, continued in New York and completed during a visit to Wellington and Gisborne, New Zealand. Thanks are due to Leni and Henry Spencer, Michael McGifford and Hugh Waltzer, and Marguerite Tait-Jamieson and Garrick Emms.

In all the variations the primary intention has not been to imitate Katherine Mansfield but, rather, to provide a modern response to the stories and the timeless themes which were their inspiration.

The Cicada

It was Saturday morning and Aroha had nothing to do. She'd made her bed, helped do the dishes, gone down to the shop to get Queenie a packet of smokes, and was now sitting at the upstairs window watching the traffic roar and *vroom* up and down the road. At the back of the flat she could hear Queenie's ghetto-blaster rocking out Michael Jackson, and Queenie singing along, 'You know I'm bad, I'm bad, you know it, you know I'm bad, I'm bad . . .' Queenie was doing the washing, the washing-machine going *shuck shuck shucks* and Queenie swearing occasionally because she hated washing clothes. Not only that but Henare had just gone down the road for a minute — and three hours had passed.

Queenie was Aroha's big sister, the eldest, and Aroha had come down from Gisborne to stay with her and Henare in Newtown, Wellington. Aroha had been excited at first, coming to the capital on the plane, and the air hostess had given her a lolly to suck. The holidays were on and Queenie had taken Aroha to the zoo, into Wellington to look at the shops and down to the video centre to get some movies out over the weekends. But Henare only liked murders or horrors and Aroha would get frightened watching them. 'Then go to sleep, babe,' Queenie would growl. But Aroha would shake her head because she was frightened that while Queenie was watching television Freddy might come up the stairs and murder her in her bed.

Then Queenie had to go back to work and Mum had rung from the Coast saying, 'You stay with Queenie for a while, babe. Me and Papa want to go to Rotorua.' Aroha's other sister, Francesca, was having her first baby and Mum wanted to be with her when the baby was born. That was two weeks ago. The holidays had finished. With Queenie at work and nobody to play with, there was nothing much else to do except watch television and to wait till six o'clock when Queenie got back home. At least at home Aroha could have played with her brother, Rangi, who was seven. Whenever she had nothing to do there was always Rangi. She had nothing to do right now; but Rangi was a long way away.

As she sat at the window Aroha heard children laughing in a house across the street. She craned her head to look and saw three little girls race out of the yellow house onto the pavement. One of the girls bent to the ground and began drawing squares with a piece of chalk. Another had a tennis ball and was bouncing it up and down. 'Hurry up! Hurry up!' the third girl yelled. Aroha knew that girl, but not very well. She had seen her across the playground at school — Queenie had taken her to Newtown Primary and enrolled her temporarily — and her name was Denise something-or-other. Aroha watched the girls and wondered whether they would let her join them if she went down. She didn't think they would; she had asked them once before and they had pretended she wasn't there. Still, there were only three girls and you needed four to play four square properly. Maybe they would let her join them this time? Should she go down now? No — she would wait. She didn't want to be hurt again. This time she'd make sure first. Perhaps they might even see her and invite her to join.

'Aroha? Aroha!' Aroha heard Queenie calling to her. 'Yes?' she yelled back. 'Come here a minute!' Queenie called. 'Okay,' Aroha responded. She leapt down from the window and along the corridor to the bathroom where Queenie was rinsing out the clothes. Over the noise of the ghetto-blaster Queenie yelled, 'I want you to help me hang out the clothes.' Aroha nodded, picking up the pegs. 'And this afternoon you can go to the two o'clock pictures,' Queenie continued. 'Are you coming too?' Aroha yelled. 'Ay?' Queenie asked, turning off the ghetto-blaster. 'ARE YOU COMING TOO?' Aroha repeated. 'Gee, babe,' Queenie said, 'you don't have to shout — ' She took up the clothes basket and went down the stairs. 'No, I'm going to have a sleep. But you'll be okay.' Queenie's slippers looked like little pink rabbits hopping from one stair to the next.

Aroha was silent as she followed Queenie with the clothes pegs. She didn't like going to the pictures by herself. She only felt lonely sitting in the middle of all those other kids. She needed someone to scream and laugh with, and to have an ice cream with at interval. And once a man had sat beside her and asked her if she wanted a lolly. So, as Queenie started to hang the clothes, Aroha screwed up her face and said, 'No, I think I'll have a sleep with you too.' Back home in Gisborne, before Queenie met Henare, Queenie would always call Aroha, 'Babe, you can sleep with me tonight.' And Aroha would run and jump in beside her sister. 'Ooh,' Queenie would sigh, 'you're better than an electric blanket!' And they would cuddle each other and go to sleep all safe and warm. Then Henare had come along and changed everything.

Over the past two weeks the two sisters hadn't had much time together. Queenie worked way over the other side of town as a secretary — everybody in Gisborne was really proud of her — but that meant leaving the house by seven thirty every morning. Henare would have gone by then — he worked for the council — and sometimes Queenie didn't have time for breakfast. 'You help yourself, babe, I gotta rush,' Queenie would say, giving Aroha a kiss and a hug. Sometimes Aroha would go to the bus stop with Queenie to be a mate until the bus came. She always felt sorry when Queenie stepped inside and waved. School didn't start till five to nine so on the first mornings Aroha would stay at the bus stop watching the people getting on and off. She would sometimes smile and get smiled back at, or say hello. But most of the people ignored her, and when one man had growled at her for being cheeky she stopped staying at the bus stop. Instead she began to dawdle-walk her way to school, looking at the shops. Sometimes some other girls would tell her to join up with them, and then she was okay. But most of the time there was just herself, looking at her reflection in the windows. Then school would start and it was okay but sometimes friends were hard to make in the playground. Most of the girls already had other friends and forgot to ask Aroha if she wanted to join them. After school was the worst because it finished at five to three and Queenie didn't get back from work until five thirty. So Aroha would have to wait on the doorstep till it was almost dark — and then, there would be Queenie, waving and grinning, 'Hi, babe, have a good day at school?' Aroha would nod. As long as her sister was *there* she was content.

'Thank goodness,' Queenie sighed as she hung the last underpants on the line. She turned the washbasket upside down, sat on it and said, 'Shucks, my hands are wet. Put a smoke in my mouth and light it for me, babe?' Aroha got a cigarette from the packet in Queenie's jeans, put it between Queenie's lips and lit it. Queenie closed her eyes, drew and 'Aaaaah,' she sighed as she breathed out. 'What are you going to do now?' Aroha asked. 'I'll go and wash my hair in a minute,' Queenie answered, 'but right now all I want to do is give my bum a rest.' Puff puff went the smoke. 'Shall I make us a cup of tea?' Aroha asked. Queenie shook her head. Then she looked at Aroha with softness and said, 'Come here, babe, come and sit by me.' And Aroha ran into her arms. Queenie stroked Aroha's hair. 'Won't be long before you have a boyfriend,' Queenie said. 'Ooo yuk,' Aroha said. 'Have you ever tried having your hair up, babe?' Queenie asked. 'My neck is too short,' Aroha said. Queenie laughed, saying, 'Better to have a short neck than a black one!' The two sisters grinned at one another. Queenie took another draw on the smoke. She noticed that one of the sheets was still a bit dirty — too bad, Henare wouldn't notice. Then she kissed Aroha on the forehead. 'You okay now?' Aroha nodded. 'You told those blues to go away?' Aroha nodded again. 'You like it here, don't you, with me and Henare?' Queenie asked.

Aroha was silent. Then she sighed. 'I miss Rangi,' she said. 'Huh?' Queenie laughed. 'You two are always squabbling!' Aroha said again, 'I miss Rangi.' Queenie paused, and then, 'Well, won't be long now before you go back home,' she said. 'Is school the trouble?' Aroha played with her hair. 'It's all right,' she answered. 'Some of the kids are funny though.' Queenie asked, 'How funny?' Aroha said, 'Sometimes I have nobody to play with me.' Queenie kissed Aroha again. 'Well, won't be long.' For a moment she was silent. Then she stood up and threw her smoke over the fence. 'No rest for the wicked,' Queenie laughed. 'And look at the time! You want some lunch?' Aroha nodded and, 'Can I help?' she asked. 'Nah,' Queenie answered. 'I'll just nuke us a pizza in the microwave.' Then Queenie reached into her jeans pocket. 'Tell you what though, babe, can you go down the dairy for me? We need some milk and — here — you get an ice cream too. By the time you get back the kai will be ready. Okay?'

Aroha took the money, ran through the house, and out the door to the gate. The three girls were still playing four square on the pavement opposite and, for a while, Aroha watched them. Then one of the girls looked back at her. 'What *you* staring at,' she yelled. Aroha looked away, embarrassed. She ran down to the dairy, bought the milk and an ice cream. Then she dawdled back along the pavement. She took the milk in to Queenie and returned to the street to watch the girls again. She saw the girls whispering to each other and, all of a sudden, Denise waved to her to come over. Aroha ran across the road, to join them but, 'We don't like people who stare at us,' Denise said. 'It puts us off our game.' The other two girls nodded in agreement. Aroha tried to brave it out. 'You're playing four square, ay?' she said. 'Isn't she clever,' one of the girls retorted. Her companions giggled. 'There's only three of you playing,' Aroha pointed out. 'So?' Denise asked. 'Nothing. I just thought — ' The girls ignored her and resumed their game. 'Do you want a lick of my ice cream?' Aroha asked. 'Ooooo,' one of the girls said, screwing up her face, 'you might have germs. All Maoris have germs.' Aroha stood her ground. 'We do *not*.' One of the other girls sniffed. 'Yes you do,' she said. At that, Aroha ran towards Denise and yanked *hard* on her hair. Denise screamed and fell to the ground, crying. The two other girls backed away from Aroha, frightened. They helped Denise up and, together, they all ran back into the yellow house. Feeling better, Aroha crossed the street to her flat and rushed upstairs. 'Is that you, babe?' Queenie yelled. 'Yes,' Aroha answered. 'Lunch won't be long now,' Queenie said.

Sitting on the window ledge, Aroha gradually began to calm down. She heard a buzzing sound and saw a cicada alight on the sill near her left hand. Breathlessly she watched it, afraid that it might fly away. But the wings folded and the cicada started to chirrup. For a while she listened to it and, as she did so, she began to remember her home in Gisborne, Mum and Dad and Rangi . . . and she reached out and enclosed the cicada in her cupped hands. The cicada felt all *tickly* inside as it tried to find a way out. It was silent and would not sing.

Still holding the cicada, Aroha saw an empty Marmite jar on the dressing-room table. She went and picked it up and brought it back to the window ledge. She imprisoned the cicada underneath the jar. 'Sing, kihikihi, sing,' she commanded the cicada. Instead, the cicada started to search for a way out, pressing its legs against the glass. Then it tried to fly, but there was no room for it to lift. 'You're a long way from home too, hikikihi,' Aroha whispered. 'I think I might keep you here for a mate, ay?' The cicada was becoming frantic, trying to fly and to find a way out all at the same time.

Suddenly, Aroha heard a door *slam* and saw Denise with a big red-faced lady. Denise was pointing up at Aroha where she sat in the window. The lady compressed her lips, instructed Denise to go inside, and began to walk across the street. Denise struck a triumphant pose before turning.

Bang, bang, *bang* went the woman at the door. Aroha heard Queenie going to answer it. There were raised voices in argument. And Aroha began to feel both frightened and lonely. All she wanted to do was to go home. Away from here. Away.

And Aroha took the glass away from the cicada and quickly said to it, 'Fly away, kihikihi, fly away.' But the cicada was so weak. It just lay there. 'Fly away, fly AWAY,' Aroha repeated. She blew softly on the cicada, trying to revive it.

The door *slammed* downstairs. 'Aroha? Pae kare — ' she heard Queenie say. 'Oh please, kihikihi,' Aroha said. The cicada's wings unfolded and blurred. And as Queenie ascended the stairs, Aroha felt herself lifting away with the cicada as it flew up into the sky.

Cat and Mouse

This was absurd. Here he was, George Campbell, thirty-three and a grown man of braw Scots descent, tiptoeing around his small London bedsitter like a — a common burglar. Yet didn't he pay the rent for this room? And shouldn't that allow him to make as much noise as he wanted to? Och, George, you're a man aren't you? Look under your kilt, there's proof enough there! Put your shoes back on and dinna ye care if the floorboards crreakk. You pay good money for the privilege of doin' what ye like in your own rrroom.

But instead here was a mouse of a man, in his little mousehole of a room, frightened to even move from the armchair: George Campbell, from New Zealand, wanting to make a cup of tea on this cold English afternoon but afraid of the noises from clinking cup and saucer. Scarcely even daring to breathe because Mavis might hear him. Mavis who was nothing but the charlady — ah, but dear, sweet Mavis! — who thought that he had gone out for the day when he had not. He was *in*.

Just fifteen minutes before, George had put on a scarf and hat, intending to take a constitutional walk in the park. He had been locking his room when Mavis's face had appeared between the banisters of the second-floor landing. She looked like a lovely marmalade cat up there, her orange hair and red lips all shining and sleak. And she had smiled at him, her little black eyes folding into the creases. 'You goin' out then?' she had asked. 'Yes, Mavis,' he had answered. 'See you later!' She had waved her dirty polishing rag at him and "ave a nice walk,' she had said. On that note, George had walked jauntily to the front door, opened it, seen what the weather was like — even the dogs were wearing jackets — and had changed his mind. Typical English weather, like dirty washing water complete with Rinso clouds.

George had let the front door *shut* and was walking back to his room — and that was when he had heard Mavis talking to that Henderson chappie on the next floor. 'Between you an' me, Mister 'enderson,' she was saying in that lovely confidential tone of hers, 'we shoulden' let all these foreigners into Ol' Blighty! Dir'y the lot ov 'em, dir'y. They come over 'ere wivvout a mind-your-leave and what do they do, eh? I'll tell you, Mister 'enderson, they stick at 'ome and just

64

lay abaht, that's what! Take that fella on the groun' floor. Now 'e's an
example ov what I'm sayin' in that dark fella. You know what 'e do?
'e lays abaht, that's what 'e do! Day and night, night and day, 'e doesn'
do nuffing. You mark my words, Mister 'enderson, 'e'll be going on the
Social Securi'y next. Just like them uvver West Indians. They
shoulden' be let in the country. I mean, it's not right, is it? We pay
for 'em out of our own taxes, Mister 'enderson! You mark my words.
We pay for the 'ole bloomin' lot of 'em.'

George had been stunned. Knocked for a six. Thrown into a tizz.
His ears had burnt down to little furry crisps. He hadn't meant to
overhear but — Mavis, who he had thought was his friend, saying such
things about *him*! And to Henderson of all people! Why, it had only
been that very morning that Mavis had confided the very latest about
Henderson to George — 'Just between you an' me, Mister Campbell,
that Mister 'enderson, oo, 'e's just dir'y, an' 'is wife is ever so common.
Common as dirt she is, an' I should know dirt when I see it 'cos I work
in it all day, don' I! If this was my 'ouse I woulden' let 'er pass fru the
front door, not me, I woulden'. Not on your Nelly! Whereas you,
Mister Campbell, you've got class.'

Mavis and Henderson had gossiped on and on. George had put the
key into his door and turned it. Had they heard upstairs? No, for dear
Mavis's voice sang on and on. George had crept softly into his bedsitter and closed the door behind him. Now, here he was, his feet up
off the floor, sitting in the armchair and trying to be as quiet as a
mouse. Och, George, where's your Scottish spirrit, man! Get up,
George, and confrront the pesky woman. Give her a piece of yourrr
mind. Let her have it with both barrrels, RRREPORRRT HER! After all,
George man, she's not a woman, she's a charrrwoman. There's a
grrreat difference, man! A common cleaner, George, that's all she is!
Och, George Campbell, dinna ye hearrr the bagpipes calling ye to
battle? Listen to ye Campbell bluid, man. Get up, George, get up.
You're a sorry excuse for a Scotsman.

George closed his eyes and put his hands to his ears to stop the
voice inside him. When he opened his eyes he caught a glimpse of
himself in the cheval mirror. He saw a small pink face, with sniffing
nose and tiny whiskers, and little paws wiggling just under the chin.
Oh, the little pink face said to itself, why didn't you go out into the
cold and rain? Why?

George was a composer of classical music for the organ. He had
come to London to further his career. He had been in the city five
months before he found the bedsitter. It had been one of a number
advertised on a small white placard in a flat-letting agency, to wit:

HIGHGATE: b/s kitch. fac., lin. supp.,
2 min. from Tube, sleep one, visitors
no ob., £5 p.w., NO MICE

For a minute, George had wondered whether NO MICE meant that mice should not apply or, perhaps, that mice — as pets like dogs, cats or goldfish — or as visitors, were not allowed. But the woman who worked in the agency soon put him right. 'Oh no,' she laughed, 'what it means is that the bedsitter doesn't *come* with mice. It doesn't have any of the little beasties running around! You know, like on four legs? But if you *want* a bedsitter with mice we can certainly let you have one — cheaper, of course — and some people don't seem to mind,' she had added. 'No? Then are you interested in the Highgate accommodation? Oh jolly good.'

So it was that George went to meet the landlord, Major Reginald Halcombe, ex-India, who acted as if he was renting Buckingham Palace. 'This is one's kitchen,' Major Halcombe said, pulling aside a curtain, behind which was a tiny stove and basin with one cold tap. 'Should one require hot water, one heats it,' Major Halcombe continued, showing George the meter, 'by inserting the correct amount of pence for the required supply of gas.' Then Major Halcombe waved vaguely and said, 'And this is one's bedroom,' his wave encompassing the entire room. 'One has a bed — here' — tapping it with his cane — 'a bedside table — here' — another tap — 'a light and mirror full-length' — two staccato taps — 'and for one's visitors one has a couch, very comfortable, seating two.' During all this, all that George could think of was that his mother would have a *fit*. She hadn't wanted him to come to London, not with all those brazen English women waiting to get their clutches on her son. Nor would she have approved at all of one small bed in an L-shaped room, a small stove and dingy wallpaper, toilet down the hall and bathroom three flights up. 'And of course,' Major Halcombe coughed, 'one's accommodation has NO MICE.' This was delivered with suitable Elgarian pomp and circumstantial swagger. 'Is one interested?' George had nodded weakly that, yes, one was. After all, one was fearful of the wee tim'rous beasties and one's mum and cat were no longer at hand to pounce.

Two weeks later, George moved in. Mavis had pounced five minutes after he had shut the door. There had been a loud and insistent rapping and, when he had opened to the caller, there she was. 'I'm Mavis,' she said, squinting through her glasses. 'Oo are you?' It was, for George, love at first sight. Stammering, he introduced himself. 'A colonial eh?' Mavis responded with a Lord-Preserve-Us-All look.

'An' wot do you do!' George told Mavis that he was a composer, and straight away she thought he was famous. 'What you say your name was?' she asked suspiciously. 'George Campbell,' George said. She digested this for a second and, her suspicions confirmed, said, 'Never 'eard of you.' Then she gave him a nod, looked in to make sure he hadn't brought a woman with him, and left.

Not, perhaps, the most auspicious start to a relationship, but matters soon became more cordial. After all, Mavis came Mondays, Wednesdays and Fridays — and George was invariably in. He would hear her *slam* the front door on entering, *mutter* as she hung up her coat, *thump* as she went down to the basement to collect mop, bucket, polishing rag and toilet supplies, and then *umph, umph, umph* as she trod her weary way past his bedsitter and up the stairs to the top, fourth, floor. This occurred on those mornings right on the dot of eleven and, 'Good morning, Mavis!' George would call. It had been obvious, in the beginning, that Mavis was unused to such courtesies because she would appear startled and clutch her purse. But after a while she had relaxed a little and, 'There's nuffink good abaht it,' she would mutter — which was at least a start.

Working from the top floor, Mavis's responsibilities were to hoover the carpet, polish the banisters, clean out the toilet (one per floor), ensure there was always a supply of pink toilet paper for each 'convenience' and do the bathroom on the third floor — the job she hated most because 'There's enough 'air in the plugholes of a mornin' for me to go into wigmakin'.' All this she did with an air of resignation and martyrdom and amid long, sighing conversations with herself: 'I 'ave to live, 'aven' I?' Mavis also supplied clean sheets, linen, tea and bath towels every Friday afternoon to all the tenants. On this day she had extra duties — she was *supposed* to make the beds and clean out the rooms. But she never had to do this for George, for his mother had brow-beaten him that if you slept in a bed you made it yourself. If you had a room you tidied it yourself. Cleanliness was next to Godliness. It was referred to in the Bible — the King James Version.

It was on this matter of Friday afternoon room cleaning that George scored his breakthrough with Mavis. Whereas George — and most of the other tenants — would tell Mavis, 'We'll do our rooms, Mavis!' there was one in particular, a certain Mr Henderson, who insisted that Mavis clean *his* room and make his and Mrs Henderson's matrimonial bed. Mavis was always complaining about it. 'I've enough to do 'aven' I? 'oovering out the 'all and polishin' all them brass fings. 'oo does 'e fink he is — the bloomin' King or somefink? 'e's jus' dir'y, that's wot 'e is, *dir'y*. An' you know what 'e does while I'm doin' 'is room? 'e just sits there in 'is armchair an' I 'ave to move 'is bloomin' feet to 'oover under 'im! Wot's 'e got a wife for, I'd like to know! Bof ov 'em are just dir'y an' worse than that, they're mean. Bof ov 'em.' Ah yes, if it hadn't been for Henderson, George and Mavis would not have got on so well. They had become conspirators, united against a common foe. But now Mavis had gone over to the other side, into Henderson's camp! What had George done wrong?

It soon became established practice for Mavis, after she had finished her work on a Friday, to drop in and have a cup of tea with George. At first she had done this with some reluctance, fearing for her womanhood and that George would serve Darjeeling, but once she realised that there was no danger of either, she began to relax. She told George that she had been born within earshot of Bow Bells and had been employed in what she called 'the secon' oldest profession in the world' all her life. She was a Cockney, of course, swallowing her aitches with remarkable relish and substituting a hiccup on almost every 'th' sound. But that only made her more endearing to George, because the Cockneys, like the Scots and Welsh, were the true sons and daughters of Albion. All in together, Scots wha hae, and all that.

Oh, and had Mavis seen *life*! 'My first place of employ,' she told George as she munched on a muffin, 'was wiv the late Major Plummer. You 'eard of 'im? Course I was young then, in me bloom. 'e was ever so nice, the old duck, but you 'ad to watch 'im all the same. You know' — and Mavis gave a knowing nod — 'always wanting to pinch me rear end, 'e was! Anyway, I was wiv 'im for, oo, six years? Then the old lad ups and dies, and I'm stuck wiv 'is two sisters. Old like. Spinsters.' This was said with another knowing look and slurp of tea. 'Well we never go' on at all. I mean they was like Mister 'enderson! And their names, 'ere's a laugh — Regina and Georgette! I used to cook for 'em too. But they could never make up their minds 'ow they wanted to 'ave their eggs — soft- or 'ard-boiled. Used to get their knickers in a twist just trying to make a decision.' Another sip of tea. 'And what's more,' said Mavis, straightening her back, '*they* had mice.' A prim expression. 'I 'ad to leave, of course. Their nephew, Martin, slipped me a fiver to come and do for 'im. So I did. Oh, those were the days!' Then Mavis would look around her present surroundings, and there was no doubt that she had fallen, really *sunk* and gone into decline from favour and grace. 'And now look at me,' she would mourn. 'But I 'ave to live, 'aven' I?'

It was always difficult for George to visualise Mavis as she said she had been — slim, well proportioned, pretty and 'wiv the best ankles this side of oranges and lemons.' For a sixty-year-old woman she was still in pretty good condition, though her proportions had all slipped below her waistline, and her ankles had gone out the window. Not that you ever looked that far, as it was her face that commanded attention — small, extremely mobile, with eyes that almost disappeared when she smiled — and the extraordinary marmalade colouring of her hair. Mavis was very particular about her hair and regarded it as her crowning glory. That may have been the case once, but no longer. Orange hair is orange hair, glorious or no.

George had become the audience of Mavis's dreams. 'Cor, Mister Campbell,' she would say, 'there's been some proper goin's on 'ere, I can tell you!' Then Mavis would look around to make sure nobody else was in the room — like the FBI or Scotland Yard — beckon George nearer with a finger and tell him all about it. 'Free people 'ave died in this 'ouse, Mister Campbell, *free*. One of 'em, poor old soul she was, I was just talkin' to 'er like I am to you an' — poof — she went just like *that*. Right in the middle of a sentence, Mister Campbell' — a giggle — 'an' I been wondering ever since what she was goin' to say!' A pursing of lips. 'An' then there was the boy in the next room before you come. 'e was on drugs. Cor, the fings we found after 'e kicked the bucket! You never seen the like — 'yperdermic needles, cotton wool, rubber tubes — 'e was an addic' you know.' A righteous look. 'And then there was 'er — with a toss of her head — 'upstairs. I took one look of 'er when she come 'ere an' I sez to meself, "Mavis, that one's on the game an' make no bones about it." Well, Mister Campbell, she was. Men visitin' day in and night out. She must have made a packet and then' — a hint of the macabre in Mavis's eyes — 'she disa*ppeared* Mister Campbell, just disappeared, and there was this awful smell from 'er room. Well, Major 'alcombe 'ad to 'ave the door broken down, didn' 'e! An' what did they find? They found 'er, lying on the floor. Dead. Oo, gives me the shivers just finkin' abaht it.'

At some point in Mavis's life there must have been a husband. Mavis always wore a cheap wedding ring and referred to herself as a 'widder'. She intimated that she had lost a daughter but, over a subsequent cup of tea, mentioned a grandson — which was most puzzling. Indeed, there were a lot of gaps in Mavis's life — and lots of colouring-in of the gaps too. George soon realised that he should not look for consistency of account or the *bald* truth. That only made him love Mavis all the more, even if the voice in his head tried to caution him. George man, the woman is a cheat, a liarr and, what's worrse, she makes up stories! Nivver have I everrr hearrrd such nonsense! Such dishonesty! Such telling of tall tales, man! Gi'e up on her, Georrrge, gi'e up on her.

The trouble was that George couldn't. George really felt that he and Mavis were getting along well. He began to look forward to her visits, and they got longer and longer. Mavis was never one to hold back, and once, in the middle of chocolate cake, asked, "ow come you're so dark?' The question was bound to come up, as Mavis's major flaw was that she didn't like West Indians. 'I have Maori blood in me,' George explained. 'Is that some sor' of disease or somefink?' Mavis asked. George told her about Polynesians. Mavis put down her chocolate cake and, 'Just like them uvver West Indians,' she said. That shocked George a bit and he asked her, 'What's wrong with West Indians, Mavis?' Mavis had the decency to look guilty. Her podgy hand, at that moment, was hovering over a piece of lemon meringue pie, and her decision was reflected in the way that hand pounced on it. 'Nuffink, really, I suppose,' Mavis said hurriedly.

It had become obvious that one should keep off the subject of race — but Lord knows, George had tried to convince Mavis that her unbelievably sweeping generalisations about West Indians (and Spaniards, Italians and everyone who was not British) marked her forever an imperialist. Being British was Better, and nothing could persuade Mavis otherwise.

But while the relationship was strained on that score, there were other 'fings' which made it happier. For instance, on one occasion, George had shown Mavis his photograph album. He had taken lots of photographs of London — to show his mum in New Zealand when he returned — and he and Mavis had spent a long afternoon viewing the album. 'Where's that, Mavis?' George would ask. 'Buckin'am Palace!' she would answer. 'Where's this?' he would point. ''yde Park!' she would say. 'And this?' George would point again. 'The Chelsea 'ouseboats!' Mavis had loved that game and it had led her to suggesting where else George should visit while in London. ''ave you been to 'ampton Court? No? Cor, you 'ave to go there! An' 'ow abaht Kew Gardens? It'll be beautiful this time of year with all them flahrs bloomin'. Me 'ubby used to take me there when we was first living togevver. An' 'ave you seen the Crown Jools? Ooh, wish they'd throw some over 'ere!' Oh, George and Mavis had been getting along so fine and — now — oh, *why* hadn't he gone out the door?

George felt shattered. He heard Mavis coming down the stairs, umph, umph, *umph*. Obviously Henderson was going out and Mavis was following him. The walls were paper-thin, and Mavis was still moaning on and on. 'They're jus' dir'y, Mister 'enderson, dir'y. Even '*im*, that calls 'imself Campbell. 'im Scots wiv all that tar in 'im? Huh! You mark my words, 'e'll be down at the Social Security, drawin' national assistance! Spongin' on us all! I mean, I know they got to live same as I do, but why don't they get themselves jobs? Why doesn't 'e' — and Mavis banged on the wall — 'get a job! 'e should go back to where 'e comes from.' Then it appeared that Henderson had got his coat on. There were mumbling sounds. Then Mavis's voice returned 'Oh, *fank* you, Mister 'enderson, ever so ta! 'ave a nice walk!' The door slammed as Henderson went out. After a while, George heard Mavis humming and — umph, umph, *umph*, — going back up the stairs.

Oh, what was George to do? *George, man, confrrront the pesky woman!* But I love her. *George, it's your last chance!* But I don't want to hurt her feelings. She's gone through so much! *But listen, man, if you don't, she'll eat you alive!* But I like her, and who else will come to tea on Friday? *Oh, George, are you man or mouse!*

George suddenly caught sight of himself in the cheval-glass again. Oh dear, oh dear. Was it his imagination or was that really a cute wee tail curling out from his trousers? And what about those long whiskers and little pink eyes? Hmmmn, squeak, squeak, he didn't look so bad after all, *squeak.*

Then it came to George what to do. He would jump off the arm-chair and scamper to the door of the bedsitting room. As quiet as a mouse, he would open it, look quickly out to see if the coast was clear and sniff his way to the front door. He should open the door, stand outside for a moment and then come in. That was it!

So, according to plan, George put on his coat, sneaked out of the house and stood for half a minute on the doorstep. Then, rattling the key in the lock and opening the door as loudly as he could, he entered. *George, man, this is your last —*

An orange marmalade cat appeared at the landing. 'Back so early?' the cat smiled. 'Yes, it's so cold out,' the little mouse squeaked. 'Will you be coming to tea on Friday?' The marmalade cat stroked her whiskers and picked at her sharp teeth. 'Oh, you couldn' keep me away,' she purred.

The Boy with the Camera

At her wits' end, the woman bought her son a camera. There, she said, go out and photograph the hills or trees or pond or birds, anything, but just *go*. The boy looked up at her with a hurt hang-dog expression. He picked up the camera and, because he loved his mother, aimed and — *click* — took his first-ever photograph — of his mother's tired, red and swollen face.

The woman had been living alone with her son for two years, her husband having deserted them both. She managed the motel that her husband had bought. In the middle of nowhere, on a cardboard plain two hundred miles out from the nearest town, the motel comprised an office and five double bedroom units — the woman and her son lived in one of the units. Apart from the motel, sitting there beside the black highway, there was nothing else to see except wave upon wave of yellow tussock grass patched with stunted trees like babies' fingers reaching up out of the parched earth. Just the motel, that black line slicing the plain in half, and the sea of *nothing*.

The motel had been built five years before by a huge brewery firm from the other side of the country. The firm had noted that the highway connected the city with a fabulous mountain resort three hundred miles away. Justifiably, perhaps, the firm had considered that a motel equidistant between city and mountains would do good business. What the firm had not counted on was that the package weekenders offered by city travel agents — including air commuter service to and from the resort — would be a more attractive, cheaper and quicker alternative for travellers. Indeed, the only people who used the road were those who did it once out of curiosity — and never again, the large service trucks taking plant to and from the resort, and itinerant Maori workers with nowhere to go. But very few people actually stopped at the motel, and if they did, they only stopped overnight — truck drivers needing a pit stop, or travelling salesmen needing a break. The television reception was poor, the units substandard, the refrigerators were not always working, there was no breakfast service — and then there were the woman and her son. There was something about both of them which was unpleasant, somehow depressing and *real*.

The Boy with the Camera

Once, the woman had worked in an upmarket bar in the city. In those days she had been as pretty as a wax doll and her figure and lascivious nature had made her popular with the local clientele. The woman had not minded being dated if the fella was good-looking, and she herself boasted that she knew one hundred and fifty-five different ways of kissing. But the woman was only attractive when she was young, and in her early thirties she began to look for some man who might marry her. She found a fine big chap with a voice on him like a trombone, but little upstairs. They married, produced a scrawny son and lived in a constant state of warfare. Her husband would disappear for nights on end and she, in retaliation, began to indulge in small infidelities. She was careless and that was when the beatings began. Nine years later she had been reduced to this: a woman who resembled a hungry bird, a thing of sticks and wires, chipped teeth and red pulpy hands. Certainly her eyes were still blue and what hair she had was as yellow as ever, but ugly. As for the boy, he looked a gangling youth, slack-jawed and dark-eyed. He followed his mother everywhere because he adored her so.

The motel was an oven in summer and a freezer in winter. Summer was worse because all day the heat was terrible. The wind blew close to the ground; it rooted among the tussock grass, slithered along the road and parched everything. Just behind the motel was a small copse of shaded trees and a little pond. Hundreds of larks shrilled there every morning, screaming a short time and shooting like poisonous darts through the slate sky.

When the woman's husband had accompanied the brewery's sales agent out to the motel, his decision to buy had been as much determined by that little copse as by the dreams of making big money — the sales agent was a slick talker and knew a sucker when he saw one. With the sale documents in his hands, the husband couldn't wait to tell his wife what he had done and that they were on their way *up*. Did you look at the occupancy rate? she asked. No. How about the monthly takings? No, but the agent assured me that the motel was a goer under the right management, and there were a lot of big trucks on the highway.

Unconvinced, the woman allowed herself to be driven across the plain. As soon as she saw the motel she knew her husband had been taken. She asked her husband to stop on a small rise just above the motel. Well, she said, looking down at the huddle of buildings which was going to be her prison, you've really done it this time. Then she started to laugh, uncontrollably, the tears rolling down her face. Her husband became mad with rage and began to beat her. In the back seat the boy closed his eyes and covered his ears so as not to hear his mother's cries.

A month later, after the sale had been confirmed, the man shifted his wife and son from their apartment in the city to the motel. The woman had grown to accept the idea and had even decided to try to make a fist of her marriage. She had also begun to dream that the motel would be successful — but the fantasy turned to dust when the car topped the rise and she saw the motel again. Nevertheless, she got herself busy preparing the motel rooms — replastering the walls and repairing the carpets, putting new curtains up, mending the linen. It was invigorating work, and during it she discovered the darkroom, just off the office, which indicated that the earlier manager had been interested in photography.

For some reason, in the first few months of ownership, the woman and her husband were lucky. They averaged at least one overnight customer a week and five or six travellers wanting to have a coffee break and to stretch their legs. The truckers took a curious interest in the couple, particularly the woman, and got on their CBs to radio one another about the motel. The woman enjoyed the company of the customers and went out of her way to be attractive and fun. She encouraged her husband to put up signs three miles on either side of the motel so that people would know that there was a really cosy rest stop just ahead with oh-so-comfortable rooms and coffee really cheap at fifty cents.

Indeed, in those initial months, the woman and her husband were the happiest they had ever been. In the mornings the woman would service the motel units and put the coffee on. Her husband would sit out front and if there was a customer, check him out. The woman would then make breakfast for her husband and son — and then give the boy his morning school lessons, the motel being too far away from any school. Around lunchtime there were bound to be people stopping for coffee, so the woman would doll herself up, put on a cute little apron — a remnant of her days as a hostess at the bar — and make the customers feel right at home. She flirted a little, but at that stage it was, Sure you can see and feel but you can't take a bite, honey. Then in the afternoon the husband would take a nap or read a magazine and the woman would take the boy through his lessons again. Come sundown, the man would switch on the VACANCY sign, and together he and the woman would wait expectantly for the headlights of a car to come down the rise, go past, and then *flash* the rear brake lights and back to the motel. Why, hello folks, the man would say, come right in, right across our doorstep. The greatest thrill came when the air commuter service between the city and resort had a break-down for five days. During the period the travel agents bussed their customers to and from the resort twice a day. The PR man for the resort contracted the husband and the woman to cater two meals per day. The woman was in her element, and the man, thinking that this was only the harbinger of greater things, beamed with pride.

Then the good luck ran out. The air commuter service resumed. Worse still, the off-season at the resort meant that service traffic dwindled to a trickle. Sure, there was still the occasional trucker or traveller, but time began to weigh heavily on the woman and her husband — particularly the husband. Nothing was worse for him than to sit out front or in his office, day by day, watching the cars go by — and waiting for one of them to stop and back up. He would brace a smile on his lips whenever a car appeared at the top of the rise and lift a hand in welcome . . . and watch as it slid past and out of his reach. He would think, The next car will stop The next car will stop The next car will stop Thenextcarwillstop StopStopStop-Stop STOPPPP — but it never did. The sight of the woman, all dressed up and waiting for customers who never came, her lips parted in expectation, only heightened his sense of frustration and failure. Nor was television or reading any help. The highway mesmerised him. It was like a long black straw, and the motel was a small illuminated mouth waiting to drink.

In this mood the man grew mean and cunning. He started to slap his son around, as if the boy were a fly. He was vicious with his wife. He watched the motel's income dwindle away, dollar by dollar, and began to panic when the bills began to pile up. One night a trucker stopped by and seemed to be interested in the woman. The husband told her to go with the man. She refused and he beat her so badly that she ended up with two broken teeth. After that her husband started to hitch rides away from the motel — anything to escape the monotony of the place and the ugliness of his wife, anything. He went away overnight. Then for weekends. Then for weeks at a time. At least the absences brought respite to the woman and her son. But on a hot Friday he would be back. The beatings became more frequent, and so did the husband's absences in the resort or the city. One evening the man took to the road, carrying with him all the savings that had ever been earned at the motel. That had been over two years ago. The boy had felt a surge of triumph because now he had his mother to himself.

The woman decided that she would have to stay because there was nowhere else to go. Battered as she was, and lacking in self-esteem, she knew that she would have to make the best of it for herself and her son. By that time, however, fortune was in a slow descending spiral. The motel had already started to show its age and, despite her attempts with her son to keep it looking nice, it started to look like her — a cheap, pathetic creature whom no amount of repair or uplift would ever improve. The signs on both sides of the motel faded in the hot sun so that travellers who may have stopped did not know the motel was there until they had passed it by. The crude paint jobs the woman tried to give the exterior peeled away one layer after another, giving the place the appearance of a diseased apple. The V in the neon sign slipped away, and then an A, so that nobody could understand the word AC NCY. Even if they had, they would not have stopped. A motel whose sign was not kept up spelt trouble. In spite of all this, there were happy times for the woman. She took up with a Maori for three weeks and enjoyed it while it lasted. Sometimes one of the truckers would bring some beer around and they would make a night of it, drinking their cares away.

The only thorn in her side was the boy — her son — who persisted in following her everywhere. No matter where she went, she felt she was never alone. The boy was always there. It was not his fault, of course, but she began to feel paranoid about him. Why don't you do something? she would scream. Go somewhere! Get out from under my feet! Give me some space, let me breathe, make me free, do anything but just GO. She would push the boy away from the motel and watch as he ran to the copse. Go hunt rabbits, take the rifle and shoot some birds, lay snares, hunt fish, anything, anything, but just get away from me. The rifle would shatter the copse, the larks shrilling and circling like a black shredded net in the sky. Make a garden, grow some flowers, plant a tree, go anywhere, collect butterflies, get out, get out oh please Get Out GET OUT GET OUT GET OUT GET OUT-OUTOUTOUT. But the boy knew that his mother did not mean it and that she loved him. After all, who else was there for her to love?

Then a travelling salesman passed by, and the woman, remembering the darkroom next to the office, bought her son the camera. From the very beginning it was a great success. The boy became camera-mad. He took photographs of his mother, her friends, the passing cars, his mother, the truckers, the larks, the motel guests, his mother, the plains, the pond, his mother, his mother, his mother. Seeing his interest, his mother decided to renovate the old darkroom. One of the truckers, an amateur photographer himself, helped her out by bringing and installing photographic equipment he no longer had any use for. He gave the boy lessons and saw the wonder on the boy's face when he developed his first photograph. The photograph had been taken by the trucker. It showed the woman with a young man. The young man's left arm was possessively around the woman's waist. When the woman saw the photograph she felt a twinge of nostalgia and fear at the sight of this young man who, despite the fact that he was still gangling and foolish, had once been her son.

Two years is a long time in the life of a boy. The body strengthens and thickens, stubble grows on the chin, the voice deepens and nocturnal fantasies are accompanied by strong surges of desire. All these symptoms of manhood descended on the boy, and the woman knew he must leave. She wrote to a brother from whom she had been estranged many years, asking if he would take her son in. A month later she received a reply saying that she should send her son for a holiday — if that worked out okay, then perhaps the boy could stay. When the woman told her son he thought he was leaving her forever. He began to whine and plead with her and, for the first time in her life, she struck him. She told him to pack and that he would be leaving the next day.

But that evening the man who had deserted her two years before returned. I thought I'd see how my wife was getting on, the husband said. Get out, she answered. That's not a nice way to welcome your man, he said. Get out and stay out, she responded. Making a go of it are you? he asked. I'm still here, she taunted. Stashing it away, huh? the husband continued. I'm doing okay, she sneered. At that point the son arrived. So the brat has grown, the father laughed. You heard her, the son said, now get out. So he's a man is he? the father asked, then take me sonny, *take me*. The father and son fought and the woman tried to help her son. The father's brutal experience gave him the upper hand. He struck his son to the ground and began kicking him. The mother managed to pull her husband away. She yelled to the boy, Go son go away go —

Bloodied and sobbing, the boy wrenched the door open and ran blindly into the darkroom. He shut the door and put his hands over his ears. He looked at all the negatives of his mother, hanging in strips around him, and pulled them all close to him, wishing they were her. He felt that he had failed her.

How long the boy was in the darkroom he never knew. But suddenly his mother was there, scratching at the door. He did not want to look at her because he was ashamed. When he did he saw that his mother's eyes had been blackened and her lips were caked with blood. The woman saw the boy's alarm. Don't worry, she said, the bastard's gone. The boy asked, How? His mother answered, He only came for the money and I gave it to him. Then, without speaking, she tended to him and told him to go to sleep. Later that night the boy heard the back door opening. He saw his mother silhouetted in the light of the naked bulb.

The next morning the woman was up early to get her son some breakfast. She wanted him out of there and on his way to his uncle in the east. She called to him, Your breakfast's getting cold. There was no answer. She shrugged her shoulders and thought that he must still be packing. She called again. There was still no answer. Angry, the mother went in search of her son. She called through the house and realised he must be in the darkroom. Don't come in yet, he said, not yet. But the woman was impatient to get rid of him. She opened the door.

The boy had just finished processing the negatives. He had blown two of them up into enlargements. The woman saw that he had used infra-red film to take the photographs. Her face grew large with grief as she realised that he had followed her the night before. Why? she asked. One of the photographs showed her dragging the body of her husband toward the copse. Because I don't want to leave, her son said. Why? she asked again. The other photograph showed her removing the knife from her husband's chest. Because I love you, her son said.

At that moment, the woman heard the sound of a car horn. It seemed to come from far away. The boy ran past her to look. He pointed to the top of the rise. Three hawks were descending out of the sun.

A Contemporary Kezia

1

Of course, looking at her now, one couldn't possibly imagine that Kataraina had once had a passion for elephants. Here she sat, waiting at Auckland Airport with her father for the flight to Tauranga to be called. At the other end, Koro and Nani would be waiting.

Kataraina's father hadn't thought about the elephants for quite some time. Garrick had offered to drive him and Kataraina to the airport, and perhaps it was the flash of a pink and green house that reminded him. 'Can you remember that pink and green elephant you had when you were a baby?' he asked. Kataraina wrinkled her eyes, thought for a moment, pushed a stray lock of hair back, and eventually nodded. 'It was blue,' she said. Her father was startled. 'Are you sure? I can remember clearly the day Jocelyn gave it to you. It was a stuffed elephant, sewn with cloth she'd kept just for the occasion. It had a pink trunk and a green floral body and a tail and — ' Kataraina interrupted him. 'It didn't have a tail,' she said, 'and it was blue.'

Well, that had really rocked Kataraina's father back on his heels. Garrick had thought that father and daughter were having an argument. After all, Kataraina, at twelve years of age, was going through that 'difficult' stage — that convenient explanation used by parents to excuse their own parental deficiencies. She certainly had grown alarmingly since the last time Garrick had seen her, sprouting up, out and sideways. There she was, ready to start high school and poised on the edge of womanhood. She was attractive like her English mother — thank God — but unfortunately just as decisive and, where memory was concerned, as unfairly accurate.

Nevertheless, in the car Garrick heard Kataraina's father trying to align *her* memory with *his*. 'Kataraina sweet,' her father said, smiling with his teeth, 'are you sure the elephant didn't have a tail? I can remember quite clearly how you used to carry it. Either by its trunk. Or its tail. You thought that elephants had two tails, one at either end!' and her father had smiled at the memory. 'No, Daddy,' the ungrateful child had said. 'There was no tail. If I didn't carry it by its tail I carried it by its ears. They were big — ' pause ' — and they were blue — '

another pause ' — just like the rest of it.' Garrick had decided to concentrate on the driving. Kataraina's father had drummed his fingers on his briefcase. 'Kataraina sweet,' he had said kindly, 'don't contradict your father.'

Kataraina was a lovely-natured girl and had always been so — give or take the occasional moment of wilfulness. Looking at her now, in the terminal building — Garrick had left in a hurry, muttering something about Margaret's keys — her father could not believe that this was the same buoyant apricot-coloured child who had once had a pink and green elephant. Why, it even looked like she had adopted the same colour scheme for life — she was wearing a green top printed with black designs (elephants perhaps?) and faded pink jeans.

The boarding call was delayed. Kataraina took out a paperback and buried her nose in it. Intently and firmly. 'Well,' her father said, 'about the elephant — ' and Kataraina rolled her eyes and muttered something horrible under her breath ' — you went absolutely overboard on elephants after that! The mobiles that we hung in your bedroom had to be elephants. Every colouring book had to be of elephants. We took you to *Aida* because there was an elephant in the triumphal scene. You never liked dolls at all, just elephants.' Kataraina sighed. 'Daddy,' she said, 'I had lots of dolls.' Her father gave her a warm hug and said 'Sweet, don't interrupt Daddy, okay? We even took you to see *Dumbo* at least six times!' Her father roared with laughter at that one. 'It was *Fantasia*,' Kataraina muttered, 'and *you* wanted to go because you liked flying horses.'

'Then your sister, Amiria, was born,' Kataraina's father said, 'and *she* caught the elephant bug as well. Can you remember?' Kataraina glared at her father and 'No,' she said, 'I had one blue elephant, not a herd, Daddy, and Amiria had a big brown teddy bear which jingled when you shook it — ' pause ' — both of which are sitting on top of the wardrobe at home — ' a slight imperious smile ' — if you want to check.' And she had the affrontery to pat him understandingly, wicked child.

But Kataraina's father went on regardless, being in the grip of his sentimental memories. 'Well!' he exclaimed. 'The love of elephants reached the point where your mother and I decided we should take you both to see one at the zoo.' Kataraina nodded, 'Yes, that's when we went to Wellington on holiday.' So she did remember *something*. 'We told you a week beforehand and you both couldn't wait — just could not wait — for the day. "When are we going to see the heffalump?"' Kataraina put her book aside. Obviously her father was going to follow this one through to the bitter end, whether she liked it or not. 'So when the day came, we piled you both into the car and off we went. We saw the rhinoceros, the emus, the snakes, the kookaburras — ' Kataraina interrupted, 'There were no snakes, Daddy, and the kookaburras were cockatoos.' Her father waved her objections aside as mere pedantry. 'Kataraina dear,' he said strongly, 'I was *there*. And there were also horses, giraffes, lions — ' Kataraina bit back on her tongue ' — and we left the elephant till last.'

The boarding call was made. Kataraina sprang up but her father called her back — she wasn't going to get away *that* easily. His eyes grew moist and glazed. 'And you and your sister just stood there, holding your — your stuffed elephants — ' he emphasised, 'and your eyes were so wide and your mouths dropped open like this — ' and he was without shame, demonstrating in public. 'It's time to go now, Daddy,' Kataraina said. 'In a second, sweet,' her father answered.

'And then,' her father said, 'you started to cry. These big BIG tears. Amiria started to cry also. Your mother and I couldn't understand why. And I asked you "Why are you crying? Don't you like the elephant?" And you rubbed your little eyes and said, "No, Daddy, this elephant's too big and it's not" — ' Kataraina mouthed the word *blue* to herself ' — "pink and green!" '

The loudspeaker crackled again. Kataraina stood up again and smiled that Yes-Daddy-anything-you-say-Daddy-but-can-we-go-now smile. Her father stood up with her. Together they walked to the plane. The hostess welcomed them. Father and daughter strapped themselves in. Kataraina took up her book again, but she could see that her father was still in a sentimental mood. 'Yes, Daddy,' she said as the plane took off, 'I do remember going to see the elephant.' And as the plane soared out and over Auckland on its way to Koro and Nani, Kataraina's middle-aged father sighed to himself. At least, thank God, he had got *one* thing right.

2

Two days later Kataraina and her father went out to Tauranga Airport to await the arrival of the younger daughter, Amiria, on the plane from Auckland. Poor Amiria had had to stay behind because she was in a school choral festival. Of course Kataraina's and Amiria's father always knew his two daughters had star potential. Despite Amiria's penchant for raucous rock music; he knew she was going to be the next Kiri Te Kanawa. As for Kataraina, she was going to win the Academy Award one day and be as great an actress as Meryl Streep, who was his idol. Right now though, Kataraina was still hung up on being a breeder of racehorses. When her father had jokingly said that he would buy her a horse Kataraina had answered, 'Oh Daddy, you need two horses to breed.' And this from his own baby's mouth.

But she was not a baby any longer. The day was hot and there Kataraina sat, sipping at a coke like a nymphet Lolita. And her father recalled that Garrick had said 'Well, it won't be long before the boys start calling.' Her father had cried 'You mustn't say that sort of thing to a *father!*' But of course they would come, he knew that, and — Kataraina's father shook his head and tried to think of something else — something in the way she was sucking through the straw reminded him of Aunt Pat. It was not unusual for Kataraina's father to make quantum leaps from plastic straws to maiden aunts, and Kataraina realised she was in trouble again when her father's eyes glazed over and he uttered those fateful words, 'Kataraina sweet, can you remember?' — Kataraina didn't mind that her father had a long memory, though that was trial enough for a young girl, but the trouble was that he remembered so *badly*. Very soon she realised that today was not going to be an exception.

'Your Aunt Pat had such a lovely house,' Kataraina's father said. 'Of all your mother's relatives, she was the one I loved most.' Kataraina slurped through the straw. 'Aunt Pat's still alive, and the house is still lovely.' Her father was gentle and 'Yes, I know, sweet. I am using the past tense because I am referring to something that happened long ago. When you were a little girl. So pay attention.' Please, God, please get Amiria's plane here early, Kataraina prayed. 'Aunt Pat was — is — the best godmother anyone could ever have — sweet, remind me to send a birthday present to Jeremy in Oxford — and she has always taken her duties seriously. When Mummy and Daddy began to see each other, Aunt Pat was very kind to me — and generous. Indeed, when I first met her, I made the mistake of admiring her huge copper fireguard. That is how it ended up in our house.' Her father paused in reverie. 'Have you seen Aunt Pat recently?' Kataraina said, 'Yes, about three weeks ago. And she still doesn't want the fireguard back.'

'Well,' Kataraina's father continued, sitting right down in the middle of his recollection as if it was a tuffet, 'your mother and I went to dinner at Aunt Pat's at least once a month. I used to look forward to it because Aunt Pat was such a splendid cook. Her meals were just sumptuous and the table was always fit for royalty. And when you were born, and later Amiria, that didn't stop our routine one bit. Every first Wednesday of the month — ' Kataraina sighed, because her mother had told her it was every third Thursday ' — we would get into the Mini and charge up to Aunt Pat's for dinner. Come to think of it, we actually bought Aunt Pat's car — I think so. Anyway — '

An announcement was made that the flight from Auckland was imminent — and Kataraina resolved that she should pray more often. ' — on every visit,' Kataraina's father said, 'Aunt Pat would have some new artistic acquisition to show us. Once it was a pair of silver candlesticks. Another time it was a new Persian carpet. But the acquisition that was the greatest success, as far as you were concerned, was the reproduction of the great Botticelli painting *Venus Arising from the Sea*.

'I can't remember how old you were at the time,' Kataraina's father said, 'three — ' Kataraina put down her coke and 'Five,' she said, because she had heard this story before. Her father laughed dangerously, 'Listen, sweet, let's split the difference then and say four.' But Kataraina stuck to her guns. 'No, Daddy, I was five. Amiria was three. And Daddy you're getting it all — ' But Kataraina's father wasn't listening. 'It was an excellent reproduction actually. The colours were very true to the original. Remarkable, really, how luminescent that painting is, even after all these years. The Venus herself is just perfect. She is pictured against an azure sea. Her hair is flowing out like a fan. And the shell she is standing in — '

From out of the sky the plane appeared. Please hurry, Kataraina prayed. 'I can't remember what we had for dinner that night,' Kataraina's father said. 'From what I recall, you had gone to sleep before we got to Aunt Pat's.' Kataraina nudged her father, saying, 'That was Amiria, Daddy. She fell asleep and you put her into the other room. I played on the floor.' Her father waved his hand. 'Well, whoever it was — anyway, there we were, having dinner. All of a sudden, Aunt Pat noticed that you had woken up and come into the diningroom. I remember it so well, sweet! There you were, standing there, and you were looking up at the Botticelli. You were simply agog, your mouth opened in amazement. And Aunt Pat thought you were admiring it and — '

'There it is, Daddy!' Kataraina cried. The plane touched down and before her father could stop her Kataraina had run out to the gate. The plane was still far away, but Kataraina began to wave and wave — and her father felt his heart lift as he observed this evidence of closeness between his two daughters. The portable stairway was wheeled to the plane. At last there were those knock-kneed chicken legs of Amiria's, skipping gaily down the stairway on to the tarmac. And there she was, the younger daughter, feeling so self-important and grown up because this was the first time she had ever flown by herself like a real adult. 'Kataraina? Oh Kataraina!' Amiria called to her sister. And Kataraina ran out on to the tarmac and hugged her sister. Then, talking the hind leg off a dog, the two sisters came to join their father.

'Hullo, Daddy!' Amiria said as she kissed her father. 'Is Koro here? Oh, he's at the farm, is he? How about Nani? Cooking our lunch? Oh, yummy, 'cos I'm absolutely starving!' — which was Amiria's constant condition. Together, father and two daughters waited for Amiria's luggage to come off the plane. Then the girls walked with their father to the ute. Lace and Keg started to bark, and Peggy Sue rolled on her back waiting for Amiria to give her a welcome scratch.

The two girls hopped into the truck, and their father saw Kataraina whispering and giggling to her sister. 'Come on,' their father laughed, 'let me in on it.' And Amiria gave a bright-as-a-button smile and said 'Kataraina told me you were talking about that time when I woke up at Aunt Pat's and saw that picture — ' and Kataraina smiled across at her father. 'You remember, Daddy,' Kataraina emphasised, 'when *Amiria* saw the Botticelli?' Their father swallowed hastily. 'Why, of course!' His eyes softened. 'Well, there you were, standing there, and Aunt Pat was waiting with bated breath to hear you compliment her. But when you spoke, you simply asked "Daddy, why is that lady being eaten by a clam?" ' Kataraina and Amiria laughed out loud. And Kataraina smiled at her father, 'We love the way you tell that story, Daddy.' Ah yes, their father thought ruefully, he had certainly remembered it well.

3

Kataraina sweet, I need to tell you about Nani, my mother. I need to do this because sometimes we take the comfort and security of our lives for granted. We forget who we are, perhaps, or where we have come from. In your case, and Amiria's, you are the inheritors of two whakapapa, one Maori and the other English. You have wonderful grandparents on both sides. And then, there is Nani.

You wouldn't believe the hard times your Nani has known. The one time I am going to tell you about happened when she was a little girl. Nani's mother and father lived on the Coast in a small whare near the beach. They were very poor and depended for food on what they could catch from the sea or the river. Everybody had a role in keeping the family alive and well. Your Nani's role was given to her when she was four. As one of the daughters in her mother's family, her job was to bury the fire at night and make it come alight in the mornings. In those days, Kataraina sweet, Maori people did not have stoves or ovens. They used to cook over open fires in the kauta, the kitchen.

Before Nani went to bed she had to cover a part of the fire with ashes, to keep it alive, so that the next dawn, when she woke up, all she had to do was to uncover the embers and blow until they were alight. That was Nani's responsibility, and it was very important because if there was no fire there was no cooked breakfast. Nani was very proud of her ability at making the fire come alight every morning. She never ever had to use a match.

Nani is seventy-one now, so what Daddy is telling you about happened sixty-five years ago. I don't quite know how it occurred but one day, when Nani was six, an auntie came to talk to her mother. Auntie said that two very old women, important kuia, one of whom Nani was named after, needed someone to blow on the fire, cook and look after them. The two old ladies were important because they were wonderful weavers, renowned for the beauty of their work. Because their work was so sacred, it was necessary for them to have a worker who could do all the common tasks — like preparing the food. The two kuia lived far away from anywhere in a remote valley — there was an old man living with them also — and, though they had their own children, who had grown up and left them, they asked for Nani. Although Nani's mother loved Nani, she must have thought that the need of the two kuia was greater than hers and, anyway, she had other daughters. So on that very day, Nani's mother said to Nani to go with her auntie. To get on the buggy with her auntie and go. Just like that. In the clothes she was wearing. No shoes. No sentimental goodbyes. No saying 'E noho ra' to the rest of the family. Just instructions from her mother to look after the old ladies, keep their fire alight, do her best, and *go*. And because Nani was obedient and loved her mother, she did as she was told.

The old ladies and the old man lived two days away by buggy. The road didn't even go to where they lived. Auntie stopped at the side of the road, pointed to a curl of smoke, and then left Nani there.

The house in which the old people lived was a small whare which was not as nice as the one Nani had been born in. Way over the other side of the paddock was the kauta, the kitchen, separated from the sacred work of the weaving. Nani was in awe of the two kuia and their art — they dyed and wove mats of all colours, reds, yellows, purples, greens, blues, you name it. As soon as Nani arrived she was treated as an adult. No excuses for being six. She was put straight to work and, because her mother had told her to be obedient, she did the work without complaint. She was shown the place where she was to sleep — on the floor at the foot of the bed of the senior woman — and that is where she slept for three years. Every morning the kuia and the old man all woke up to say karakia, prayers. Straight afterwards, Nani would run over to the kauta, barefoot in all weather, to blow on the embers. The kauta was in bad condition, with rain coming in through the roof, and Nani had a lot of trouble when she first got there keeping the rain out. But she figured it all out for herself and patched the roof and holes with pieces of wood cemented with clay. The first few months, though, she got a lot of punishment from those two old ladies. I guess they wanted Nani to learn faster.

Once the fire was going, Nani got the bucket and went to the spring to get water. The bucket was as big as she was. But she figured that one out, too, and made a sled out of two planks of wood. She then made a harness for herself. After a while, though, she made friends with the old people's pet dog — it was old too — and she taught it to take the harness in its teeth and pull the sled. That dog was your Nani's best friend and they loved one another very much. Together the dog and Nani would take the water back to the kauta, where Nani would fill the pots and bring the water to the boil. All this, Kataraina sweet, before it was light.

Now. The two kuia and the old man didn't have any money. Their main diet was eels and dried shark meat. The senior of the two old women showed Nani how to catch the eels — only *one* time — and then your Nani had to do it by herself from then on. No excuses. No 'Can you show me again?' Just the once. Nani would gather worms — under dried cowpats was the best place to find worms — and thread them on to a whitau, a flax thread. Then she would get her dog to drag an old tin basin down to the river. There she would sit, dangling the whitau into the water, waiting for the eels to bite. Once an eel did this it wouldn't let go of the worm and *flick*, Nani would pull the eel out and into the basin. *Flick*, and she would pull the eel out. *Flick*, another eel. *Flick*, another. And in all that time, the dog would sit silent because the dog knew that its life, and those of the old people, depended on Nani's fishing skills. As for shark meat, Nani was the one responsible for curing and drying the meat — a hard job which used to make her hands raw. Sometimes people would bring a bag of flour or tinned food, in exchange for the woven mats. The old ladies would give the flour to Nani and say, 'E Hera, make us a Maori bread.' The old people never had butter with their bread. But as a special treat they would sometimes get some dripping for Nani, for they soon grew to love her. Your Nani was obedient and she did her work well.

Very soon your Nani had all the household tasks well under control. Her one dress was falling apart and she decided she'd better learn how to weave so she could make a new one. She asked the senior kuia to show her, but the old lady said, 'No, Hera, your job is to keep the fire alight.' Nani felt very sorry for herself and was very embarrassed because her body was showing through her dress. You know your Nani still has great modesty — she would hide whenever visitors came because she was so ashamed that she didn't have a nice dress. Then one night the two kuia surprised her. They said, 'This is for you, Hera.' They had woven her a beautiful cloak, so soft on her shoulders that it made her feel like a million dollars.

Nani has never spoken ill of those three old people, Kataraina sweet. She has told me that they were as kind as they could be. But she was always wondering when her mother was coming to get her. She would go out to the road with the dog and sit there, waiting, looking up the road. One day she saw two older children coming along the road, but she was so shy that she hid in the grass. When they drew abreast she saw that they were a brother and a sister of hers. She sprang out and ran to them, saying, 'Have you come to get me? Have you come to take me home?' But they didn't know who *she* was and, frightened, ran away. Nani has often said that she never ever realised how hard she was working until she left. She just didn't have any comparisons to make. But when she did find out, I think it took her a long time to understand it all.

Well. The old people did their best. Sometimes they got sick. Nani was sent out to gather herbs to make them better. She and her pet dog began to do more and more heavy work. Your Nani loved that old dog. She depended on him. He was obedient to her. Then one day, when Nani and the dog were returning with the water from the spring, the dog began to pant in a strange way. It lay down. When Nani saw that her dog was going to die she got so *wild* that she got a stick and started to beat it, trying to make it stand up. 'Get up, kuri,' she yelled. 'We have to get the water back to the kauta.' But the poor dog just couldn't do it. Quietly it began to whimper, almost as if it was asking Nani's forgiveness for leaving her alone, and then it died. Just like that. No excuses. One minute there, next minute gone.

Your Nani cried, of course, though she knew it was a sign of weakness. When the dog died she didn't want to go on herself. Blowing on the fire every morning. Covering the fire every night. Cooking. Sleeping on the dirt floor.

Nani was nine when she left. She has never spoken about why. She insists she never ran away. She has always said, 'I just left.' Daddy doesn't even know where she went to, but I think it was to stay with one of her older sisters. When she arrived there, her sister was so surprised because she didn't know Nani was still alive. Shortly after

Nani left, one of the old ladies died. The old man was next. Then the second kuia went. She was found two days later, sitting naked in front of the cold fire in the kauta, dead. Your Nani never knew any of this until much later in her life.

Kataraina sweet, and you too, Amiria, this is only one of the experiences your Nani had when she was a little girl. She had to be responsible from a very early age, and she expects others to be responsible also. She has taught her own children and I, in turn, try to teach you and Amiria, Nani's grandchildren. It's strange, really, but all her life your Nani has been the one who always looks after the fire and blows on the embers and brings us life every day.

Nani went up to that old place in the bush not long ago. Of course it's all changed now. Good roads. Most of the bush gone. But she found the place where the old kauta had been and where she had buried her pet dog. She cried for those old people, for her dog and for those three years she had lived there. She cried so hard that she could have flooded the whole world.

So now, Kataraina, do you understand? When your Nani talks to you and Amiria she wants you to listen *hard* because she feels we all have a responsibility to each other. And remember, Kataraina, and you too, Amiria, that you have had the benefits, as I have also, of a good life. Most of this we owe to Nani, yes *owe* her, because she has been determined that none of us will ever need to want for anything. When you two get older, you will be modern women living in a modern age. But when you both become the somebody your Nani wants you to become, don't you ever forget Nani. Her worth is beyond price.

Now, Kataraina sweet, you must go over to your Nani and give her a big hug. Hold her tight and don't let her go because sometimes, no matter how adult a person is, you can still get frightened of nothing and of everything. And Nani is not always able to be strong. Worse, is that sometimes Nani blames herself for leaving that place when she was nine. She doesn't want you to ever be in the position to have to make such a terrible choice. So kiss her gently, Kataraina sweet, and tell her that you will indeed become the woman that she wishes you to be — the possessor of *all* her strengths, of all the determination of the Maori ancestry that she has bequeathed you. Tell her, 'It's all right, Nani,' and convey to her, through the strength of your love, that she does not need to forgive herself for being a nine-year-old girl. After all, how was your Nani to know that those old people would get so feeble that they wouldn't be able to blow on the embers and make a fire to keep them warm?

Country Life

1

Whenever Mama played the grand piano in the evenings, she always played in darkness or by moonlight. She would tell Miranda and her two younger sisters to turn the lamps down low or to blow the candles out and open the curtains. Then, as Mama played some piece by Chopin, Ravel or Liszt, she would tell the girls about the Maestro who had taught her pianoforte in London. 'Come, my darlings,' she would call in her thrilling voice. 'Come to me and I shall tell you more about the Maestro. Oh, I do believe he was half in love with me but — ' and she would listen to the wekas calling outside and giggle ' — such is life.'

'The Maestro was the pupil of the great Paderewski,' Mama would say grandly. 'I was the first pupil he had ever had from New Zealand. "Vere iz zis New Zaylan?" the Maestro asked me. "Zomvere in ze Baltic?" ' The girls would always giggle at Mama's mimicry. 'Oh, he was a gentle, gentle man, the Maestro, but very strict. It was he who said, "Ma cherie, ven you play you should not ze look take at ze keez. You should know vere zay are. Only zen vill you be able to conzentrate on ze intentioni of ze compozere." I have never forgotten that. Never.' And to prove it, Mama would proceed to coax strings of glistening pearl-like notes from the darkness — the haunting 'Undine' or the virtuosic 'La Campanella' — her slight form dipping and swaying and giving its strength to interpreting the music.

The most magical evenings were when the moon came out and flooded through the window. Mama would exclaim, 'Ah,' and begin to play Debussy's very simple 'Clair de Lune'. It was all so terribly romantic really, to sit there, watching as the moon limned Mama and the piano with light. 'The Maestro said that "Clair de Lune" should only be played by moonlight, " — for zen, ma cherie, you hear ze muzic of ze heavenz".' It was only later, much later, when Miranda and her sisters began to go to school in the city, that they started to suspect that playing 'Clair de Lune' by moonlight had less to do with Debussy and possibly more to do with the fact that the farm had no electricity.

Mama was a romantic and prone to romantic effusions, but people in the valley were always so forgiving of her — and had been ever since she had come as the wife of its favourite son, Andy Bell. Despite the fact that Andy had forsaken all the local girls, any wife of Andy's was good enough for them. Not only that, but any famous New Zealander — even if she was simply a 'pianner' player — who was big enough to give away Fame and Fortune for life in Waikeri must be doing it for Love. More important, Andy had written that his new missus wouldn't stand in the way of his playing footie for the local side on Saturdays.

Papa snared Mama when he had been on a rugby tour of England. Mama was giving a recital at a concert hall in Bournemouth and Papa, noting that she was from good old Enzed, decided to have a listen in. Surely no chap could resist the magic of Mama, in white flowing silk, playing the Romantics — even if the critics complained she was rather heavy on the pedal and employed too much rubato. Papa had wooed her, won her, survived the wrath of the Maestro, and shipped her and her grand piano to the valley. The locals had never seen the like of Andy Bell's missus. She wasn't quite their cup of tea, being from Christchurch and all, but she didn't put on airs — you had to say that for her. And although she was an ethereal little thing, surely there was something sweet about hearing a pianner drifting its notes, out of complete and utter darkness, across the valley. 'Ah yes, I gave it all up,' Mama would sigh, 'but look at my audience now! My three lovely daughters, a wonderful husband and' — Mama would give a delicious giggle — 'the occasional swaggerman, sheep and wekas!'

Indeed, the only people who appeared intolerant of Mama were those who lived outside the valley — and Grandmama and Aunt Ida, Mama's sister. The only living relatives of Mama, Grandmama and Aunt Ida had uprooted themselves from their comfortable life in Christchurch to be near her — not in the valley, thank you very much, but in the nearest civilised town. There, every Saturday, Miranda and her sisters would be left to visit while Papa played rugby for Waikeri Old Boys and Mama attended, as a committee member, the weekly meetings of the local musical society.

'Your mother was always mad,' Grandmama would invariably tell Miranda and her sisters, usually while taking tea on the terrace. 'I don't know where it came from, really I don't. Certainly not from my side of the family and surely not from your grandfather's either. Though — ' Grandmama was prone to memory lapses ' — I do recall a cousin who ran away with a Lithuanian — but she was twice removed.' In most cases, whenever Grandmama was holding forth about Mama, all that was required of the girls was just to sit still and listen. Originally, the girls had considered Grandmama to be most unfaithful — until Mama explained that this was Grandmama's *way*, and that Grandmama was really conducting a conversation with herself. Indeed: 'Take your names, girls,' Grandmama would say, with her eyes fixed not at them but some point just past her nose. 'Now I know that devotion to Shakespeare is very laudable but — Miranda, Ophelia and *Desdemona*? My dears, the deed poll was designed for children like yourselves whose parents have shown such disregard for common sense. Desdemona, change your name to Mona as soon as you can. Miranda? Mary perhaps. It is so simple, dear, and has such a nice virginal ring to it. I am afraid, Ophelia, that you will have to think of something — but do make it plain. Something like Ann or Joan. And to the point. Try not to choose something hyphenated and too American.' Then Grandmama would pause and sigh deeply. 'Luckily your dear brother, Richard, escaped your mother's penchant for the idiotic. But to name him after a crookback? Really! Better Richard, however, than her first choice — Oberon.'

'Now I know,' Grandmama would continue, 'that I might be accused of lack of imagination, but thank God for that. Your mother has enough for all of us. Did you know, girls — and please sit up, Ophelia — that your Mama went through a biblical phase? Dreadful! She named her dolls Bathsheba, Hepzibah, Abigail and Delilah. I suppose we should be thankful for small mercies.' Then Grandmama would close her monologue with, 'You will have to do the best you can, girls. You have my support.' She would concentrate on Miranda. 'I fear for you, Miranda, my dear. You are so like — ' a shudder — 'her. If you have any notion of using your Mama as an exemplar, please don't. It would be easier on all of us. Oh, are your parents here already? Goodbye then, my dears. You know that you were the reasons Ida and I came here, don't you? After all, somebody has to protect you and guide you. Give Grandmama a kiss. Bye bye.' And with a peck on Grandmama's scented and powdered cheek, the girls would depart. Grandmama always smelled so wonderful.

3

Of course, Mama's romantic effusions and the lack of electricity on the farm were two entirely different matters. All the same, when the subject became the hot news in the playground of the school the children attended — a school not in the village but in the city, where Mama considered the academic prescription and social standing of the children were a little more desirable, but not much more — the children did not know what to think.

It all came about because Ophelia had invited a friend, Linda Potts, to stay the weekend at the farm. In retrospect, Ophelia realised that Linda was awfully common — Like her mother, Mama had said — but Ophelia had hoped to ingratiate herself with Linda's group. Ophelia didn't know, of course, that Linda's inclination to gossip — Just like her mother, Mama might have said — would mean that everybody would know by playtime. The first to confront Ophelia was smart-alecky Kevin Da Costa, who yelled out, 'Hoi, Feely-meely, is yer old man so hard up he can't afford 'lectric powah! Ya got none, have ya.' Da Costa's mates tittered behind him, their eyes agog at the news. What was that? The snotty Bells had no electricity? No electric lights? No power for the radio? Not even an electric oven! Oo, how did they heat their water! What fun! What fun! Poor Ophelia was so embarrassed that she turned red and could have died on the spot. Luckily Desdemona, who was made of sterner stuff, saw her sister's plight and ran to her rescue. 'You smelly piece of dung,' she said, an endearment that attested to a good vocabulary, 'why don't you go and flush yourself down the loo!' Then, before Da Costa had time to figure out what she had said, she shepherded Ophelia away. Together they sought out Miranda to take counsel with her. They found that Miranda was maintaining a very haughty estate — whenever faced with a challenge of an unanswerable nature, Miranda would always adopt a lofty, unattainable, above-it-all posture and think of Anne Boleyn. Miranda was never good at confrontation, only disdain. In this case she considered that damage limitation was called for. 'Ophelia,' she instructed, 'you must have it out with Linda Potts.'

Like Miranda, Ophelia had a lot of the wilting violet in her, but instruction from her older sister was always to be heeded. She saw Linda hanging upside down on the jungle gym with some other girls. She ran over and swung herself up beside Linda. Tucking her dress in so that the boys wouldn't see her panties — Linda Potts wasn't so modest — Exactly like her mother, Mama would have said — Ophelia took a deep breath and said 'I thought you were my friend, Linda Potts' Startled, Linda Potts pushed her dress up from her face to see who was talking to her. Linda knew her goose was cooked but 'nuffink' 'I never told nobody' she said, the lie so transparent on that grubby little face. To prevent further discussion on the matter, Linda swung herself up and, eyes squinting at the sun, pointed to some unfortunate patsy. 'It was her,' she told Ophelia, fingering shy Hariata Jones who was both deaf and mute, 'Yes,' said one of Linda's cronies, because Linda had promised her a ride on her new bike after school. But Ophelia surprised them by sticking to her guns. 'No, it was you, Linda Potts,' she said. 'And — ' although Ophelia had wanted to be one of Linda's group the right thing was called for here ' — I don't want you to be my friend any longer.' The other children gasped because this certainly devalued Linda's status. Feeling brave and self-sacrificing, Ophelia swung herself down and started to walk away. 'Who cares!' Linda Potts yelled after her for it was not in her nature — Most definitely like her mother, Mama would have said — to let anyone else have the last word. 'Who cares, you — ' apart from which, Linda Potts could not afford to be faced down by Ophelia ' — you ding dong Bell!' The children scattered then, screaming this witticism to each other across the playground.

4

That afternoon the three children were very subdued when George, the Maori handyman who took them to and from school every day, came to pick them up. 'Did the little misses have a bad day?' George asked. He always called them the little misses, a term Miranda had always found condescending. 'Or did the little misses get the strap?' George seemed to find this notion absurdly funny and threw back his head in a roaring snorting sneezing sort of a laugh, ha-ha-ha-ha-*hawww*. Really, one could not be too cross with George for too long; one could only sympathise with him, given this dreadful affliction. 'Never mind, little misses,' George continued, 'it'll all be better tomorrow,' which was George's unfailingly cheerful philosophy.

The drive from school to the valley — and vice versa — normally took an hour and a quarter, or an hour and a half on Fridays when traffic was busy. Sometimes the children felt embarrassed about not going to the village school, but whatever Mama wished was usually what Mama got. Not that Mama minded shepherds' children or the dark-skinned Maoris who predominated at the valley school, but what did they know of Latin, French, the Classics, MUSIC; ah, there was the rub. Then, of course, Mama had considered that the expense of sending one daughter to a city school should be undercut by sending the others also. And after a short discussion with Papa — who always concurred where the girls were concerned but demurred on any

93

question of Richard until all the facts were presented — it was done.

The tarseal, or, as Mama used to put it, 'The Last Sign of Civilisation', stopped around fifty minutes from the Seddon Bridge. Normally, by this stage, before the car hit the dusty gravel road to the valley and the farm just beyond, the three girls could be counted on to have fallen fast asleep. They had early learned that the best way to fight utter boredom was to sleep through it — something they had occasionally done when listening to Grandmama and Aunt Ida. Miranda, by virtue of her status as the eldest, always sat up front with George; her two sisters, leaning against each other, were propped up in the back. On this particular afternoon, Ophelia and Desdemona had retreated into dreamland but Miranda was wide awake. She was feeling cross and irritated, and she blamed it all on Mama. Over the course of the afternoon she and her sisters had been subjected to embarrassment and vilification for something quite outside their powers to control — the possession of electricity. It was just not fair for Mama to deny them all light bulbs simply because *she* had to play 'Clair de Lune' only by moonlight. It was unfair and — and — it was too selfish.

In this mood it was, therefore, not unexpected that Miranda would jump from the car, on its arrival at the farm, in search of Mama. Ophelia and Desdemona ran into the house, stopping long enough in the kitchen to ask Heni, George's wife and the cook, what they were going to have for dinner. 'Eel steaks and huhu grub pudding,' Heni said as usual. 'Oh goody,' Ophelia said, 'mince pies and jelly.' She and Desdemona ran to their room to change — they had to share a room because Ophelia was afraid of the dark. It wasn't too long before the two girls were in farm clothes and dashing down to collect the eggs, feed the ducks and watch the Maori workers at the shearing shed — Papa was down there directing the work. 'Are you coming?' the girls asked Miranda. 'No,' Miranda said. 'Well,' Heni interrupted, 'don't you go disturbing your poor mother, she's tuckered out. She's not a strong lady. I told her to take her nap.' Heni idolised Mama and was in awe of her musical abilities. She never allowed Mama anywhere near the kitchen. 'Miranda? You just listen to me, Deaf Ears — ' But it was too late. When Miranda's mind was made up, nothing could stop her.

'Mama? Mama!' Miranda called as she entered the dimly lit bedroom. Mama was like a Sleeping Beauty and, for the first time ever, Miranda realised what Papa meant when he said that nothing was more wonderful than waking up next to Mama. She was just like an Aubrey Beardsley illustration, her hair so black against her translucent skin. Her lips were as red as an open rose. 'Mama,' Miranda said again as she sat on the bed. Mama's eyelids flickered. 'Mmmnn? Oh,

Miranda — ' And Mama raised a finger to trace her daughter's chin. 'Mama,' Miranda said, 'I have a question to ask.' Mama sighed and a look of irritation crossed her clear brow. 'Now, Miranda?' Miranda was firm. 'Yes, Mama,' she said, 'I would like to know if there was any electricity in Debussy's time.' Mama blinked her eyes rapidly. 'Mmmmmn, electricity? They had gas lamps, I think. Yes, gas.' Mama turned, but, 'There then,' Miranda said, 'but times have changed, Mama. I'm sure Debussy wouldn't mind if you played 'Clair de Lune' by electricity. Mama?' But Mama had returned to sleep.

At that moment Heni came in. She grabbed Miranda, none too gently, and tried to pull her out of the room. 'If you persist,' Miranda said, 'I shall SCREAM. Then Mama would really wake up. And we — ' she smiled dangerously ' — wouldn't want that, would we!' Heni glared at Miranda, let her go and waited until they were in the kitchen. Then Heni boxed Miranda's ears. 'You watch out, Miss High and Mighty,' Heni said, 'you're not too old to be spanked.' Miranda was uneasy. 'You wouldn't dare,' she said. 'Oh, wouldn't I just,' Heni answered, raising a large wooden mixing spoon. Miranda decided a prompt departure was called for. She skipped down the steps and decided to seek out Papa. Far away she saw her two sisters calling, 'Where's the ducks! Where's the ducks! Here ducks! Here ducks!' The ducks seemed to come from everywhere, half waddling half flying to scoop up the bread and other leftovers from the kitchen.

Miranda waved to her sisters as she headed for the shearing shed. Usually, Miranda disliked going into the shed. It was smelly, dirty and the wool was greasy. What she particularly didn't like was seeing the poor defenceless sheep during the shearing. She felt so sorry for them as they lay there, between the shearers' legs, bleating, 'Help! Help! We want to keep our woollen coats on! Help!' The poor things looked so undressed when they were shorn, jumping down the race and out the pens baa-ing, 'Oh no! Oh no! We've been robbed of our longjohns!' Apart from that, the Maori workers were always busy and Miranda often felt in the way. The Maoris belonged to another, less-privileged world, which she could never comprehend. Worse, some of the younger Maori workers were about the same age as Miranda. That made Miranda feel very embarrassed, and not even Anne Boleyn could enable her to rise above it all.

'Papa?' Miranda called. Papa was in one of the outside yards with Barry, the head shepherd. They had just brought in more sheep for the shearing tomorrow. 'Hullo, Miranda,' Papa said. 'How was school today?' Miranda had to shout above the noise of the sheep and the barking of the dogs — especially Soot, who hated her. 'That's what I've come to tell you about,' Miranda answered. 'It was awful, Papa.' Papa cupped his ear and Miranda had to shout. 'Papa, why can't we have electricity?'

5

The answer was very simple really. Papa had just laughed and replied, 'Because electricity hasn't reached us yet.' He had, however, told Miranda that he had seen a plan put out by the Electricity Department which indicated that the valley would soon receive some magical process called 'Electrical Reticulation'. At dinner that evening Miranda asked, 'How soon?' Mama chided her. 'Tiresome child.' Then to Papa, she added, 'Miranda woke me up on this same subject of electricity. Debussy got involved, though how I just don't know.'

At that moment Heni came in to take the plates away. 'You listen to me, Mr Bell,' Heni said. 'You should disciple Miranda before she gets too hoha.' Mama winced and said, 'The word is discipline, Heni dear.' Heni put a prim look on her face. 'Same thing, Mrs Bell, same thing. Miranda's been uppity ever since her auntie, you know, *her* — ' Heni didn't like Aunt Ida one bit — 'took her to see that *Gone with the Wind.*' Heni went all self-aggrieved. 'Well, I ain't no Mammie, and Miranda sure isn't any Scarlett O'Hara.' At that, Mama gave her gorgeous giggle. 'Oh Heni, the things you say.' And Papa, recalling Miranda's question, said, 'I don't know, Miranda dear. But great days are ahead. The country's on the march — national airline, railway communications, commerce, agriculture, industry — and Waikeri Valley will be next.'

But what was 'reticulation'? George had put his finger on it, in his own inimitable way, when he drove the girls to school the next morning. 'How many power lines you counted on our way to school?' he asked. Miranda looked out the window. 'There's lots,' she said. 'Nah, little misses,' George said. 'Those are for the telephone! There's no power poles at all. That's what reticulation do. It brings the power poles from the dam to the switch on the wall. George is cleverer than you little misses! Ha-ha-ha-*haw.*'

That morning at school Miranda, Ophelia and Desdemona went on the attack. The first strategy was designed to outflank the enemy. 'Hullo, Linda Potts,' Ophelia said to her once-friend in the playground. 'How's your mama?' Linda Potts screwed up her eyes suspiciously. 'What's it to you then?' Ophelia responded, 'Oh my papa wondered if she would like to come and work for us on the farm — as our housemaid.' The cronies standing with Linda went *ooh errr.*

Linda sniffed and stabbed her sharp nose in the air. 'My mum wouldn't never be a housemaid.' Ophelia smiled. 'Oh really? Well who is this then?' She reached into her skirt pocket and pulled out a photograph. Evidence. There was Linda Potts's mum, standing with Heni in younger days in the front yard of what was clearly the Bells' farmhouse. Linda's friends gasped with horror and edged away from her. 'Gimme that,' Linda hissed. 'Gimme that!' But too many children had already seen the incriminating photograph and they scattered. Very soon the news had spread that 'Potty's mum once used to *clean* for the Bells'. This was called Creating A Diversion, and no better diversion could have been chosen than to re-establish financial and social status by deflating the reputation of the enemy. By lunchtime poor Linda Potts was eating her sandwiches by herself, her fair-weather friends having deserted her, wailing loudly about unfair Fate. Just like her mother, Mama would have said.

The next strategy was then to go in under cover and *hit* the enemy with all your firepower. Desdemona delivered the *one, two* to Kevin Da Costa with 'You, Heapa Composta! Of course my papa can afford electricity! *And —* ' if all else fails hurt a boy where it pains him most ' — he's got three cars, one truck, two tractors and a bulldozer!' Indeed, this was enough to shrivel Da Costa in his socks, for Da Costa's father was supposed to be owner of a garage station. Then it was left to Miranda to Recapture The Ground. 'Of course Papa can afford any-thing,' Miranda said to anybody in hearing distance. Sweet Miranda could be such a snob, pulling rank whenever it was required. 'How-ever, if one has not electrical reticulation — ' this said with appropriate dramatic emphasis ' — what can one do? One must consider building one's own *private* dam — ' She didn't really say that Papa was going to do this, only implied it. 'Or — ' and it was here that Miranda had a masterstroke ' — one writes to the Prime Minister to complain!' The others in Miranda's class gasped in awe. 'You wouldn't *dare!*' they said. 'Yes she would!' chorused Ophelia and Desdemona. 'Yes I *shall*,' said Miranda the Magnificent. And, while the playground resounded with this new development that 'Miranda Bell is writing a letter to GOD', she sat down to compose her complaint.

Dear Prime Minister

I am a pupil at this school and am in Miss Grayson's class. Every-body here has got electricity, but not us. We live in Waikeri Valley and must use candles and lamps. As a consequence, my sisters, Ophelia and Desdemona, and I sometimes cannot finish our homework, especially in the winter when it gets dark quickly. And

Mama has to play 'Clair de Lune' by moonlight.

I am therefore writing to ask when you are opening a new dam? May we have electricity in Waikeri Valley soon, please? Thanking you in advance.

I remain,
Your obedient servant
(Miss) Miranda Bell

'Of course, Miranda dear,' Grandmama said that afternoon when the girls went to visit, 'you may have an envelope and a stamp for your letter! Ida? Would you fetch my purse from the bedroom?' The girls were taking tea on the terrace and, as Aunt Ida walked inside, Desdemona, who was always forward, said, 'There's something the matter with Aunt Ida's hair.' Grandmama leaned forward. 'Sshh, girls, we mustn't let Ida know that we have noticed. She went to see Joan Fontaine in a Technicolor motion picture two nights ago. *Well*, I have no good words for the Technicolor process.' The girls commiserated with Grandmama. Aunt Ida was just mad on the movies and went at least twice a week. She would go in one woman and come out *transformed* into Vivien Leigh in *Waterloo Bridge* or Joan Fontaine in *Frenchman's Creek* or Ingrid Bergman in *Spellbound*. Between one movie and the next, Aunt Ida would become an imitation of one of the above or, on bad days, all of the above. This time she had dyed her normally black hair a reddish sort of tinge — with the result that she looked like a brindle cow. 'Ah, thank you, Ida,' Grandmama said when Aunt returned. Then, turning to Miranda, Grandmama said, 'Oh, I thoroughly approve of your sending a letter to the Prime Minister. A person in government is a servant of the people, prime minister or no. I once knew a prime minister. Odious little man he was, too. *There.*' Grandmama sealed the envelope. 'Ida? You might care to take Miranda's letter to the post office. You've some letters of your own to post, haven't you? Miranda, you go with your aunt. As for you two smaller girls, let me give you some advice. Now, my dears, your mama always had a penchant for dressing you girls in the worst possible fashions. Look at you both! You look like a pair of Parisienne courtesans — no, I shall not explain that word, Desdemona dear, but to be one is to suffer a fate worse than death. When you are older, girls, do try to dress sensibly. Like Grandmama, for instance, in tasteful colours and *not* cerise or vermilion — '

'Come along, Miranda,' Aunt Ida called. Ida had put on a yellow picture hat and changed into a pretty yellow frock. The outfit would have looked lovely on Mama, but on Aunt Ida — oh *dear*. 'Who have you written to this week?' Miranda asked as Aunt Ida drifted along in a dream. 'What was that, Miranda?' Aunt Ida answered. 'Oh, Leslie Howard. He was so divine as Ashley in *Gone with the Wind*.' Miranda had thought he was a drip. 'And Laurence Oliver — ' big nose and fat lips like Kevin Da Costa ' — and Robert Taylor' — stiff as a board and crooked of nose. 'What about Clark Gable?' Miranda asked, which was mean of her, because she only wanted to see Aunt Ida go into her Vivien Leigh impersonation. Sure enough, Aunt Ida stopped and began to drum her heels in the dust and wave her fists against an invisible Rhett Butler. 'Oh I hate Clark Gable, I hate him, he's beastly, just *beastly*.' Then, just as suddenly, Aunt Ida stared at her surroundings. '*Everything's* beastly,' she said. 'Being stuck here in this awful town. With these awful people. Oh, I wish I was back in Christchurch with my boyfriend Simon — ' that had been a long time ago when Aunt Ida had been twelve ' — instead of here in this — this — backwash of civilisation.'

Miranda and Aunt Ida arrived at the post office. Aunt Ida pursed her lips and kissed each of her letters on the left corner of the envelopes. Miranda simply popped hers into the slot. 'It's all your mother's fault,' Aunt Ida said, 'that I'm stuck here.' And Miranda replied, 'I know exactly how you feel, Aunt Ida. We should have had electricity years ago.' The two patted each other conspiratorially as they left the post office.

6

Three weeks is a long time in a school playground. Friendships wax and wane, fortunes rise and fall, alliances change at the swap of peanut butter sandwich with shortbread biscuit or grapes — and today's piece of amazing gossip is yesterday's old hat. It was not unexpected, therefore, that Desdemona and Kevin Da Costa should be seen on the same longball side — Kevin knew a winning batsman when he saw her — nor that Ophelia and Linda Potts should hang upside down on the jungle gym like pigtailed bats, discussing the colour of their teacher's knickers. Electrical reticulation paled into insignificance when compared with longball or pink panties. Even Miranda, who was usually conscientious about such things, had quite forgotten that she had posted a letter to the Prime Minister in Wellington — it may just as well have been to the other side of the world, really — until the reply came, addressed to Miranda Bell, in a white envelope bearing the telltale letters OHMS.

George was the one who told the girls. On their way home from school he said, 'What you little misses been up to, eh? I just picked up the mail and there's one for you, Miranda.' Miranda's heart went bumpity *bump*. 'For me? It must be from the Prime Minister!' George scoffed, 'What's a big boss like that doing writing to a little miss like you!' Miranda said authoritatively, 'George, please give me the letter.' But George shook his head. 'Oh no, little Miss, I give this letter to Mrs and *she* give it to you. Otherwise George might be — ' and he drew a finger across his neck.

When the children arrived at the farm Mama was playing some Chopin *études*. Ophelia and Desdemona ran in to her crying, 'Mama! Mama! Miranda's had a letter. From the Prime Minister!' But Heni stopped them. 'I don't care if it's the King himself,' she said, 'your fella's letter will have to wait until your mama has finished her practice.' Heni was always a dragon as far as Mama's practice was concerned. 'But this is important,' Miranda wailed. 'Uh huh,' Heni answered. 'Well, I can't see any lightning in the sky and I can't feel any earthquake either. In other words, Smarty, you can *just* wait.' That really made Miranda's temper flare. She and her sisters got out of their school clothes and went down to the shearing shed to petition their papa. 'Hullo, girls,' Papa said. He was doing a tally on the bales of wool produced from the year's shearing. 'Papa,' Miranda said, 'I insist that Heni be sacked.' Papa was amused. 'Heni? What has she done now!' Miranda drew herself up to her tallest height. 'Papa, Heni refused to let us in to see Mama! Our *own* mother, Papa.' Papa took his hat off and wiped his brow. 'Hmmmn — ' he said. But before he could go any further, a bell started to ring at the house. 'Must be more serious than I thought,' Papa said. 'Come on.' Mama only rang the bell in cases of emergency.

When the girls arrived at the house they found that Mama had stopped playing the piano. She sat in the sitting-room together with George, cap in hand, and Heni, who glared at Miranda disapprovingly. Mama had Miranda's letter in her left hand. 'Dear,' Mama said to Papa as he entered, 'Miranda has received — ' she waved the offending envelope ' — this.' Papa smiled at Miranda, 'Well, Miranda?' Desdemona and Ophelia interrupted, saying excitedly, 'Miranda wrote to the Prime Minister! She asked him when we were getting electricity!' Mama raised an eyebrow. 'To the Prime Minister? About electricity? Tiresome child!' And Heni nodded, saying, 'You have to disciple kids early, Mr Bell. I should know.' Miranda averted her eyes. 'Grandmama felt it was all right to write to the Prime Minister,' she said. Mama drummed her fingers. 'I should have realised,' she said, 'that Mother would have something to do with this.' Papa put a stop to the discussion. 'Miranda dear, you may open your letter,' he said. He passed the letter to her. Miranda slit the envelope and, letter in hand, read it aloud:

Dear Miranda,

I have welcomed the opportunity to put aside matters of State to reply to your letter about the electrification of Waikeri Valley. Most of the people who write me letters are much older than you are and their letters are generally uncomplimentary. Thank you for providing me with a light interlude to my day.

I have consulted my colleague, the Minister of Electricity, and I have welcome news. Waikeri Valley will be brought into the national grid next year. The work of putting up power poles will begin in a month. You and your sisters will have all the electricity you wish to finish your homework next winter.

Kindly convey my good wishes to your parents. I have followed your father's rugby career with some interest. I can also recall having the pleasure of listening to your mother playing at a recital in London. I do hope it will not be too long before I have the pleasure of hearing her again.

I remain
Your humble servant,
Prime Minister of New Zealand

For a moment there was silence. Then, 'Well blow me down,' Papa said. And, 'Goodness,' Mama tried to laugh. Miranda's eyes were shining. 'Oh, Mama, you won't have to play 'Clair de Lune' by moonlight ever again,' Miranda said.

That evening Miranda could hardly sleep for the excitement. Over dinner Papa had started to talk about getting an electrician and a plumber in, and Mama discussed just where the light fittings and power points should be. Even Heni got into the act, telephoning everybody in the valley on the party line. 'Get off the line, Gabby Don!' she would shout whenever she suspected the valley's gossip was listening in. 'And I'll be able to get a fridge and a real oven,' Heni sighed, 'and George will be so pleased not to have to heat up the water for everybody's baths. Just imagine! Hot water from a *tap*.'

Later Papa, Ophelia and Desdemona listened to Mama playing Sibelius. Miranda, however, drifted from room to room, oil-lamp in hand, whispering to the house as she did so. 'Hullo, kitchen. Guess what! Very soon you'll have a new stove and a refrigerator instead of a safe. In the evenings you'll be lit by a bright sun and you will shine *everywhere.* Not like now, when you are lit only by candlelight, lamplight or firelight. I can only see spots of you but not all of you. You will be *wonderful.* Hullo, dining-room. Papa is going to put a light fitting just above you, table, and three more along the wall. You are also going to have a heater to keep us all warm. You will look gay and *bright.* Hullo, living-room. Are you still up there in the corner, Mr Spider? Electricity is coming to light up your world too! Mama will have a large chandelier just over the piano and she won't ruin her beautiful eyes. Papa wants to get a wireless and a phonograph. You will look so *heavenly!*'

And it seemed to Miranda, as she wandered with her lamp, that she was seeing the house for the very first time. Every greeting she made seemed to turn the house from an edifice of brick, wood, tin and mortar into an utterly magical kingdom. Of course she knew it was all an optical illusion — that the flickering of the lamp's flame kept on changing the perspectives, enlarging dimensions and instilling life into shadows — but, nevertheless, she felt a mood of awe come over her. She felt like Ali Baba commanding 'Open Sesame' or Alice falling down the rabbit hole — or as if Rapunzel had let down her hair so that she, Miranda, could climb into a golden tower. Yes, it was just like that, and watching the house come alive filled Miranda with a sense of exultation. She had never noticed before how warm and golden firelight made the kitchen, nor heard the manuka crackle and hiss in conversation. Nor had she expected to see the flowered wallpaper in the hallway suddenly blossom with petals — to drink the light from the lamp as she approached — and to sigh closed again when she had passed. The corners of the living-room where lamplight simply *touched* were bejewelled and glowing spaces — like remote and fantastic worlds filled with unicorn, dodo, phoenix, Pegasus and other fabulous creatures. The lamplight made of the oak staircase a living tree, its trunks and branches constantly moving as Miranda ascended it. The equestrian mural in the hallway moved in obeisance as Miranda passed by. And the carpet beneath her feet was not some thin fabric but a loom of sumptuous purple and red Persian jewels strewn before her. Everywhere she went, Miranda felt she was in the presence of magic.

Then the house seemed to creak with old voices and sing in soprano whispers, dancing to Mama's limpid music. And the house seemed to speak of days gone by. Of how it had been built by Great-Grandpa Bell, those many years ago, with fine silk curtains and strong mellow wood, all to receive the generations of the Bell family. Grandma Bell, for instance, had been delivered of four sons in the conjugal bedroom and, in that same bedroom, Papa had taken Mama to wife. The song of the house was a gentle and sweet one, filled with childish laughter and fond memories of three little babies growing into three sisters. The house had seen it all, been marked by it all and blessed by it all. Nothing, the house whispered, is more precious to me than to serve and protect the children of this house. And Miranda felt a *splash* on her cheek and knew that this was a benediction.

The excitement lasted well after Mama had finished playing the piano for the evening. Ophelia and Desdemona came into Miranda's bedroom. 'We'll have our own bedside lights,' Desdemona said excitedly, 'and we'll be able to read all night.' Papa and Mama heard her and 'Oh no you won't,' they laughed. Later, when the house was quiet, Mama called, 'Miranda? Time to put out your lamp and go to sleep, dear.' At that moment Miranda heard the opossum come harshly chattering to her window. Although it wasn't a pet, the opossum seemed to like saying goodnight to Miranda. There was a rustle in the lemon tree and a thump as the opossum landed on the window sill. 'Soon, Mister Possum,' Miranda promised, 'your life will change also.' The opossum's eyes were like golden orbs, and trapped in each iris was a perfect miniature of the lamp in Miranda's room. *Rack a cack cack*, the opossum answered as the lamps in its eyes slowly gutted, dimmed and died.

7

The announcement POWER COMING TO WAIKERI was published in the city newspaper at the very end of that summer. Miranda cut the announcement out of the newspaper and pinned it to the wall next to her calendar. Oh, it was so frustrating to see how slowly the days went by! She had, at that point, more than a vested interest in the advance of electric reticulation — her notoriety as 'the little girl who wrote a letter to the Prime Minister' had given her a reputation that needed to be kept up. Indeed, some people credited her fully with the coming of electricity to the valley! 'Don't ever let that talk go to your head,' Grandmama cautioned, 'otherwise you might end up — ' an exquisite shudder ' — like your mama.' Not only that, but Miranda's stocks were never higher in the playground. She gave up Anne Boleyn for a more triumphant queen — Elizabeth I — and despatched her enemies with the same vigour and panache as Elizabeth had the Spanish Armada. And ha ha haha, that copycat Linda Potts hadn't received *any* reply from the Prime Minister to *her* letter asking for his autograph. Common, Mama would have said of that request!

Autumn came early to the valley, harbinger of a long hard winter. The leaves turned yellow and red, falling in swathes across the valley. George was forever chopping firewood and saying 'Pae kare, little misses, George will be glad when that 'lectricity comes and he won't have to chop no more wood!' Even Heni, who was usually happy with her lot, would go on and on about having to bake in a wood oven and use a hand eggbeater. She soon brightened up, though, when Papa brought home a new electric stove. 'Well, Heni,' he told her, 'you may have to wait a while before you start to use it, but it's all yours.' Heni gave a cry of delight and started to talk to the stove as if it was a real person. 'Yessirree,' the girls would hear her, 'you and me are going to cook till the cows come home! Blancmange. Sponge cakes. Maori bread when the missus isn't looking. Potatoes cut into chips. We're going to fry, boil, steam, grill, bake, poach and jump over the moon if we have to!' And when Papa brought home the refrigerator, Heni was in Seventh Heaven. 'We've still got so much to get,' Mama cautioned, 'but I'll leave that up to you, Heni.' Heni's eyes grew shiny just *thinking* about electric toasters, eggbeaters, jugs, coffee percolators, not to *mention* washing machine, drier, vacuum cleaner, electric wall clock and a kitchen radio! She got on the telephone to all her friends. ' — and we're going into town next week to have a big spend. We'll buy the whole town out, whooo! So you fellas better watch out, else there'll be nothing left when we've finished! And get off the phone, Gabby Don! Take your big ears somewhere else!' But Heni was always secretly pleased when Gabby Don was listening because she knew he was better than a newspaper at making sure her good news got around.

Then, in the fullness of autumn, important-looking people could be found parked on the side of the road to and from the valley. 'Surveyors,' George said. Following them came great big trucks bearing earth-moving equipment, long concrete electric poles and huge rolls of wire like oversized Catherine wheels. The poles lay on the sides of the road for quite some time — or so it seemed to Miranda — until, one day, truckloads of men descended. From then on, every day brought new sights — one was never too sure just what you would come across around the next corner. There were always signs on the road — MEN WORKING, PROCEED WITH CAUTION, or SLOW — and the valley resounded with the grunt of grader and whump of ditch-digger. All at once the electric poles began to be lifted into the sky, stringing the valley with man-made flowers — metallic stalks and ceramic electric knobs like buds that would never bloom. Soon the clear space that had once been blue sky started to be webbed by the wires that would bring the electricity from the dam, way down south, to the valley.

Winter came and the days fell alarmingly away under the onslaught of that juggernaut — electrical reticulation. Electricians and plumbers came to the house to prepare it for electricity. Mama was driven to distraction by the noise and clutter that surrounded her. Her music, when she played the piano during the evenings, became angular, aggressive and full of discords. But Mama, Miranda — everybody — knew that personal discomfort was but a small price to pay for the glory that was electricity.

The invitation finally came. 'The Minister of Electricity is pleased to invite Mr and Mrs Andrew Bell and family to a special ceremony marking the introduction of electricity to Waikeri Valley. The ceremony will take place on Friday 14 November in Waikeri, at 3 p.m. Guests are requested to take their seats by 2.45 p.m. Afternoon tea will follow. RSVP.'

'Well now,' Papa said. The time had almost come. The family was filled with anticipation, but, now that electricity was almost *here*, they were at a loss for words. And then, before Miranda even realised it, the very day was *there*, and she had no time — no time at all — to take a last look at the house and say, 'Thank you!'

8

Afterwards Miranda realised that her life before electricity had been rather like one of Mama's pieces — Liszt's 'Les Préludes' — full of sweetness, bravura, sentiment, pyrotechnics, nostalgia, brilliance and lyricism. All her life, electricity had been waiting and, when it had come, nothing was ever the same again.

The girls were let off from school early that afternoon. How ironic it was that, on the very day that electricity was due to be introduced to the valley, the playground was a-buzz with the news that the new miracle of communications would soon be playing nationwide — Cinemascope movies! Beside that, pooh, who would want to be bothered by the addition of Waikeri to the national electric grid! Grandmama was decidedly dubious about the new movie technique. 'Knowing what your Aunt Ida did to her hair when the Technicolor process was introduced,' Grandmama said, 'I fear the worst. Of course Ida was always as mad as a hatter. She must have caught it from your mother. This new process — ' Grandmama looked at some space equidistant between herself and the girls ' — makes the screen wider and delivers something called stereophonic sound. Three cameras are required to put the film on the screen. The mind boggles, my dears, simply *boggles*. And what will Ida make of all that, I wonder? I dread to think. 'Just — ' Grandmama wiggled her fingers distatefully — 'dread it!' Then she had sighed and sat up straight in her chair. 'But that is my cross,' Grandmama continued with strength and resolution, 'and, after all, Mama and Ida are my daughters. Is that your papa already? Give Grandmama a kiss, my dears. And remember that I am always here, always ready to uphold those values young girls like yourselves should pursue. Oh, I do hope you *all* grow up lacking in imagination!' And with a flutter of her white handkerchief, as if she were waving from a sinking ship, Grandmama had sent the girls on their way. 'Enjoy the ceremoneeee — ' she called, her voice fading as she disappeared beneath the waves.

And after all that, the ceremony had to be delayed owing to the late arrival of the Minister's plane from Wellington. Nevertheless, that enabled all the residents of Waikeri to have a good yarn to one another about the valley, how great it was to be living in these Modern Times, blah blah blah blah *blah*. Mama was in her finest Spanish lace, holding a parasol against the sun. Heni was like a queen in blue dress and white gloves, greeting her Maori relatives with a dignity and unspoken authority that belied her everyday existence as cook for the Bell family. In a sudden insight Miranda realised that George and Heni, in the fluency of their own culture and language, were different from the George and Heni who worked and cooked and spoke in fractured English. And, looking at the Maori villagers as they sat there, Miranda felt ashamed at the great gulf that existed between herself and them. She wanted to fly across the gulf to Heni and say, 'Oh, Heni, I'm sorry, I just didn't understand — ' But George began signalling from the gate of the post office — the ministerial cavalcade was approaching. You could see them miles away, like the cavalry in one of Aunt Ida's movie magazines.

You could tell easily which gentleman the Minister was. He was so clean-looking and as red of face as a ripe tomato. He smiled at everybody, shook hands with whoever put their hands out and said, 'Nice to see you again' — even if he'd never set eyes on them ever. The postmistress and local councillor escorted the Minister up the steps of the dais. Waikeri had done itself proud — there were ribbons and pennants flying in the breeze and a special *red* tape which was to be symbolically cut. The Minister looked at his watch, nodded in agreement with the postmistress, and stood to deliver his speech. 'Ladies and gentlemen,' he said into the microphone — but it was dead. The Minister laughed out loud and said, 'Well, ladies and gentlemen, perhaps I can use the microphone *after* the ribbon is cut and the power can be turned on!' Everybody laughed at that one, and the mood quickly turned affectionate. 'Ladies and gentlemen, it is my pleasure to represent the Government on this auspicious occasion. I only wish I had brought the Minister of Transport with me but — ' the Minister pretended to dust his suit off ' — you can be assured that I will advise him that I have done my duty but *he* still has to tarseal your road!' That caused another laugh and choruses of *Hear, hear*.

All of a sudden Miranda began to feel terribly sentimental — and she didn't know why. Perhaps it was the sense of occasion or sense of inevitability. It was like Christmas or New Year — one looked so forward to them and then, when they were there, one didn't want them to end. Miranda was so sentimental that she stopped listening to the Minister until Mama elbowed her gently. 'Sit up, Miranda dear,' Mama said, smiling behind her glove. 'The Minister is talking about *you*.' Miranda gasped, wide-eyed, and, 'Oh, there she is,' the Minister said. 'Come up, little girl, would you please?' Everybody began to clap as Miranda walked up to the dais and took her place by the Minister's side. The Minister put a hand on her shoulder and Miranda coloured. 'Young girl,' the Minister continued, 'the Prime Minister told me about your letter. He was charmed by it. Both he and I would be honoured if — ' and Mama smiled with pride as the Minister passed the scissors to Miranda ' — you would cut the ribbon signifying the introduction of electric power to Waikeri Valley.' And amid much clapping and foot stamping, the deed was done. The Minister raised a hand, the lights went on in the pavilion and along the main street, and the microphone went *live*. 'Ladies and gentlemen,' the Minister's voice BOOMED across the valley, 'welcome to the world of ELECTRICITY!' Then he began to clap into the microphone and the sound was like approaching thunder.

Well. What a turn-up that was for the books! And the girls could hardly wait, not another *minute*, before asking Mama and Papa, 'Please may we go home now?' But the Minister had taken Mama's arm and escorted her to the pavilion, where the cups of tea and biscuits were waiting. 'Hush,' Mama said. 'There are duties to perform.' So the children had to cross their legs and hope that the tea urn would run out — or that the Minister would fall dead or something. Grown-ups were so *mean* — all they could think of at moments like this was *food*. Naturally, of course, Mama whispered to the Minister that Heni had made the pikelets. The Minister complimented Heni, who simply *beamed* — not just because the Minister had praised her cooking but also because Gabby Don had been in hearing distance. 'Please, Mama, now?' Miranda asked again. 'Oh, impatience thy name is Miranda!' Mama chided. 'It is improper to leave before the official party.' Mama was clearly enjoying herself. So it was not until very late, when darkness had fallen like a heavy curtain, that Mama said, 'Come along! Come along all!' Laughing and singing, the family all hastened to the car, Heni squeezing in beside George and counting the electric power poles as they bent past. And, for the first time ever, Miranda noticed lights stabbing the darkness of the valley. Electric power was irrevocably here.

In a mood of elation and excitement the family arrived at the house. The wekas were calling and the noise of the bush was so magical. George almost went to light a lamp — how everybody laughed at that! Then Papa told everybody to go into a room each and, at his command, depress the light switch in that room. Heni chose the kitchen, Mama the sitting-room, Ophelia the dining-room, Desdemona her bedroom and Miranda the hallway. 'Are we all at our stations?' Papa called. Yeesss!' everybody responded. 'Then ONE — ' The house began to sigh and creak and whisper. ' — TWO — ' The flowered wallpaper started to blossom, the petals reaching out for the light. ' — THREE — ' And as the light switches were depressed, the magic kingdoms began to glow and come to life. ' — NOW!'

The cheer that Miranda had intended to give caught in her throat. The light flooded in, spilled over, invaded every corner, *exposed* everything. And it seemed to Miranda that the house *screamed* and she felt like — like she had murdered something very precious. The flowered wallpaper just *died* there, its petals cracking and splintering and flaking off the walls. The staircase was no longer a living trunk but a horrible warped piece of wood, stained with rain and twisting in agony. The glowing spaces where once lamplight had only *touched* were revealed for what they really were — gone were the magical kingdoms and, in their places, were cobwebs, black spiders and the shells of dead, feasted-upon flies. The equestrian mural was nothing more than a fading pattern of browns and blacks. Nor was there any Persian carpet on the floor — rather, a nondescript roll of cheap cloth. The magic had gone. No Open Sesame or other incantation would ever bring it back.

All around her, Miranda heard the sound of laughing and excitement. Heni was banging pots in the kitchen. Papa was twiddling with the knobs on his wireless. The refrigerator started to *hum*. Things began to tick, spring, tock, buzz, click, crackle, whirr and hiss. A monster had come into the house, eating up all the silence. 'Isn't electricity wonderful?' Ophelia yelled. 'Isn't it marvellous?' asked Desdemona. And then, there was Mama, looking so wan and pallid, and Miranda knew — just *knew* — that Mama was feeling exactly as she was. 'Oh, Mama,' Miranda cried, 'it's all a mistake — ' But Mama had become rather like a mechanical doll. 'Oh dear,' Mama said to herself, 'I hadn't realised how stained the wallpaper had become. And look at the ceiling! We must get a tradesman in immediately. Andrew? Andrew!' Mama went into the kitchen. Miranda followed her. There was Papa, switching the lights on and off, and George roaring with laughter and pointing at the oven, 'No more chopping wood!' and Heni making the eggbeater whir and —

It was all too much for Miranda. She ran into her bedroom and put her hands over her eyes and ears. But she knew that the prelude was over. Even when she felt the wetness splash on her cheek she knew it was not a benediction but, rather, the rain coming in. 'Goodbye, house,' Miranda said, 'oh, *goodbye*.' But she knew with a certainty that the house had already gone and, with it, all the magic it had once possessed. Nor would the dear, *dear* opossum ever come again to scratch at the window sill. And nor would sweet, imaginative Mama ever again play 'Clair de Lune' by moonlight.

The Affectionate Kidnappers

The two kuia began to weep when their rangatira came in. They wept not because they were frightened but because they were ashamed that their big chief should see them like *this*, in the whareherehere. For a long time they sat there, not looking at him, faces downcast, grieving with one another, and the tears were like wet stones splashing in the dust at their feet.

'Hei aha,' the chief said after a while. Then he turned to the sergeant standing behind him and said, 'Can I speak to my women alone, boss?' The sergeant knew that Hasbrick, the Maori guide, was a good and trustworthy fellow, but the law was the law and the two women might still be capable of some treachery — still waters ran deep among the Maoris. Nevertheless, while putting on a stern appearance, for at Police School he was always told that Appearances Must Always Be Maintained, he responded, 'Well, just this once, Hasbrick. But no funny business, mind.' As he left he closed the door to the cell and with an obvious gesture, all the more melodramatic because it was so ludicrously lofty, turned the key in the lock.

The rangatira sighed as he sat down beside the two women. 'You two are old enough to have more sense,' he said. At that rebuke the kuia redoubled their tangi, turned away and tried to press themselves into the corner. 'Well,' the chief said, insistently, 'it's your own fault, ne?' The kuia were silent, their lips quivering. 'Kati,' the chief relented, 'enough. You two are just like the two birds making your roimata toroa on the ground.' The women smiled at their chief's remarks. He proffered a handkerchief but, shaking their heads, the women used their own scarves to dab at their eyes. Then, hesitantly they reached out for their chief to hold his hand tightly. 'Kei te pai,' he said. 'You should leave us in the jailhouse,' they answered. 'You should tell them to shut us away forever.' But 'Kei te pai, Kuini,' the chief soothed the kuia in the red dress. 'Kei te pai, Puti,' he said to the old lady in the yellow and green. 'I know you two didn't mean to do wrong.'

'She was such a pretty little blondie girl,' Kuini said. 'She was swinging on a gate, all by herself, you know, down there by the hotera. As soon as I saw her I knew she was the Buttons' little girl. You know, they come every summer to the Sounds and me and Puti, we did some work for Mrs Button last summer, cleaning and that. Ay, Puti?'

'Ae,' Puti agreed. 'Kua mahi maua mo te wahine Pakeha. A strict lady that lady.'

'Oh, and Pearl had grown,' Kuini said. 'The year before she only came up to here and *this* year — ' Kuini's eyes softened with tenderness. 'And her teeth were so white. But it made us sad to see her all alone. A tamariki all alone — no good. Especially near a hotel with all those boozers around. So I said to her, "You want to come with us, Pearl Button? Haere mai koe ki te marae?" And she nodded. And I saw Mrs Button in the window — '

'Ae. We waved and waved at her,' Puti said.

'And when she saw us she waved back. So we made signs that we would take Pearl with us for our mate. We pointed to the marae. And Mrs Button waved her apron at us as if to say, "Go right ahead!" So we did.'

'We told the pirihimana this,' Puti said. 'We told him loud but he didn't want to hear us, I reckon. What did we do wrong?' Her face screwed up as if she had tasted a lemon and she started to quiver. The tears started again, as if she was a bottle of aerated water that had been shaken too hard.

The rangatira kept a calm face. This was a no-good business this. 'Didn't you stop to think that this was a Pakeha little girl?' he asked gently, 'a white girl?' Kuini was offended. Her eyes opened wide. 'Kaore,' she said. 'This was a tamariki. Pearl.' Hasbrick's eyelids flickered, betraying his incredulity. Not only was this a white girl but this was also a pretty as a picture blondie girl. Pakehas didn't like their girls being messed around by Maoris. The idea of a pretty curly-headed white girl being taken away by Maoris brought all sorts of pictures to their minds — of sacrifices to idols, cannibalism, of white girls being captured and scalped by Red Indians — and *he* knew because these were the sorts of questions tourists asked him. 'Do you worship these wooden gods?' 'Are there still headhunters in New Zealand?' 'Do you have tomahawks?' No wonder the pirihimana had raised such a big posse. 'This was Pearl,' Kuini said again, emphatically. 'What's the fuss? Maori tamariki wouldn't have such a fuss for them.' At this, Puti smiled. 'Maybe because a Maori mother would be glad to get rid of her kids for the day,' she joked.

'So we took Pearl down to the marae,' Kuini continued, 'and she was as happy as anything. Everybody was helping to get kai ready for our hui today. Lots of people. They all made a fuss of Pearl. Old Joe, he said to me, "You're too ugly to be this kid's mother!" Then he made a pukana at her and gave her a peach to eat. "Kei te matekai koe?" he asked her. And, boy, she was hungry all right. She started to hoe in and the juice ran down her front. It made us feel very happy, ay, Puti, to see that kid eat so much. Too skinny, the Pakeha children, but,' she sighed, 'that's the Pakeha way.'

'Didn't it ever pass through your minds,' Hasbrick asked, 'how her mother would feel about her daughter eating the Maori kai?' Kuini looked startled. 'What's wrong with the Maori kai?' And Hasbrick knew they wouldn't understand the violence of the reaction of Pearl's mother. *Oh, Pearl, did you eat something from the floor? John, darling, did you hear what the Maoris did? They forced food on her. There's no telling what sorts of diseases she got down there. All those dogs they have. And no hygiene. The place should be burned down. Harbouring diseases and diseased people. Oh darling, she drank some water too. Some filthy Maori water. Oh. Oh.*

'Then all of a sudden,' Puti said, 'the koroua, Rangiora, came in, cracking his whip. "Haere mai koutou ki te ruku moana," he shouted. "Kia tere, kia tere." And before we knew it, old Joe had snatched Pearl up and put her in his green cart. He said, "You can drive the trap, tamariki," and Pearl just loved it. Kuini put her on her lap, and old Joe gave Pearl the reins, and we were off. You should have seen those ponies of Joe's. They knew they had a little Pakeha on board. The red pony trotted along with a high proud step and the black pony tossed its mane as if to say, "Anei! Titiro koutou ki ahau!" And Pearl also played with Auntie's pounamu. She was very happy, and that made us happy.' Puti fingered her kete nervously. 'I suppose that is where the wrong lies,' she said in a small voice. 'Making her happy. And we shouldn't have taken her to the sea.'

'What's done is done,' the rangatira said. But in his ears he could still hear the burning words of Pearl's mother. *How dare they. How dare they take her to the sea. She could have drowned. Haven't they got any sense? Not only that, but they were all naked down there. And they unbuttoned Pearl's drawers. My little daughter, defenceless, in the midst of savages. It is too horrible for me to contemplate. Touching her rosy skin with their dirty hands.*

'She'd never seen the sea before,' Kuini said. 'Fancy a kid never seeing the sea! She was frightened at first. But we showed her that it wouldn't hurt her — not the Kingdom of Tangaroa. We took her over to Maggie's place first and then across the paddock to the beach. There we started digging for the toheroa. And soon Pearl started to dig too. Ka nui tana mahi! Oh it was such fun to have a Pakeha tamariki. A Pakeha moko. And *then*, when she felt how warm and tickly the sea was, she started to scream with delight. "Oo, oo! Lovely! Lovely!" She was so excited that she threw herself into my arms, kicking and screaming, oh, the joy of it! Feeling that little body having such fun!'

But that's not what the policemen saw, Hasbrick thought. He conjured the event up in his mind — a little naked girl, kicking and screaming, beating her fists against two black women, a Pakeha blondie girl, looking for all the world as if she was going to be drowned by two black women —

The sergeant reappeared, rattling his keys in the lock. The two women shrank into the shadows. Their eyes were like glowing paua. Then Kuini said, with dignity, to her rangatira, 'E koro, kei te pirangi maua ko Puti ki a hoki atu maua kia maua whare. Puti and I wish to return to our homes.' The rangatira felt anguish in his heart. 'Kei te pirangi maua ko Puti ki a maua wharemoe,' Kuini said. 'We also wish to sleep in our own beds. Not here, in this place of shame.' Her voice trembled with the words.

'Aue, kui,' Hasbrick answered. And the two women realised by the tone of his voice that they would be lost — gone into the darkness, gone into the stomach of the Pakeha, gone into the realm of the night, eaten up by the white man. 'You are facing a serious charge,' Hasbrick continued. 'The Pakeha think you kidnapped the little girl.' And Puti cried out, and Kuini began to grieve, not because of the charge but because she had never slept anywhere else but in her own bed in her own house. And here, for the first time, she would have to lie down on a foreign mattress in a strange room which was noa and could not give her any protection. At that moment, something died inside her, something that had been her strength all her life. She felt it ebbing away, slipping away, leaving her a mere husk. Dimly, she heard Puti say, 'But Mrs Button knows. She knows us.' And she heard her chief reply, 'No. Mrs Button doesn't remember either of you.' And it came to Kuini, with blinding clarity, that Mrs Button was to be felt sorry for — it was not Mrs Button's fault that she couldn't tell one Maori apart from another. And Kuini reached for Puti's hands and face and pressed her face against Puti's saying, 'Never mind, kui. You and I will be mates for each other, just like the two birds.'

'I will be back in the morning,' the rangatira said. 'But you will not be alone. Some of the people have already gathered outside and will stay there to keep you company through the night.' And sure enough, as he was speaking, the two women heard soft singing drifting through the window. 'After all, you two are our kuia.'

Then the rangatira was gone. The two women sat in the gathering dark. Puti thought, *I will never forget. All those little men in blue coats. Little blue men. With their whistles. Running, running towards us. With their police batons raised. It was* — Suddenly, she felt Kuini nudging her and pointing down to the floor. Kuini's voice was still and drained of life. 'Anei,' she whispered. Although the light was waning, the pattern in the dust could still be seen. 'Anei, te roimata toroa.' The soft sounds of waiata swelled in the darkness like currents of the wind holding up Kuini's words. 'E noho ra, Pearl Button,' Kuini said, 'taku moko Pakeha.' The syllables drifted like two birds beating heavily eastward into the night. Then the light went, everything went, life went.

This Life is Weary

1

The little cottages were in a lane to themselves at the very bottom of a steep rise. At the top was the house that the children called *The Big House* — everybody called it that because it was oh so lovely with its lovely house and gardens lived in by its lovely owners — like another world really, one much nicer than down here below the broad road which ran between. But Dadda would always laugh whenever the children were too filled to the brim about the goings on up there, and he would remind them that 'We are all equal in the sight of God' or 'Remember — the lilies of the field — ' This was Dadda's way of saying that no envy should be attached to *The Big House*, nor malice against its gilded inhabitants.

The children loved their Dadda so much, especially Celia the eldest, who thought he was the most wonderful, most handsome, most perfect man in the whole world. Truth to tell, Celia was not far wrong about him — Jack Scott was a fine man. His face was strong and open and was topped with blond curly hair. His shoulders were broad and, altogether, he was a fine figure of a man. But Dadda was more than physically attractive — he possessed a sense of goodness and wholeness, as if his physical beauty merely reflected an inner purity untouched by coarseness. 'When I grow up, Dadda,' Celia would say, 'I shall marry someone just like you.' To this Jack Scott would laugh again — her dear, laughing Dadda — and caution Celia that beauty or handsomeness faded with years and, 'Oh, my sweet Celia, follow your heart and, wherever it leads, to ugly plump thin or brown, there lie you down.'

This kind of simple honesty was what made Dadda so greatly loved in this land of chocolate-brown houses. Although the very smoke coming out of the chimneys might be poverty-stricken — not at all like the great silvery plumes that uncurled from *The Big House* — one could hear the larks sing whenever the carter, Jack Scott, was around. ''ere you, Old Faithful,' the washerwomen would call as Dadda whistled past. ''ow come you're always so 'appy of a mornin'?' Dadda would answer, 'God has given us another beautiful day, ladies, and there are so many beautiful things in it.' And the washerwomen would blush, for they took his remarks as declarations of romance and they loved him all the more — not lasciviously, mind, because they were decent women and beyond the age of temptation. 'Oh my, Jack Scott,' they would call, 'you 'ave a way with the words, but be off with you!' Ah yes, and the men loved Dadda too because of his uprightness and fairness. 'You're a good lad, Jack,' the old pensioners would tell him whenever he was able to spare them some victuals. 'Yes, you're a good mate,' the young men agreed. There was not a finer friend to the young men than Dadda.

He was not old, was Dadda, being only twenty-nine, and his responsibilities as a good husband and father had not brought weariness to him. In the case of Mam, though, Celia could see that life's travails had changed her greatly from the little slip of a thing whom Dadda had met on the ship bringing settlers from England. Romance had blossomed below decks between Jack and Em — and Em's parents had not put a stop to it, for they could tell that Jack would make honest passage through the world and, given his good head for business, a profitable one. Nobody could want better for a daughter of fifteen years. So, on arrival in Wellington, Jack and Em had become man and wife, and they had fulfilled God's commandment to be fruitful by producing Celia, Margaret and Thomas within the first three years of marriage. The doctor had cautioned Jack, saying, 'Give Em some peace now, lad, and let her body recover from the childbearing.' Dadda had laughed and said, 'It's not for my want of trying, Doctor, but the babies just seem to come and, if it is God's will — ' And God willed that there should be two more, the babes Matthew and Mark.

The Big House was regarded with simple awe by many who lived in the little cottages below. Others were not so awestruck, looking upon *The Big House* with a sense of grievance, for it represented everything that they had hoped to escape from when they had left England. Even Dadda was not untouched by the angry murmurs of the working men at meetings of an evening. But above all else, he truly believed that Work and Self-Improvement would win the changes that all strived for.

Dadda went to work every morning before dawn. He would slip out of bed and creep with candle up into the loft to see his little ones. 'Blessed be the new day,' he would whisper, 'and God keep you all safe and well.' Then he would be gone, often not returning until long after dark. Mam had the babes to tend to and, whenever she could, she took small mending work from *The Big House* — she had artistic fingers for embroidery. As for the children, they went off to school during the week. Mam was very firm about this and did not want them swarming in the little crowded lanes like many of the other children who were kept at home.

However, Saturday afternoons were free for the children to do as they pleased and, without fail, this meant going up to *The Big House*, crossing quickly over the broad road between, to watch the house and the comings and goings of the lovely people who lived or visited there. Celia had found a special place — you had to slip between the rose bushes and under the karaka trees to get to it — right by the tennis court. Under the trees was an old wrought-iron loveseat, just ideal for the children. The seat had obviously been thrown out many years ago but it was comfortable enough — once you wiped away the birds' droppings — and perfect to observe from. There was the house, side on to the sun, gleaming like a two-storeyed dolls' house. The driveway was at the front with a circle of green in the middle. Oh, what excitement was occasioned whenever the front gateway opened and a carriage came in! There was a back gateway also and, there, the delivery vans and storemen would enter, bringing the groceries, meat and other supplies to Cook. Once, the children had seen the familiar figure of Dadda himself, and that night they couldn't wait to tell him, 'Dadda, oh Dadda! We saw you at *The Big House* today!' — as if grace and divinity had been suddenly bestowed on him. The house was surrounded with broad swathes of bright green lawn bordered by daisy plants. Just beyond the borders were the roses — hundreds and hundreds of glorious dark red roses of the kind that the children had seen on chocolate boxes.

It was Celia, of course, who thought of keeping notebooks on *The Big House*. Celia had always been an imaginative child and it only seemed natural that simple observation should lead to something more formal — like setting it all down in writing. Dadda and Mam were amused at first but grew to be thoroughly approving. 'Better that the children should be constructive,' Mam would say, 'than down here wasting their lives away.' And Dadda had said, 'Who knows? Some of what they see might rub off on them!' So it soon became part of the Saturday routine for Mam to sharpen pencils and, when the children became more serious about keeping notebooks, to let them take a simple lunch — a crust of bread each and a bottle with water in it — with them. 'Be back before dark!' Mam would cry as the children scampered off. 'We will, Mam, we will!' Celia would reply — because telling Mam and Dadda, right after supper, about what they had seen at *The Big House* became part of the Saturday excursions also. And the children knew that Mam and Dadda welcomed their reports, taking them as signs that their children would do better than they had to make good lives for themselves.

Although Celia had never been to any theatre, watching *The Big House* was just as she imagined a play would be. Like all theatrical settings, the weather was always ideal up there and the days perfect and made to order. The backdrop was windless and warm, with a light blue sky flecked with gold. It was all so unlike the dark and dirty eyesore which cluttered the area the children came from. Indeed, sometimes it was difficult for the children to accept that this world was as real as their own — it really was as if they had paid a penny to go to His Majesty's Royal Theatre for a few hours of a drab Saturday afternoon. But what fun! Naturally, the house itself was the main stage prop, particularly the verandahs, top and bottom, and the french doors on to the verandahs. From out of these doors would come the lovely people of *The Big House*, the main actors of every Saturday afternoon performance. Head of the Household was Mr Sheridan, who worked in the city and never seemed to be around very much. He generally slept late on Saturdays, sometimes not appearing until 2 p.m., all hairy and drumming his chest after a wash. Mistress of the House was Mrs Sheridan, prone to sitting on a chair off the main bedroom and fanning herself like a lady in a magazine. Once, so Margaret swore, Mrs Sheridan actually waved to the children where they sat. 'Impossible,' Celia replied. Her version appeared that night, after supper, when she produced a sketch of Mrs Sheridan trying to swat at something going bbbzzzz — Mam and Dadda thought that was very funny, but Margaret was cross.

Mr and Mrs Sheridan had three daughters, Meg, Jose and Laura, and a son, Laurie — and it was on these four fascinating golden creatures that the children focused all their attention. Celia would scribble like mad in her notebook as Margaret and Thomas described every appearance: 'Meg has just washed her hair,' Margaret would say, in awe, because washing one's hair in the afternoon was the prerogative of the wealthy. 'Oh, look, there's Jose! She has put on her lovely silk petticoat and the kimono jacket.' And Thomas would reflect, 'Do you think she got the jacket from the Chinamen who play pakapoo?' To which Celia, the expert on fashion, would say, 'Kimonos come from Japan, Thomas, not China.' But Margaret might interrupt, 'Oh, quick, here comes Meg again! Doesn't she look pretty? I'll bet a beau is coming to call.' And sure enough, half an hour later, the gateway would open and a fine hansom would deposit a grave but hopeful young man. 'Oh, he's not right for Meg,' Celia would say. 'Pooh, no!'

Thomas and Margaret would agree, for they knew that without doubt Meg was going to be a famous pianist. Her life was not to be squandered away on silly young men! Wasn't it true that every afternoon Meg practised the piano and showed signs of improving? — why, only four mistakes in the 'Für Elise' last Saturday! As for Jose, oh dear, she would just have to give up any thought of an operatic career. While her voice was strong enough, alas, her sense of timing was woeful. Worse still, she could never hold the tune. Apart from which, nobody could sing 'This Life is Weary' better than Dadda —

> This Life is *Wee*-ary,
> A Tear — a Sigh.
> A Love that *Chan*-ges,
> This Life is *Wee*-ary,
> A Tear — a Sigh.
> A Love that *Chan*-ges,
> And then . . . Good-bye!

No, Jose would be better off receiving silly young men herself. In this manner, the children would observe, ponder, dream and hope that the characters whom they had come to love would grow, prosper and make the right decisions.

The children's main interest was in the heroine of the Sheridan family, the one whom they thought was most like themselves — Laura. Her every entrance was greeted in the same way as a diva by a starstruck audience — with a hushed indrawn breath, moment of recognition, long sigh of release and joyous acclamation. Laura was Celia's age — at least, that's what Celia insisted — and could do no wrong. She was the one whom the children most wanted to have as a friend, if class would ever allow it. Their notebooks were filled, positively to the very margins, with anecdotes, drawings and notes about Laura in all her moods. To even get a good likeness was difficult enough, for Laura was always flying in and out, here and there, to and fro. Often the children would have to compare their drawings for accuracy and, 'No, she didn't look like that,' Celia would say, 'she looked like this.' Then Margaret would interject, 'But she wasn't wearing the blue pinafore, she was wearing the yellow one with the tiny wee apron.' To which Thomas would respond, 'Well, she was just perfect as she was, a perfect little princess.' This was, in fact, patently inaccurate, because perfect little princesses were not tomboys — and there was a streak of this in Laura. Perfect little princesses did not do cartwheels on the front lawn or thumb their noses at beaux they didn't like. Oh, she was such a character sometimes! 'I wonder what her bedroom is like?'

Margaret would wonder. 'Does it have a huge bed and are all her dolls propped up on the pillows?' Interrupting, Thomas would venture, 'And would there be a rockinghorse?' To which Celia would purse her lips and say, 'Perhaps. Rockinghorses are really for boys but — yes, Laura is bound to have one.'

On most occasions, the appearances by the Sheridans were seen from afar. There was one magical moment, however — the children had to pinch themselves to make sure they weren't dreaming — when Hans, one of the servants, brought a small table and four chairs on to the tennis court right in front of the children. Laura appeared with three of her dolls, placed them on chairs and proceeded to have afternoon tea with cakes and biscuits. 'Lady Elizabeth,' Laura said, 'would you care for some milk? Sugar? One lump or two?' Then, with a laugh, 'Oh, quite, Countess Mitzi, quite.' And Celia almost fainted away with pleasure when, turning to the third doll, Laura said, 'Princess Celia, how was your last visit to Paris?' For the rest of the afternoon the children were just transported, bursting with ecstasy — and they could hardly wait to tell Mam and Dadda. 'Oh, slow down, lovey,' Mam said to Celia. 'Do slow down!' And that put the seal on the entire afternoon, for it was exactly the sort of comment that the children were constantly passing about Laura herself.

2

One day, the children came running back from an afternoon watching *The Big House* with the news 'Oh, Mam! Dadda! There's going to be a garden-party! At *The Big House*! We heard Mrs Sheridan reminding Cook! Next Saturday! Oh, can we go for the whole day? With our notebooks? In the morning? So many people have been invited! Please, Mam! Please, Dadda!' As it happened, Em had hoped the girls would mind the babes while she visited her parents but, 'Let the little ones go,' Dadda said, adding with a wink, 'and I shall try to come home early in the afternoon, eh, Em love?' Trying not to blush, Em said, 'All right, children, you may go,' and the children clapped their hands together with glee. Then a thoughtful, twinkling look came into Mam's eyes and she suddenly left the kitchen to rummage in the glory box in the bedroom. When she came back she had some velvet and other material in her arms. 'Come here, Celia lovey,' Em said. 'My, you've grown —' and her eyes sparkled with sadness, mingled with pride, at the thought of her eldest daughter growing into womanhood. 'What are you doing, Mam?' Celia asked. 'Why, measuring you, your sister and brother, of course,' Mam said. 'You can't go to a garden-party in your everyday clothes.' And Margaret said, 'But Mam, we're not invited — ' To which Em said, 'Hush, child. We can dream, can't we?' And Jack came to hold Em close and kiss her. 'That we can, Em love,' he said, 'that we can.'

The children could hardly contain themselves. All that week they conjectured about the garden-party — who would come, what food would be served, what Laura would wear, would there be a band, how many waiters — and they were so fidgety that Mam had to say, 'Do keep still, Margaret, or else your dress will not be ready in time!' Then Margaret would stay very still indeed, hardly drawing breath, because green velvet was her favourite colour and she wanted to look her very best — and Mam even made a green bow for her hair! Thomas, reluctant at first, also got into the swing of things. He knew that he was going to look a proper guy — and how was he going to get up to *The Big House* and back without the other swarming children seeing him — but, oh, there was such a delicious silky feeling to the new shirt! As for Celia, she had determined, 'Mam, I can make my own dress and hat.' So while Mam stitched costumes for Margaret and Thomas, Celia worked on a cloth that had once been a curtain. When Celia completed her dress Mam trimmed it with a lace ribbon she had been saving for herself.

Then, when all the stitching and sewing was completed, didn't the children look just lovely, parading in front of Dadda and Mam that Friday night before the garden-party? Hardly a wink was slept, so that when Dadda came to wake them, why, the children were already dressed and waiting! And wasn't Dadda the most perfect man? He had transformed the cart into a carriage and placed cushions on the seats. Then, bowing, he handed the children up, saying, 'Lady Margaret, if you would be so kind — Princess Celia, charmed — Sir Thomas, delighted — ' And Mam, trying not to laugh too much, came from the doorway with a hamper of cordial, sandwiches and a dear wee cake. 'Oh, Mam. Oh, Dadda,' was all that Celia could say because the words got caught in her throat. 'Have a lovely time, children,' Mam said. 'And Thomas, don't worry — your Dadda will pick you all up before dark from the gateway of *The Big House*. Byeeee — ' And she blew a kiss as they left.

And after all the weather was ideal. When the dawn came creeping across the sky, the children knew it was going to be a perfect day for the Sheridans' garden-party. From their position under the trees they saw the garden-party from beginning to end. They saw the Maori gardener already at work mowing the lawns and sweeping them. 'Oh, he's missed a piece!' Margaret wailed but, joy, he returned to sweep the swathe so that the lawn looked all combed the same way — not a lick out of place. 'Nothing must go wrong,' Celia nodded. Then the children saw movement in *The Big House* and knew that Mr and Mrs Sheridan, Meg, Jose, Laura and Laurie were at breakfast. Mr Sheridan came out the front door with a BANG to go through the gateway. At the same time the men came to put up the marquee. And who else but Laura, the little princess herself, should appear to give the men their instructions! 'Oh, she's so pretty!' Thomas said, 'and look, she's eating bread and butter — just like we do.' The next few moments, though, were anxious ones for the children because at one point, Laura pointed to the tennis court. Yes, it was certainly the most appropriate place for the marquee but, 'It will spoil our view,' Celia whispered. And, why, Laura must have heard, because the workmen set the marquee near the karaka trees instead!

'Message, Laura!' a voice cried from the house, and away the little princess skimmed. But what was happening at the back door? Why, the florist had arrived and just look at the pots and pots of canna lilies — so radiant and frighteningly alive on their bright crimson stems! And then, from the drawing room, was that Meg on the piano? Pom! Ta-ta-ta Tee-ta! Oh dear, was Jose really going to embarrass herself by singing at the garden-party? There she was, warming up — 'This Life is *Wee*-ary, A Tear — a Sigh — ' Oh dear, dear, dear. But now look! Someone else had arrived at the back door. Surely it was the Godber van, clattering into the yard, bringing lovely cream puffs! And there was the man from Godber's talking to Cook, and —

Suddenly the sky was filled with a soft radiance and it was almost like — like a shooting star, in the daytime though, going UP into the sky — and Celia felt such sweet pain that she wanted to weep. Her heart was so full, so overflowing, so brimming over, and in that same instant she thought of her Dadda.

Strange really, but for a while after that the house fell into silence. Laura's voice could be heard piping and alarmed. 'What is happening now?' Margaret asked. 'I'm not sure,' Celia said. 'Perhaps it is lunch-time already.' Indeed it was — hadn't time passed quickly? So Margaret opened the hamper, Celia laid the food out, and Thomas said, 'Lady Margaret, would you care for some wine?' Margaret clapped her hands together and, 'Thank you, Sir Thomas,' she said as Thomas poured some cordial into her glass. 'And you, Princess Celia?' Celia inclined her head. And oh, it was so much fun to be sitting there sipping wine on the perfect day.

Lunch in *The Big House* was over by half past one. The green-coated bandsmen arrived and established themselves right next to the children near the tennis court. The man on the tuba saw them and gave a cheery wave. Would he tell? No — he was too jolly to do that. Soon after, the guests began coming in streams — one carriage after the other — the women so lovely, oh so *lovely*. The band struck up. The hired waiters ran from the house to the marquee. Wherever the children looked there were couples strolling, bending to the flowers, greeting, and gliding across the lawn. The children were enchanted, transported, transformed — in Heaven — by it all. There in the shadows they imitated the movements of the guests, and sometimes when the band played, Sir Thomas first asked Lady Margaret and then Princess Celia to dance with him, on and on and on. The man on the tuba smiled when he saw them dancing and, oh goodness, when the waiters came to offer the band refreshments he must have pointed out the children! Over came one of the waiters with a tray of delicious cakes and cream puffs, and he bowed gravely, saying, 'Mesdames? Monsieur?' And always, far away in the sunlight was dear, darling Laura. Something was bothering her, but she was so gracious, wasn't she? 'Oh, I must sketch her,' Celia cried. And the perfect afternoon slowly ripened, slowly faded, slowly its petals closed. And soon it was all over.

The children were in ever such an excited state as they waited for their Dadda to pick them up. They had stayed beneath the trees until the very end when the last bandsman had packed his instrument and left. The man with the tuba had given a very cheery wave. By the time the children reached the gateway it was almost dark. 'Wasn't it wonderful when — ' the children would reminisce to one another. They wanted to savour every minute of the garden-party and, 'Oh, write that one down, Celia,' Margaret would cry. 'We forgot about that moment.' So for a while they sat scribbling away in the gathering darkness. 'Weren't the guests all so lovely?' Margaret whispered. On and on the children chattered.

The darkness deepened. The children couldn't wait for Dadda to arrive so that they could get home quickly and tell him and Mam about the garden-party. When the night fell like a cloak, Celia said, 'Dadda must be delayed. Come along, let's go on home. Like as not we'll meet him coming up the hill.' Thomas was so happy that he didn't even think to be embarrassed should they meet any swarming children. Down, down, down into the sordid lanes the children descended. The lights were on in some of the houses. People were like silent wraiths slipping into and out of the light. All of a sudden someone came running from behind the children, passing them and turning the corner. When the children rounded the corner themselves, they saw a young man with a girl. The girl was pressed against him and she looked as if she was crying. Celia overheard the young man say, 'Was it awful?' The girl shook her head — and there was something terribly familiar in the motion — but it was so dark, so dark.

Then the children were in sight of their own house and they started to run towards it. But what was this? Lamps were shining in the front parlour. A dark knot of people stood outside. Women in shawls and men in tweed caps were gathered there. Without knowing why, Celia felt an awful feeling inside her heart. She saw Gran, Mam's mother, sitting in a chair beside the gate. As the children approached, Gran gave a cry. The knot loosened and voices came out of the darkness at the children, 'Oh, the poor wee children.' Gran kissed the children and held them tight. 'What's wrong, Gran?' Celia asked. 'There's been an accident, Celia dear,' Gran answered. 'Your father — '
Celia pulled Margaret and Thomas quickly through the crowd and into the house. Auntie May was there in the passageway, but Celia didn't want *her*.

'Mam? Dadda?' Celia called. 'Mam?' Then another woman was there. Her face was all puffed up and red, with swollen eyes and swollen lips. 'Mam?' Celia whispered, because it was indeed her mother. But she looked so — so — *awful*.

'Your Dadda's gone,' Mam said. 'He's gone.'

Margaret started to wail and Thomas bit his lip and screwed up his eyes. The two children ran to the comfort of their mother's arms. But Celia just stood there. *Oh, Dadda, was that you, that soft radiance? Was that your soul coming to say goodbye before going to Heaven?* Then, in the corner, Celia noticed a basket of fruit — the fruit looked so lovely, oh so very lovely — and she remembered the garden-party. 'I must tell Dadda,' Celia thought. Her heart was breaking into a thousand pieces. 'Where's Dadda?' she asked. Mam motioned toward the bedroom.

For a moment Celia was too frightened to go in. She didn't want to *know*. She didn't want to *see*. All of a sudden, she felt a fleeting sense of unfairness that *The Big House*, with its gilded life, should be so impervious to all the ills of the world. But no, she shouldn't think like that. Dadda wouldn't want her to think like that, would he? 'Dadda?' she called from the doorway. 'Dadda?' She took a step and, why, there he was in his bed, and she had caught him asleep! There he was, glowing in the light of the smoky lamp, her handsome laughing Dadda. And fast asleep he was, sleeping so soundly that he didn't even stir when she knelt beside him. Curly headed Dadda, deeply, peacefully sleeping.

'Oh Dadda,' Celia whispered. She put her head against his, and the first glowing tear dropped down her cheek like a golden sun. 'It was a lovely garden-party, Dadda, just *lovely*,' she said.

His First Ball

Just why it was that he, Tuta Wharepapa, should receive the invitation was a mystery to him. Indeed, when it came, in an envelope bearing a very imposing crest, his mother mistook it for something entirely different — notice of a traffic misdemeanour, a summons perhaps, or even worse, an overdue account. She fingered it gingerly, holding it as far away from her body as possible — just in case a pair of hands came out to grab her fortnightly cheque — and said, 'Here, Tuta. It must be a bill.' She thrust it quickly at her son before he could get away and, wriggling her fingers to get rid of the taint, waited for him to open it.

'Hey — ' Tuta said as he stared down at the card. His face dropped such a long way that his mother — her name was Coral — became alarmed. Visions of pleading in court on his behalf flashed through her mind. 'Oh, Tuta, how bad is it?' she said as she prepared to defend her son against all-comers. But Tuta remained speechless and Coral had to grab the card from his hands. 'What's this?' she asked. The card was edged with gold:

> The Aide-de-Camp in Waiting
> Is Desired By Their Excellencies

'Oh, Tuta, what have you done?' Coral said. But Tuta was still in a state of shock. Then, 'Read on, Mum,' he said.

> To Invite Mr Tuta Wharepapa
> To A Dance At Government House

Coral's voice drifted away into speechlessness like her son's. Then she compressed her lips and jabbed Tuta with an elbow. 'I'm tired of your jokes,' she said. 'It's not my joke, Mum,' Tuta responded. 'I know you, Tuta,' Coral continued. 'True, Mum, honest. One of the boys must be having me on.' Coral looked at Tuta, unconvinced. 'Who'd want to have *you* at their flash party?' she asked. 'Just wait till I get the joker who sent this,' Tuta swore to himself. Then Coral began to laugh. 'You? Go to Government House? You don't even know how to bow!' And she laughed and laughed so much at the idea that Tuta couldn't take it. 'Where are you going, Your Highness?' Coral asked. 'To find out who sent this,' Tuta replied, waving the offending invitation in her face. 'By the time I finish with him — or her' — because he suddenly realised Coral herself might have sent it ' — they'll be laughing on the other side of their face.' With that, he strode out of the kitchen. 'Oh, Tuta?' he heard Coral call, all la-di-da, 'If you ore gooing pahst Goverment Howse please convay may regahrds to — ' and she burst out laughing again.

Tuta leapt on to his motorbike and, over the rest of the day, roared around the city calling on his mates from the factory. 'It wasn't me, Tuta,' Crazy-Joe said as he sank a red ball in the billiard saloon, 'but I tell you, man, you'll look great in a suit.' Nor was it Blackjack over at the garage, who said, 'But listen, mate, when you go grab some of those Diplo number plates for me, ay?' And neither was it Des, who moonlighted as Desirée Dawn at the strip club, or Sheree, who worked part time at the pinball parlour. 'You couldn't take a partner, could you?' Desirée Dawn breathed hopefully. 'Nah, you wouldn't be able to fit on my bike,' Tuta said — apart from which he didn't think a six-foot transvestite with a passion for pink boas and slit satin dresses would enjoy it all that much. By the end of the day Tuta was no wiser, and when he arrived at Bigfoot's house and found his mate waiting for him in a tiara, he knew that word was getting around. Then it came to him that perhaps the invitation was real after all. Gloria Simmons would know — she was the boss's secretary and knew some lords.

'Oh,' Mrs Simmons whispered reverently as Tuta handed her the crested envelope. She led Tuta into the sitting-room. 'It looks real,' she said as she held it to the light. Then she opened the envelope and, incredulous, asked, 'You received this?' Tuta nodded. 'You didn't just pick it up on the street,' Mrs Simmons continued, 'and put your name on it?' Offended, Tuta shook his head, saying 'You don't think I want to go, do you?' Mrs Simmons pursed her lips and said, 'Perhaps there's another Tuta Wharepapa, and you got his invitation in error.' And Mrs Simmons's teeth smiled and said, 'In that case, let me ring Government House and let them know.' With that, Mrs Simmons went into another room, where Tuta heard her dialling. Then *her* voice went all la-di-da too as she trilled, 'Ooo, Gahverment Howse? May ay speak to the Aide-de-Camp? Ooo, har do yoo do. So sorry to trouble you but ay am ringing to advayse you — ' Tuta rolled his eyes — how come everybody he told about the invitation got infected by some kind of disease! Then he became acutely aware that Mrs Simmons had stopped talking. He heard her gasp. He heard her say in her own lingo, 'You mean to tell me that this is for real? That you people actually sent an invite to a — a — boy who packs batteries in a factory?' She put down the telephone and returned to the sitting-room. She was pale but calm as she said, 'Tuta dear, difficult though this may be, can you remember the woman who came to look at the factory about two months ago?' Tuta knitted his eyebrows. 'Yeah, I think so. That must have been when we opened the new extension.' Mrs Simmons closed her eyes. 'The woman, Tuta. The woman.' Tuta thought again. 'Oh yeah, there *was* a lady, come to think of it, a horsey-looking lady who — ' Mrs Simmons interrupted him. 'Tuta, dear, that lady was the wife of the Governor-General.'

Dazed, Tuta said, 'But she didn't say who she was.' And he listened as Mrs Simmons explained that Mrs Governor-General had been very impressed by the workers at the factory and that Tuta was being invited to represent them. 'Of course you will have to go,' Mrs Simmons said. 'One does not say "No" to the Crown.' Then Mrs Simmons got up and telephoned Tuta's mother. 'Coral? Gloria here. Listen, about Tuta, you and I should talk about what is required. What for? Why, when he goes to the ball of course! Now — ' *Me? Go to a ball?* Tuta thought. *With all those flash people, all those flash ladies with their crowns and diamonds and emeralds? Not bloody likely — Bigfoot can go, he's already got a tiara, yeah. Not me. They'll have to drag me there. I'm not going. Not me. No fear. No WAY.* But he knew, when he saw the neighbours waiting for him at home that, of course, his mother had already flapped her mouth to everybody. 'Oh yes,' she was telling the neighbours when Tuta walked in, 'it was delivered by special messenger. This dirty big black car came and a man, must have been a flunkey, knocked on the door and — ' Then Coral saw Tuta and, 'Oh Tuta,' she cried, opening her arms to him as if she hadn't seen him for days.

After that, of course, there was no turning back. The boss from the factory called to put the hard word on Tuta. Mrs Simmons RSVPeed by telephone and — 'Just in case, Tuta dear' — by letter and, once that was done, he had to go. The rest of his mates at the factory got into the act, also, cancelling the airline booking he made to get out of town and, from thereon in, followed him everywhere. 'Giz a break, fellas,' Tuta pleaded as he tried to get out, cajole or bribe himself out of the predicament. But Crazy-Joe only said, 'Lissen, if you don't get there then I'm — ' and he drew a finger across his throat, and Blackjack said, 'Hey, man, I know a man who knows a man who can get us a Rolls for the night — ' and Bigfoot just handed him the tiara. And boy, did Coral ever turn out to be the walking compendium of What To Do And How To Do It At A Ball. 'Gloria says that we have to take you to a tailor so you can hire a suit. Not just any suit and none of your purple numbers either. A black *conservative* suit. And then we have to get you a bowtie and you have to wear black shoes — so I reckon a paint job on your brown ones will do. You've got a white shirt, thank goodness, but we'll have to get some new socks — calf length so that when you sit down people won't see your hairy legs. Now, what else? Oh yes, I've already made an appointment for you to go to have your hair cut, no buts, Tuta, and the boys are taking you there, so don't think you're going to wriggle out of it. By the time that dance comes around we'll have you decked out like the Prince of Wales — ' which was just what Tuta was afraid of.

But that was only the beginning. Not only did his appearance have to be radically altered, but his manners had to be brushed up also — and Mrs Simmons was the first to have a go. 'Tuta dear,' she said when he knocked on her door, 'Do come in. Yes, take your boots off but on THE NIGHT, the shoes stay *on*. Please, come this way. No, Tuta, *after* me, just a few steps behind. Never barge, Tuta and don't shamble along. Be PROUD, Tuta, be HAUGHTY' — and she showed him how to put his nose in the air. Tuta followed her, his nose so high that he almost tripped, into the dining-room. 'Voila!' she said. 'Ay?' Tuta answered. Mrs Simmons then realised that this was going to be very difficult. 'I said, "Ta ra!" ' She had set the table with a beautiful cloth — and it appeared to be laid with thousands of knives, forks and spoons. 'This is what it will be like at the ball,' she explained. 'Oh boy,' Tuta said. 'Now, because I'm a lady you must escort me to my seat,' Mrs Simmons said. 'Huh? Can't you walk there yourself?' Tuta asked. 'Just *do* it,' Mrs Simmons responded dangerously, 'and *don't* push me all the way under the table, Tuta, just to the edge will do — ' and then, under her breath ' — Patience, Gloria dear, *patienza*.' Once seated, she motioned Tuta to a chair opposite her. 'Gee, thanks,' he said. Mrs Simmons paused, thoughtfully, and said, 'Tuta dear, when in doubt don't say *anything*. Just shut your mouth.' She shivered, but really, the boy would only understand common language, '— and keep it shut.' Then she smiled. 'Now follow every action that I make.' Exaggerating the movements for Tuta's benefit, Mrs Simmons said, 'First, take up the spoon. No, not that one, *that* one. That's for your soup, that's for the second course, that's for the third course, that's for the fourth — ' Tuta looked helplessly at her. 'Can't I use the same knives and things all the time?' he asked. '*Never*,' Mrs Simmons shivered. 'Well, what's all these courses for?' Tuta objected. 'Why don't they just stick all the kai on the table at once?' Mrs Simmons deigned not to answer. Instead she motioned to the glasses, saying, 'Now *this* is for white wine, this for red wine, this for champagne and this for cognac.' Tuta sighed, saying 'No beer? Thought as much.' Refusing to hear him, Mrs Simmons proceeded, 'You sip your wine just like you sip the soup. Like *so*,' and she showed him. 'No, Tuta, not too fast. And leave the bowl *on* the table, *don't* put it to your lips. No, *don't* slurp. Oh my goodness. Very GOOD, Tuta! Now wipe your lips with the napkin.' Tuta looked puzzled. 'Ay?' he asked. 'The paper napkin on your lap,' Mrs Simmons said. 'This hanky thing?' Tuta responded. 'Why, Tuta!' Mrs Simmons's teeth said, 'How clever of you to work that out. Shall we proceed to the second course? Good!' Mrs Simmons felt quite sure that Professor Higgins didn't have it *this* bad.

Then, of course, there was the matter of learning how to dance — not hot rock but slow *slow* dancing, holding a girl, 'You know,' Mrs Simmons said, '*together*,' adding, 'and young ladies at the ball are never allowed to decline.' So Tuta made a date with Desirée Dawn after hours at the club. Desirée was just overwhelmed to be asked for advice and told her friends Alexis Dynamite and Chantelle Derrier to help her. 'Lissun, honey,' Desirée said as she cracked her gum. 'No matter what the dance is, there's always a basic rhythm.' Chantelle giggled and said, 'Yeah, very basic.' Ignoring her, Desirée hauled Tuta on to the floor, did a few jeté's and, once she had limbered up, said, 'Now *you* lead,' and 'Oo, honey, I didn't know you were so masterful.' Alexis fluttered her false eyelashes and, 'You two don't need music at *all*,' she whispered. Nevertheless, Alexis ran the tape and the music boomed across the club floor. 'This isn't ball music,' Tuta said as he heard the raunch scream out of the saxes. 'How do *you* know?' Chantelle responded. And Tuta had the feeling that he wasn't going to learn how to dance in any way except improperly. 'Lissun,' Desirée said, 'Alexis and I will show you. Move your butt over here, Lexie. Now, Tuta honey, just watch. Can ya hear the rhythum? Well you go *boom* and a *boom* and a *boom boom boom*.' And Alexis screamed and yelled, 'Desirée, he wants to dance with the girl, not *make* her in the middle of the floor.' And Chantelle only made matters worse by laughing, 'Yeah, you stupid slut, you want him to end up in prison like you?' At which Desirée gasped, walked over to Chantelle, peeled off both Chantelle's false eyelashes, said, 'Can you see better? Good,' and lammed her one in the mouth. As he exited, Tuta knew he would have better luck with Sheree at the pinball parlour — she used to be good at roller skating and could even do the splits in mid-air.

So it went on. The fitting at the tailor's was duly accomplished ('Hmmmmnnnn,' the tailor said as he measured Tuta up. 'Your shoulders are too wide, your hips too large, you have shorter legs than you should have but — Hmmmmnnnn'), his hair was trimmed to within an inch of propriety, and he painted his brown shoes black. His lessons continued with Mrs Simmons, Tuta's mother, the workers from the factory — even the boss — all pitching in to assist Tuta in the etiquette required. For instance: 'If you're talking you ask about the weather. This is called polite conversation. You say "Isn't it lovely?" to everything, even if it isn't. You always say "Yes" if you're offered something, even if you don't want it. The man with the medals is *not* the waiter. He is His Excellency. The lady who looks like a horse is not in drag and you should *not* ask if her tiara fell off the same truck as Bigfoot's.'

Then, suddenly it was time for Tuta to go to the ball. 'Yes, Mum,' he said to Coral as she fussed around him with a clothes brush, 'I've got a hanky, I've brushed my teeth three times already, the invite is in my pocket — ' And when Tuta stepped out the door the whole world was there — the boss, Mrs Simmons, Crazy-Joe, Blackjack, Bigfoot and others from the factory, Desirée Dawn and the neighbours. 'Don't let us down,' the boss said. 'Not too much food on the fork,' Mrs Simmons instructed. 'The third boom is the one that does it,' Desirée Dawn called. 'Don't forget the Diplo plates,' Blackjack whispered. 'And don't drink too much of the beer,' Coral said. Then, there was the car, a Jaguar festooned with white ribbons and two small dolls on the bonnet. 'It's a ball I'm off to,' Tuta said sarcastically, 'not a wedding.' Blackjack shrugged his shoulders. 'Best I could do, mate, and this beauty was just sitting there outside the church and — ' He got in and started the motor. Tuta sat in the back and, suddenly, Bigfoot and Crazy-Joe were in either side. 'The boss's orders,' they said. 'We deliver you to the door or else — ' Outside, Tuta saw the boss draw a line across their necks. The car drew away and as it did so, Mrs Simmons gave a small scream. 'Oh my goodness, I forgot to tell Tuta that if Nature calls he should not use the bushes,' she said.

Looking back, Tuta never quite understood how he ever survived that journey. At one point a police car drew level on the motorway, but when they looked over at the Jaguar and saw Tuta he could just imagine their disbelief, Nah. Couldn't possibly . . . Nah. His head was whirling with all the etiquette he had learnt and all the instructions he had to remember. He trembled, squirmed, palpitated and sweated all over the seat. Then he was there, and Blackjack was showing the invitation, and the officer at the gate was looking doubtfully at the wedding decorations, and then 'Proceed ahead, sir,' the officer said. *What a long drive*, Tuta thought. *What a big palace. And look at all those flash people. And they're all going in.* 'Well, mate,' Blackjack said, 'Good luck. Look for us in the car park.' And Crazy-Joe said, 'Hey, give the missus a whirl for me, ay?' and with that, and a squeal of tires (Black-jack was always such a show-off), they were gone.

He was alone. Him. Tuta Wharepapa. Standing there. At the entrance way. Inside he heard music and the laughter of the guests. Then someone grabbed his arm and said, 'Come along!' and before he knew it he was inside and being propelled along a long hallway. And the young woman who had grabbed him was suddenly pulled away by her companion, and Tuta was alone again. *Oh boy*, he thought. *Look at this red carpet.* He felt quite sure that the paint was running off his shoes and that there were great big black footmarks all the way to where he was now standing. Then a voice BOOMED ahead, and Tuta saw that there was a line of people in front and they were handing their invitations in to the bouncer. Tuta joined them. The bouncer was very old and very dignified — he looked, though, as if he should have been retired from the job years ago. *Nah*, Tuta thought. *He couldn't be a bouncer. Must be a toff.* The toff looked Tuta up and down and thrust out his white-gloved hand. 'I got an invitation,' Tuta said. 'True. I got one.' The toff read the card and his eyebrows arched. 'Your name?' he BOOMED. 'Tuta.' Couldn't he read? Then the toff turned away in the direction of a huge ballroom that stretched right to the end of the world. The room seemed to be hung with hundreds of chandeliers and *thousands* of people were either dancing or standing around the perimeter. There were steps leading down to the ballroom and, at the bottom, was a man wearing medals and a woman whose tiara wasn't as sparkly as Bigfoot's — *them*. And Tuta felt *sure*, when the Major-Domo — for that was who the toff was — stepped forward and opened his mouth to announce him, that *everybody* must have heard him BOOM —

'Your Excellencies, Mr Tutae Tockypocka.'

Tuta looked for a hole to disappear into. He tried to backpedal down the hallway but there were people behind him. 'No, you got it wrong,' he said between clenched teeth to the Major-Domo. 'Tutae's a rude word.' But the Major-Domo simply sniffed, handed back the invitation, and motioned Tuta down the stairs. Had *they* heard? In trembling anticipation Tuta approached the Governor-General. 'Mr Horrynotta?' the Governor-General smiled. 'Splendid that you were able to come along. Dear? Here's Mr Tutae.' And in front of him was Mrs Governor-General. 'Mr Forrimoppa, how kind of you to come. May I call you Tutae? Please let me introduce you to Lord Wells.' And Lord Wells, too. 'Mr Mopperuppa, quite a mouthful, what. Not so with Tutae, what?' *You don't know the half of it*, Tuta thought gloomily. And then Mrs Governor-General just *had* to, didn't she, giggle and

pronounce to all and sundry, 'Everybody, you must meet Mr Tutae.'
And that's who Tuta became all that evening. 'Have you met Mr Tutae
yet? No? Mr Tutae, this is Mr — ' And Tuta would either shake hands
or do a stiff little bow and look around for that hole in the floor. He
once made an attempt to explain what 'tutae' was but heard Mrs
Simmons's voice: 'If in doubt, Tuta, *don't*.' So instead he would draw
attention away from that word by asking about the weather. 'Do you
think it will rain?' he would ask. 'Oh, not inside, Mr Tutae!' — and
the word got around that Mr Tutae was such a wit, so funny, so quaint,
that he soon found himself exactly where he didn't want to be — at
the centre of attention. In desperation, he asked every woman to
dance. 'Why, certainly, Mr Tutae!' they said, because ladies never said
no. So he danced with them all — a fat lady, a slim lady, a lady whose
bones cracked all the time — and, because he was nervous, he went
boom at every third step, and *that* word got around too. And as the
Governor-General waltzed past he shouted, 'Well done, Tutae, jolly
good show.'

No matter what he tried to do Tuta could never get away from
being at the centre of the crowd or at the centre of attention. Instead
of being gratified, however, Tuta became more embarrassed. Everybody seemed to laugh at his every word, even when it wasn't funny,
or to accept his way of dancing because it was so *daring*. It seemed
as if he could get away with anything. At the same time, Tuta suddenly
realised that he was the only Maori there and that perhaps people
were mocking him. He wasn't a real person to them, but rather an
Entertainment. Even when buffet dinner was served, the crowd still
seemed to mock him, pressing in upon him with 'Have some hors-
d'oeuvres, Mr Tutae. Some *escalope* of veal, perhaps? You must try the
pâté de foie gras! A slice of *jambon*? What about some langouste? Oh,
the raspberry gâteau is just divine!' It was as if the crowd knew very
well his ignorance of such delicacies and, by referring to them, was
putting him down. In desperation Tuta tried some caviar. 'Oh, Mr
Tutae, we can see that you just love caviar!' Tuta gave a quiet, almost
dangerous, smile. 'Yes,' he said. 'I think it's just divine.'

So it went on. But then, just after the buffet, a Very Important
Person arrived and, relieved, Tuta found himself deserted. Interested,
he watched as the one who had just arrived became the centre of
attention. 'It always happens this way,' a voice said behind Tuta. 'I
wouldn't worry about it.' Startled, Tuta turned around and saw a huge
fern. 'Before you,' the fern continued, 'it was me.' Then Tuta saw that
a young woman was sitting behind the fern. 'I'm not worried,' he said
to her, 'I'm glad.' The woman sniffed and said, 'You certainly looked

as if you were enjoying it.' Tuta parted the fronds to get a good look at the woman's face — it was a pleasant face, one which could be pretty if it didn't frown so much. 'Shift over,' Tuta said. 'I'm coming to join you.' He sidled around the plant and sat beside her. 'My name is — ' he began. 'Yes, I know,' the woman said quickly, 'Mr Tutae.' Tuta shook his head vigorously, '*No*, not Tutae. Tuta.' The woman looked at him curiously and, 'Is there a difference?' she asked. 'You better believe it,' Tuta said. 'Oh — ' the woman sniffed. 'I'm Joyce.'

The music started to play again. Joyce squinted her eyes and Tuta sighed, 'Why don't you put on your glasses?' Joyce squealed, 'How did you know?' before popping them on and parting the fronds. 'I'm a sociology student,' Joyce muttered. 'Don't you think people's behaviour is just amazing? I mean ay-*may*zing?' Tuta shrugged his shoulders and wondered if Joyce was looking at something he couldn't see. 'I mean,' Joyce continued, 'look at them out there, just *look* at them. This could be India under the Raj. All this British Imperial graciousness and yet the carpet is being pulled from right beneath their feet.' Puzzled, Tuta tried to see the ball through Joyce's eyes, but failed. 'Ah well,' Joyce sighed. Then she put her hand out to Tuta so that he could shake it, saying 'Goodbye, Mr Tuta.' Tuta looked at her and, 'Are you going?' he asked. 'Oh no,' Joyce said, 'I'm staying here until everybody leaves. But *you* must go out and reclaim attention.' Tuta laughed. 'That new guy's welcome,' he said. 'But don't you want to fulfil their expectations?' Joyce asked. Tuta paused, and 'If that means what I think it means, no,' he said. 'Good,' Joyce responded, 'You are perfectly capable of beating them at their own game. Good luck.'

Then, curious, Tuta asked, 'What did you mean when you said that before me it had been *you*?' Joyce shifted uneasily, took off her glasses and said, 'Well, I'm not a Maori, but I thought it would have been obvious — ' *Oh*, Tuta thought, *she's a plain Jane and people have been making fun of her*. 'But that doesn't matter to me,' Tuta said gallantly. 'Really?' Joyce asked. 'I'll prove it,' Tuta said. 'How about having the next dance.' Joyce gasped, 'Are you *sure*?' Taken aback, Tuta said, 'Of course, I'm sure.' And Joyce said, 'But are you *sure* you're sure!' To show her, Tuta stood up and took her hand. Joyce sighed and shook her head. 'Well, don't say I didn't warn you.' Then she stood up . . . and up . . . and UP.

'Oh,' Tuta said as he parted the fronds to look up at Joyce's face. She must have been six feet six at least. He and Joyce regarded each other miserably. Joyce bit her lip. *Well you asked for it*, Tuta thought. 'Come on,' he said, 'let's have a good time.' He reached up, grabbed her waist, put his face against her chest, and they waltzed into the middle of the floor. There, Tuta stood as high on his toes as possible. *Oh, why did I come?* he thought. Then the music ended and he took Joyce back to the fern. 'I'm sorry I'm such a bad dancer,' she apologised. 'I always took the man's part at school.' Tuta smiled at her, 'That's no sweat. Well — ' And he was just about to leave her when he suddenly realised that after all he and Joyce were both outsiders really. And it came to him that, bloody hell, if you could not join them — as if he would really want to do *that* — then, yes, he could beat them if he wanted to. Not by giving in to them, but by being strong enough to stand up to them. Dance, perhaps, but using his own steps. Listen, also, not to the music of the band but to the music in his head. He owed it, after all, to generous but silly wonderful mixed-up Mum, Mrs Simmons, Desirée Dawn, and the boys — Crazy-Joe, Blackjack and Bigfoot — who were out *there* but wanting to know enough to get *in*. But they needed to come in on their own terms — that's what they would have to learn — as the real people they were and not as carbon copies of the people already on the inside. Once they learnt that, *oh, world, watch out, for your walls will come down in a flash, like Jericho.*

'Look,' Tuta said, 'how about another dance!' Joyce looked at him in disbelief. 'You're a sucker for punishment, aren't you!' she muttered. 'Why?' Tuta bowed, mockingly. 'Well, for one thing, it would be just divine.' At that, Joyce let out a peal of laughter. She stood up again. 'Thank you,' Joyce whispered. Then, 'You know, this is my first ball.' And Tuta smiled and 'It's *my* first ball too,' he said. 'From now on, balls like these will never be the same again.' He took her hand and the band began to wail a sweet but *oh-so-mean* saxophone solo as he led her on to the floor.

Summons to Alexandra

Barbara eased the car to a stop outside the gate. She had left the hotel early that morning. The hour was just past seven. The sky was empty and grey, waiting to be coloured in with birds, clouds, movement but, for the moment it looked gravid. Waiting.

She was here. At Anna's place. Beyond the gate a muddy road slipped across the paddocks to a small stain of trees where the farmhouse was. For a while Barbara simply sat there, looking for signs of life in the house — a curl of smoke, a flash of movement in the window perhaps, the lifting of a blind, the wave of a white hand. But there was none. She reached for a cigarette, placed one in her mouth and lit it. Everything she did was deft and delicate. She was anxious that she may have come too early. But Anna had said seven or thereabouts. Anna was never precise. It was one of her failings and always had been.

Well, let's get it over with, Barbara thought. She stubbed the cigarette out, opened the door of the car and walked quickly to the gate. It was heavy and difficult to move, splashing mud on her feet. She had to shove and push very hard before there was enough room for the car to pass through. When she had finished she saw that her beige suit had spots on it. Her shoes were flecked with mud. Damn, and a lock of hair had loosened from its pins. Couldn't be helped. Barbara rested a while, breathing heavily. This kind of exertion was not good for a city woman. Then she shivered and walked back to the car.

The car was a small rental that Barbara had hired on her arrival the night before in Alexandra. She had checked into her hotel and then rung Anna. 'Hullo? Oh it's you, James. May I speak to Anna?' She had tried to lighten her voice so that no sign of tension would be detected. She didn't want Anna to find any chink, any opening, anywhere. 'Anna? Is that you? Yes, the flight was fine. I left Auckland just after three. The hotel? Oh, it's very attractive. Anna, I just rang to confirm arrangements for tomorrow. Seven or thereabouts? Yes, that would suit me well. My flight leaves at ten thirty. That will leave enough time. Yes. So am I. Looking forward to seeing you. And — and the baby. Until then? Yes. Bye bye.'

There was a bump as the car moved through the gateway. Barbara stepped out to close the gate. She placed the latch and had a fleeting feeling of terror. Almost as if she might never be able to leave. She shrugged the premonition off, stepped back into the car, and put it into first gear. The car had to negotiate a slight dip, and for a while the house was lost to view. Sheep scurried away from the road, then looked back at her, silently. Then the car was going up the other side and — there it was, the house, seeming further away than ever. And suddenly the morning sun dazzled on the windows so that the house looked like a huge golden honeycomb.

Barbara brought the car to a stop outside the front door. She tooted the horn — it was intended to be a gesture of friendliness — and was alarmed at how aggressive and alien it sounded, like a warning. The curtains billowed. Behind them Barbara saw movement and heard the sound of low, almost angry, buzzing. Then the door opened and James was there, pulling on gumboots and a jersey, and coming down the steps to meet her. Barbara opened the door and smiled valiantly. 'Good morning, James,' Barbara smiled. She put her hand out — he looked at it — and then he put his arms around her and kissed her on the mouth. She was too shocked to struggle. She felt his tongue trying to sting through her lips. She looked into his eyes — they were open, taunting, lusting, delirious, burnt out. He let her go. 'Anna's still in bed,' he said. He turned, opening the front door for her and, when she had entered, shut it with a slam.

The room Barbara had entered was long, low and dark. Like most old-fashioned farmhouses, the room combined dining-room and kitchen. Right in the middle was a huge oak table and, to the right, a stove, oven, refrigerator and bench space. The bench was piled high with unwashed dishes. A door led off beside the bench to the laundry and downstairs bathroom. There was an alcove at left and beyond it was the sitting-room. A fire was glowing in the open hearth.

'Say hello to your aunt,' James said. Three children were sitting at the table having breakfast. They had crusts spread with honey. 'Hello, children,' Barbara said gaily. Another two older children appeared at the alcove, and looking up from the stove was the eldest girl. The six children took no notice of their father — it was almost as if he was a stranger too — and they made a soft murmur like the blurred sounds of whirring wings. They came towards Barbara and with a grateful smile on her face she opened her arms to embrace them. But when they pushed their faces against hers, their mouth parts scratching at her cheek, she had the feeling that they were not greeting her at all but seeking some recognition that she should be there. They seemed to find none and began to shove and push against her, circling her and forcing her back towards the front door.

James pulled Barbara towards him. 'You kids go and get dressed,' he said. He motioned Barbara to follow him up the circular staircase. The children fell back, murmuring furiously. 'However does Anna negotiate the stairs?' Barbara asked. 'She hardly ever comes down now,' James said. Astonished, Barbara asked, 'Do you mean that she stays upstairs all the time?' James did not reply. At the top of the stairs was a vestibule, like an antechamber. Leading from it was a long passageway and on either side were the children's bedrooms. The whole upstairs area was coated in heavy yellow paint. The air was heavy with some sweet, cloying deodorant. As Barbara walked behind James she began to feel faint. There was something in the smell which bothered her and something about the colour yellow which frightened her. But before she could turn back, 'Anna's in here,' James said. Barbara made as if to go back down the passageway. But she saw the children coming up the staircase. There was nowhere else to go but forward. Before her was a curtain, and James had pulled it to one side. Barbara dipped and entered and the curtain fell like a heavy drape behind her. Closing everything out. Closing her *in*.

'So you're here,' a voice said. Mesmerised, Barbara tried to see where she was. The blinds were still down and the room was dark. It was a big room cluttered with furniture and strewn with clothes. The smell was stronger here at the source. 'Anna?' Barbara asked. She saw a slim white hand reaching up to the blind to let the light in. And the light, when it came, seemed not to emanate from outside at all but from within the honeycomb. And it *flashed* and *glowed* in the many mirrors in the room. And reflected in every mirror was Anna, triumphal, like a glorious queen bee pulsating on a large yellow bed.

At the sight of her younger sister, Barbara forgot her fears. She walked toward Anna and did not see the other three children until they were almost upon her, buzzing furiously. 'It's only your aunt,' Anna commanded, and the children retreated to watch from the shadows with wide green eyes. Barbara sat on the bed beside her sister. She felt a rush of tenderness, mixed with relief, and 'Oh, Anna,' she said. For a long moment the two sisters just looked at each other, Barbara with love and Anna with amusement. Then, 'How are you feeling?' Barbara asked. 'Empty!' Anna laughed, and the rings on her fingers glittered yellow and black. 'I don't know how you do it,' Barbara said. 'You still look so — so — slim. How is the baby?' Anna shifted her head a little and directed Barbara's attention to a small white crib in the far corner. The three children were hovering above it. 'He's sleeping right now,' Anna said. 'Wait till he wakes up.'

Barbara turned back to Anna. There was no doubt that the two sisters had come from the same hive. They had the same golden, textured hair, the same flawless skin, the same perfect oval chin. When they were younger and closer they had been inseparable. Only at adolescence, when Anna had feared her transition from girl into woman and Barbara revelled in it, had they begun to break apart. Indeed, in those days Barbara's awareness of her sexuality had made her into a being of brilliance, completely overshadowing her younger sister. Barbara had led all her men on a merry dance and spread her glory wide through the summer sky. James himself had been one of Barbara's conquests, and when he fell from grace he had turned to the woman who reminded him of her — Anna. As for Barbara, she had flown higher and higher, and an investment banker by the name of Harry had caught her. Barbara and Harry had married in one of the society weddings of the year. Barbara had been pleased when her little sister and James had married early in the following year. Some of James's Maori friends had come along. The wedding had been a wonderful and spirited occasion.

'It's lovely to see you,' Barbara said, and she really believed it. Yet there had been one period in their lives when the sisters had been estranged. 'I know it has been a long time,' Barbara continued, apologising. The estrangement had occurred because foolish, foolish James had told Anna, in a pique of anger, that he still loved Barbara. 'But when you telephoned me that the baby had come and asked me down here, well, here I am.' Barbara tried to make light of it, but she knew that she had purposely stayed away, not only because of James but also because of Anna's obscene — in Barbara's eyes — capacity to produce children. For fifteen years after their marriages the balance had changed between Barbara and Anna. The one who had denied her sexuality — Anna — had become the one who produced the children, ten in all, growing more and more beautiful with each child. And the one who had once been in the ascendant — Barbara — had had one child, a daughter, who had died in infancy and then, no matter how hard she had tried, no further children. Although the premium in girlhood was on beauty and sexuality, the premium in womanhood was on homebuilding and motherhood. There was no way out. And who could blame Harry — who wanted children desperately — for his little infidelities? Certainly not she, Barbara, who took the blame entirely on herself.

Up to this point Barbara had not realised that she had been carrying on a monologue with herself. Nor had she noticed how contemptuously Anna was watching her. But she should have known that her sister realised why, in fact, she had come. Yet Anna was devious, maintaining the pleasantries between them. 'How is Harry?' Anna asked. 'Harry?' Barbara repeated. 'Oh, prospering as usual. Making lots of money. He wants to build an extension on the house.' And Anna smiled and said, 'Goodness. All that money. All that effort on the house. Whatever for?' And Barbara felt her heart thudding against her ribcage and she wondered, *Shall I ask her now? Is it too soon to say, By the way, Anna dear* — But Anna went on quickly, teasingly, 'Of course, with all that money and just you and Harry, what else can you spend it on? You could always go around the world, of course.' Yes they could, Barbara thought to herself, and they had — many times since Little B had died. And they had hoped for more children, and the doctor had said that Barbara and Harry were both perfectly healthy. But when Little B went, something had gone wrong inside Barbara. After a while she realised that she was afraid and that she didn't want to bring another child into the world, invest emotionally in it, only to see it wither and die also. Very soon Harry had read her fear and unwillingness. He had turned, as he had always done, to pallid pearl-like women. And whenever he and Barbara had made love, it had become an act of accusation on his part and an acceptance of punishment on hers.

Anna's eyes glittered again. 'You've come all this way,' Anna said, 'and I haven't offered you a cup of tea!' She called to the three children in the room, 'Bring a cup of tea for your aunt.' The children shifted indecisively in the shadows and then one of them lifted away leaving the other two on guard. *I could say, now, Anna dear, you know that since Little B went away we have wanted children. And it just hasn't worked out. And then we thought about adoption* — 'Some people have all the luck,' Anna said. 'Going round the world, attending parties. I saw your photograph in *Metro* magazine, and here I am with James and the children in Alexandra! But I'm happy.' And Anna lifted herself into a sitting position and the light from the windows gilded her with gold. 'Oh yes,' Barbara replied, distracted. 'The photograph was taken at La Divina, wasn't it? Harry knows one of the owners. The food is gorgeous.' Poor Harry, it had been his idea to adopt. He had become all fired up about it, put himself on cloud number nine, foolish man. What had the woman at the agency said? Something about their both being too old? Too old, too OLD. He had all the money in the world but he was too old. THEY were too old. Biologically. And by legal definition, according to adoption procedure. Adoption was the prerogative of the young.

The tea arrived. One of the children poured two cups and handed one to Anna and the other to Barbara. Anna sipped the golden liquid blissfully. As she did so, the children crowded around her and began to brush Anna's hair, softly, lovingly. Anna fell almost into a trance, hardly breathing, and it was such an affecting scene. Barbara stirred her tea and raised the cup to her lips. She noticed something gossamer in the liquid. Then, as the tea swirled and circled she saw a wasp, a large shining wasp, and it was drowning. And, as she put the cup down, Barbara knew that the children had done this — this — cruel *thing*.

Suddenly the baby began to cry. Anna's eyes flickered and she started awake. She saw Barbara sitting there and said, 'Would you like to see the baby now?' Barbara's throat was dry and aching, and she nodded. 'Children — ' Anna commanded. But the children were reluctant and Anna had to order them again. Barbara watched as they lifted the baby from the cradle and brought it to their mother. As soon as the baby was placed in Anna's arms, the baby's crying stopped. And Anna's eyes flickered for the third time as she handed the baby to Barbara.

'Oh, Anna,' Barbara whispered as she loosed the soft folds of cloth from around the baby. 'He's just — just — such a royal little thing.' And she held the baby's cheek next to hers to feel its softness, and closed her eyes with the ecstasy of it. She began to cry, her need spilling out of her and, because her tears curtained away everything else, she did not see that all the children had come into the room, watching every move she made, waiting for their mother's sign, watching Barbara, watching Anna. And Barbara felt so open and so sure that her sister saw her openness and would be generous and, *The time has come and all I need to do is ask, after all Anna has so many children, so many, and surely* — And, 'Anna dear,' Barbara began.

And Anna lifted, curved her golden body, and *struck*.

'Poor Barbara,' Anna said. 'Poor sister. Perhaps you should have taken James after all. You'll never have a child like this, will you, dear?'

Barbara cried out. She stood up. Her tears blurred her vision and it seemed that thousands of wings glistened and roared around her, hemming her into a small circle. She looked down at the golden apparition that was her sister. 'Even after all these years?' she asked. 'Goodbye, Barbara,' Anna said.

The curtain was behind Barbara as she backed out of the room. Down the long passageway she went, into the antechamber to where the circular staircase was. She felt as if she was in a maze, a giant hexagonal maze, golden gleaming. The maze was dark, and shining shapes rushed up to smother her with stings. She descended the circular staircase and James was there, trying to embrace her. She pushed him away, ran to the front door, opened it and fell into the sunlight. The footpath was slippery and she almost lost her balance. A cloud of angry wings enveloped her. Frantically she pushed them aside, stumbled to the car and started the motor. Behind she caught a glimpse of golden bees, but as the house receded into the distance she saw that they were simply children waving farewell.

The car dipped and for a while the house was lost to view. Then there it was again, dazzling in the sun. Barbara began to feel ashamed. What would Anna and James think about her sudden exit from the house? She would ring them from the hotel before she left for the airport. She would tell them about the strain she had been under lately — with Harry, life, home, everything. Goodness, and she had forgotten to leave the gift she had brought for the new baby. How careless! Yes, that's what she would do. She would ring to say, *Anna dear.*

The gate was in front of the car. Barbara got out and opened it. She drove the car through and, for a while, just sat there. Traumatised. She felt tears coming again and, quickly, reached for a cigarette. She closed her eyes and inhaled deeply. There would never be any more children. Not for her. Harry perhaps —

Barbara finished her cigarette. She looked at her watch. She went to close the gate. As it clicked shut Barbara saw a blur of black and gold on the top railing. Resting on the gate was a bright golden insect scattering light from its wings. Beneath it was another of its kind, dying. The golden insect pulsated gently, almost sweetly, its poisoned tip deep within the other. Then suddenly its wings caught flame, and Barbara watched as it lifted and flew in the direction of the hive that she knew lay not very far away.

On a Train

Frank Saunders was one of those middle-aged men whom other commuters travelling from Lower Hutt to Wellington on the train took an instant aversion to. It wasn't that he looked disreputable — indeed, in his grey suit and tie he was every inch the typical insurance broker — it was just that he was always so darned cheerful. Nobody had a right to be jolly, particularly at that time of the morning, and with the prospect of a long and boring day ahead, but he was. Standing there on the platform, waiting for the unit from Trentham, he looked the odd man out — and he knew it. The other commuters appeared to be still lobotomised from lack of sleep. There they were, standing each with a careful margin of space between them. And if a new arrival stood too close to one of them, that person would sidle a few surreptitious steps away to keep his margin intact, causing everyone else on the platform to re-adjust their positions and define their own margins again and again down the platform. It was like watching a line of soldiers constantly dressing to the right.

Quite amusing really, Frank Saunders thought. People just didn't like being too close to one another. They felt invaded, offended even, that they might have to get involved. And woe betide any cheery 'Good morning!' to this lot. That would be an invitation to instant assassination. People just didn't like to talk in the mornings. They needed to be cajoled into their day, wooed out of their Monday morning doldrums by a cup of coffee and the *Dominion*, and seduced into a week of work by the prospect of the Thursday morning pay-packet.

The unit from Trentham arrived, an aged silver bullet which looked like a German flying bomb. The usual rush of commuters to claim window seats began. Not that they would ever see the view, Frank Saunders thought. No, there was something comfortable, something secure about a window seat. It was one's own private space and, if you were powerful enough, you could send out vibrations so that nobody would sit next to you. Should anybody be foolish enough to do so all they got was a forbidding 'How dare you' look and a snap as a paper or magazine was opened, forming an instant barrier to conversation or intercourse of any kind. What on earth was wrong with people, Frank Saunders wondered. How ever did the human race survive!

Humming, Frank Saunders decided that it was time that he boarded the train. He walked along the platform towards a non-smokers' compartment. It was then that he saw them. A boy and a girl, both teenagers, both Maori. They were a slight couple. The girl was shading the left side of her face with a hand, as if she was hiding something. The boy muttered to her. *We gotta go, Roha. No use staying here. We'll be okay.* The girl pulled her collar up around her neck. The boy nodded and then jerked her toward the unit. As she stumbled after him, her hand fell away from her face. For a brief second Frank Saunders saw that her left cheek and her neck were raw and bloodied, and that her eyes were red and swollen. Her bottom lip had been totally skinned and was purpled and mashed like the inside of a bruised fruit. The couple stepped into a smokers' compartment. For a moment Frank Saunders watched them, wavering. On a sudden whim he followed them, and the girl, catching the flash of his coat as he entered, gave a whimper of helplessness. *That man, Hemi. He's following us.*

The boy and girl took a seat together. A young executive sitting opposite suddenly noticed the girl's wounds. His newspaper was not an adequate barrier and he soon muttered under his breath and left. Whatever had happened to the girl and boy, he wanted no part of it, no way. Frank Saunders, too, was having second thoughts. He began to be angry with himself. For one thing, he hated the smell of cigarette smoke. For another, the couple might simply have had a domestic dispute — and if they were in bigger trouble than that, the likelihood was that he would not be able to help them anyway. He made as if to step out of the compartment, but it was too late. The doors snapped shut. The train began to move. Ah well. He may as well take a seat. And with that, Frank Saunders moved to the seat opposite the young couple.

Frank Saunders was not a small man by any means. But it was his large purposeful actions, rather than his size, that alarmed the girl. She caught the flash of his coat again and she stifled a cry. *Hemi. It's him. That man on the platform.* At that, Frank Saunders made a gesture of assistance. 'Please don't be afraid,' he said, 'but is there anything I can do to — ' The boy recoiled from the Pakeha's voice. 'Shove off, mister,' he said. Frank Saunders tried to calm him. 'Look, boy,' he said, 'if you two need any help — ' The boy bunched his fists. 'Don't call me boy,' he said. 'Now shove off.' Frank Saunders shrugged his shoulders. *I want to get out of here, Hemi.* Suddenly the girl leapt up, pushed past Frank Saunders and moved to the front of the compartment. The boy followed her.

They — the girl and the boy — must have been either seventeen or eighteen, Frank Saunders guessed. They seemed no different to the hundreds of others whom he had seen crowding in the Hutt Valley. They'd probably dropped out of a dull school existence into a dull, no-prospects, out-of-work life. Some people survived or made the effort to survive. These two kids looked as if they were the kind who didn't. What was it like not to have work? Not to have a place to go during the daytime? Not to have a pay cheque coming in, proving your worth to society? It must be soul-destroying, Frank Saunders thought. All over the country youth unemployment was the worst it had been since the Depression. And all this in the midst of seeming plenty. *Is he still staring at us, Roha? The bastard, he's hassling us.*

The train stopped at Petone. There was a rush of people getting on and only a few who alighted. Petone was 'coming up', as the land agents liked to describe it, but nothing would ever improve its ramshackle, down-at-heel, seaside look. Indeed, although some attempts had been made to improve the foreshore, Petone remained as ridiculously pathetic as the risible and unfair nickname given it by residents from Wellington City — Costa del Petone. Like so many dormitory suburbs, Petone was one of those places which snooty Wellingtonians passed through on their way to more 'respectable' destinations. One only actually stopped to buy second-hand cars, second-hand furniture or old-fashioned manufacturing seconds.

Then the train was on the move again. The door between one compartment and the next opened behind Frank Saunders, and a uniformed railway attendant was there. 'All tickets,' he called. 'All tickets.' As he clipped Frank Saunders' pass, Frank Saunders asked him when the new timetable was due. *Oh, Hemi. Look. That Pakeha is telling the guard about us. We've got to get off the train.* The conductor moved on through the crushed compartment. Suddenly Frank Saunders was aware of a tussle further in front. It was the girl again. She was struggling with the boy. Alarmed, people around the couple were trying to edge away. *For Chrissake, Roha. Don't clap out on me. Not now.* 'Tickets,' the railway attendant demanded. 'Tickets.' The boy took two passes from his jacket. The attendant inspected them and then said to Hemi, 'You and your lady are making everyone nervous, mate.' His words were a warning. Then, as he passed through, the conductor announced, 'Next and final stop, Wellington Station. Wellington Station.' *Hang in there, Roha. Hang in there.*

Ahead was Wellington City, the Capital, gleaming like a huge wedding cake in the blue sky. A plane was circling, preparing to land at the airport. The sea was like a pond and the only ripples were being made by the departing morning ferry. But Frank Saunders was not looking at the view. He was, rather, becoming increasingly concerned for the girl and the boy. For some reason the notion that the couple were drug addicts crossed his mind. There was a lot of addiction in the Hutt. People were turning to drugs in the same way as they turned to alcohol or sex — as a soporific for all the ills of the day to day grind. Yes, that must be the couple's problem. Hard drugs. Or perhaps they were victims of violent crime? There was always someone, some woman usually, splitting the night with her screams. Wife bashing, child bashing, poofter bashing, had become the favourite New Zealand sports. *He's staring at us again, Hemi.* Frank Saunders made up his mind to try a second approach to the boy and the girl. *Just let him go me, Roha. I'll smash his face in.*

And all of a sudden the train was there, pulling slowly into Wellington Railway Station. The commuters began to surge towards the doors, waiting for the train to come to a stop. It was all ironic when you thought about it. Most people were reluctant to go to work, but when they got to the end of the ride all they wanted to do was get off the train. There was a hiss and a slight jolt — a moment of quiet — and the doors opened. *Quick, Roha, now's our chance.* Frank Saunders saw the girl and the boy leap from the train. 'Hey — ' a bystander yelled as the boy pushed him aside. Frank Saunders went to run after them, but it was too late. Well if that was the way they wanted it, all he could do was to wish them luck.

Then, above the melee of the milling platform, he heard a scream, curling like a wounded bird. He knew it was the girl. He saw a crowd gathering. He shoved through it. The girl had tripped and fallen. The boy was trying to help her up. A platform attendant was coming, his whistle in his lips, ready to be blown just in case of danger. Quickly Frank Saunders bent toward the boy to warn him. 'Listen, boy, you need help,' he said. *Hemi. It's that Pakeha.* And the boy turned, pushing Frank Saunders away. 'Get off our backs, man,' he raged. 'Shove off, Pakeha. Leave us alone. Stop hassling us.' Pushing Frank Saunders back. Hitting him. Forcing him along the platform.

The platform attendant blew on his whistle. The sound was shrill. Shocking. At its sound the boy pulled a knife. It flashed in the air. Then the police were there, pulling the boy back. The girl was screaming and yelling and trying to help him. The last that Frank Saunders saw of them was when they were being restrained and taken into custody.

White-faced with shock, Frank Saunders allowed himself to be seated in the stationmaster's office. He was given a cup of tea. A police officer came into the room. 'Sir, we require a statement,' he said. For a moment Frank Saunders stared at him. 'I only wanted to help,' he said. 'Why did he pull the knife on me?' The police officer shrugged his shoulders, saying, 'We dunno, sir. Perhaps they were running.' Frank Saunders persisted. 'But where to? Or where from?' Then he realised that the questions were academic really. For kids like that, there was nowhere.

Royal Hunt before the Storm

Peter lay on his back in the little wood. He was feeling deliciously alive, so full of sap that to keep it all in he had to stretch wide, extending his feet and arms as far as they could go. There was such ecstasy and wonder and incredulity in knowing that another person actually loved him! Nor was this just another 'person', but the most wonderful most perfect girl in the whole world. Giggling at the thought of it, Peter ran his fingers through his thinning hair. To top it all off, Anne was such a tremendous catch, a prize beauty with such grey eyes, such a white swan-like neck and oval chin, such marigold-coloured hair . . . . That such a girl as she could ever see anything in such as he, a great fellow for books, was beyond comprehension. And last night, while listening to the orchestra at the concert playing Berlioz's *Royal Hunt before the Storm*, Anne had actually whispered to him, 'I don't like the music, Peter, too overt for me, but I do like you.' Why, a fellow needed to be carried out on a stretcher after that! Peter's ears had burned with pleasure all night, and he had not minded at all when, seeing Anne to her flat, his intentions to kiss her had been thwarted. 'Oh no, please don't,' Anne had said. 'The evening has already been perfect as it is. Dear Peter — ' She had touched a gloved hand to Peter's cheek and gone inside, her touch lingering with him on the steps.

Reaching over, Peter plucked a long strand of grass and held it against the sun. Of course, Anne was a sensitive girl, which was only to be expected from someone recently emigrated from England to New Zealand. Why, there was a vast difference in culture and society between the Home Country and the colonies! New Zealand was a very rough and ready country for such a rose as Anne. Peter had realised this when he had first met Anne. Indeed, she was so sensitive that she never liked being touched. In particular, she hated anyone, even him, touching her hair. It was as if her hair was something sacred, something not to be handled in any familiar manner. When he had first tried to do so, Anne had been so panic stricken that the ring on his finger had caught in her hair and pulled some out by the roots. 'Oh, now see what you have done!' Anne had said, and she had run to the mirror, crying, 'Oh, look. Just look.' There had only been one or two strands involved but, through her eyes, Peter had seen total devastation. He had learnt a lot about Anne at that moment. Not that she was vain — there was not a vain bone in her body — but that her sense of self, of possession of herself by herself, was not something that she could or would ever give away. He would need to be patient. He had all the time in the world, really. And if there had happened to have been another girl in his life — which there wasn't, so the question was academic — Peter knew that there was only one person he wanted. His body and heart told him so. Keeping herself sacrosanct was Anne's little piece of magic — it was the way in which she kept her world safe — and that made her all the more precious to him.

'Peter? Peter,' Anne called. 'You can come now.' She looked down into the little wood from the top of the hill and waved to him. He looked so far away, like a prince. He sat up and she saw him shade his eyes. 'Over here!' she called. He waved back and, standing up was no longer a prince but a thin young man, unattractively red from too much sun, striding toward her — and she felt, all of a sudden, a shiver of apprehension, like a comb through her hair. No other person had ever been here with her. She had never allowed it, being afraid that they would not see the beauty that was here untouched.

For a moment Anne almost regretted her decision. But it was too late, for there he was, Peter, smiling through the sun. 'Oh, Peter,' Anne said to cover her confusion, 'you've got grass stains all over your shirt. Here.' She began to brush him down and was instantly shocked at the heat she felt beneath his shirt. He gasped at her cool touch and she coloured. Impulsively he bent down to her, his lips so red and swollen, opening to show his white teeth and his darting tongue — and she pushed him away.

'Anne, my love,' Peter cried. 'I'm such a stupid idiot. I could kill myself. Oh, my stupid, stupid clumsiness.'

'No,' Anne replied. 'It's not your fault. It's mine and it's me who should be sorry. When you tried to take me into your arms last night I tried to explain then. I'm not afraid of you, Peter, it's not that. But somehow I feel that if we held each other's hands and kissed it would be all changed. We wouldn't be — ' she fluttered her hands, helplessly ' — free.'

'My darling,' Peter said, 'I love you.'

'Yes, I know,' Anne said, 'and that only makes it worse. Can't you see? There is so much in life that can be *sublime*. I want that more than anything else — '

'Anne, my sweet,' Peter interrupted. 'Please don't torture yourself.' He modulated his voice with tones of understanding. 'Please, show me this place of yours. I promise I shall be good.' His words were coy and playful, like a small boy asking for cake, and Anne, lulled by the child-ishness of the words, nodded. She led Peter through the wood and under the dappled sunlit canopy. There was an apple tree on the knoll and the apples shone with rich carnality. But beyond the wood the sky stretched out to the end of the universe. 'Here we are,' Anne said, and her voice was grave like a prayer. And Peter looked down upon the garden.

For a moment Peter didn't know what to think or how to react. He had the preposterous notion that perhaps he had stepped over a gilt frame into a large landscape painting, one in which all the elements of balance, symmetry, line, form and perspective had been dictated by a master artist. Right in front of him, sloping down to an egg-blue lake, was a broad swathe of bright green lawn, so artificially green and clipped that it could well have been made of porcelain. The lawn was bordered on both sides by English trees, quietly splendid and so taste-fully arranged that if you closed one eye and then the other you saw the left border mirrored exactly by the right. A path ran like white piping on a wedding cake — 'There! This is where the lawn ends and the lake begins.' And, oh, the lake itself was just utter tranquillity. Not a breath nor stray wind — not a scratch — disturbed the glassy surface — and even it conspired to balance the panorama, for reflected in it were the white-capped mountains and impossible aquamarine of sky.

'What is this place?' Peter said after a while. 'I don't know,' Anne replied. 'I think it has been here forever.'

But the crowning glory was the formal garden. Set in the middle of the lawn, it looked like an exquisite Fabergé brooch. Right in the centre was a marble fountain with paths like silver filigree radiating from it. The paths were bordered with topiaried bushes, and each bush was in turn mounted in a setting of rhododendrons and azaleas. The paths themselves terminated at small neo-Classic pillars.

'Who did this?' Peter whispered. 'I don't know,' Anne replied. 'But what is it doing here — in New Zealand?' Peter laughed incredulously. 'Oh, please don't ask such questions,' Anne pleaded. She skipped away from him, down towards the garden. She raised a hand to Peter, 'Come.' As he ran to join her, Peter could not help but think how pretty she looked. And as she went ahead of him it seemed as if she really belonged in the garden, a flawless shining diamond to set off its beauty and lustre.

Anne was waiting for him at one of the pillars. He made as if to speak and she raised a finger to her lips. She gave a serious little smile that curled just slightly at the edges and then entered the garden. Peter followed and, as soon as he placed his feet on the path, realised with surprise that proximity to the garden had not destroyed its perfection. From afar you would have expected faults of balance or rough execution to be obscured by distance, but surely as one got closer, would you not expect to see the brush marks or overpainting of the artist? An inconsistent gap in one of the gardens perhaps, or a careless curve in the otherwise mathematical linear precision of the path? A few fallen leaves or petals, at least, to blur the outlines? There were none, not a one. And it came to Peter — he had to giggle at the heresy of the thought — that if one considered God to be the Master Gardener then this would be how His garden would look. And he thought again that it was no wonder than Anne hadn't liked the Berlioz last evening. There was no room for bombast here or for the pungent passions of any *Royal Hunt* — the smell of horses, howls of the hunting pack and flaring terror of the hart.

'Well, what do you think?' Anne said in a hushed way. 'Isn't it beautiful?' She had led Peter to the middle of the garden where the fountain gently played. She was pointing to the centrepiece statue of a young, nude male, unreachable because of the moat of water surrounding him.

There was no doubt that the figure had been well executed, but statues of young males, no matter how beautiful, were not Peter's sort of thing. He remembered how once in Florence he had waited for hours to view the Michelangelo *David* and, after twenty minutes' serious study, had remained singularly unimpressed. It was not that he didn't appreciate the artistry, but rather the subject — the figure was beautiful, true, but too much so. Yet, 'Yes, he is beautiful,' he said to Anne. His experience in Florence, where a gaggle of girls had oohed and aahed over the *David*, had made him suspect that women defined masculine beauty in their own way. It was obvious that, like the group of girls, Anne's appreciation inclined to the classical — the tight curls, the aquiline nose and romantic cast of the face, the strong neck and upper torso pinched with nipples, the chest narrowing into a small waist, the strong thighs and calves and — quite out of character really — the huge sculpted hands. The statue in the garden was of this same mould. It could have been brother to the *David*. It could have been Adam. But it was not a man, not with that perfect but small genitalia. Why was it, Peter wondered, that sculptors who paid such attention to musculature would be so puritan? That was why Peter felt no jealousy about the statue. Nevertheless, when he saw the look of adoration on Anne's face he was surprised by his sudden rush of anger. She was running her fingers again and again through her hair.

'He's so perfect,' Anne said. 'Oh, he is — *perfect.*'

She led Peter away then, to a shaded place in the garden, over-looking the lake, where she had placed the picnic hamper.

It was about half an hour later than Anne heard the sound. At first she thought it was a wasp. She gave a small cry, 'Oh!' and put her hands to her hair. Peter, curious, asked, 'What is it?' Then he, also, heard the sound. He tried to pinpoint it. He and Anne had returned from the garden and were now lying in the shadow of the apple tree on the rise above the garden. Laughing, he said, 'Over there, Anne!'

Far away a crack was developing on the mirror surface of the lake. As it splintered nearer, Peter saw that it was being caused by a small dinghy with an outboard motor. There were two people in the dinghy, a man and a woman, and they were both laughing, their laughter pricking the exquisite peace.

'They're not going to land here, are they?' Anne asked. She had to squint against the sun and, in that moment, Peter saw a kind of childish petulance he had never seen in her before. 'You mustn't be so proprietorial,' he said. He looked again, shading his eyes, and saw that the dinghy had changed course and was heading for an area of bush further along from the garden. 'There!' he said, 'gone!', as the dinghy disappeared from sight.

Anne sighed with relief. 'You'll think me foolish, Peter,' she said, 'but I didn't want anything to disturb our day together. Here. In my garden.' There was an air of satisfaction in her tone as if she herself was pleased about how things had gone. 'Oh, my dear, I so wanted you to see me — the way I am — how our life together should be.'

At that, Peter's heart lifted, because of the strength of Anne's endearment. He was lying in the grass at her feet and he reached up with one arm to embrace her. She caught his wayward hand and, smiling firmly, held it at her side. He tried to lace his fingers through hers but she resisted. When she spoke, though, her words were romantic and her manner abstracted.

'Do you remember when we first met?' Anne began. 'On the ferry? You were so ridiculously endearing, and so polite. You couldn't stop apologising — and that's how I saw you — as an apologetic young man.'

'Oh, Anne,' Peter responded.

'There were times, however,' she said, 'when I thought you were too forward and too passionate — ' she coloured at the words ' — so impatient you seemed! But I trusted in your goodness and respect of me.'

Peter tried to interject. 'But I would never, Anne, never have done anything to — '

'No, let me finish,' Anne said firmly. She paused, choosing her words carefully. 'I want' — she closed her eyes as if making a wish — 'I want, above all else, for us to be friends. I want us to be like children,' she said with emphasis, 'in a garden of innocent delights. Like brother and sister, if you like.' She saw a flicker pass through Peter's eyes, of puzzlement tinged with hurt, and went on in a rush, trying to press home her point. She felt it was important for her to do so — she had chosen him, after all, because she had discerned a gentility — a passivity almost — in him which, she hoped, would make him accept what she had to say. 'Oh, Peter, I want to have a friendship with a man — to have a man as a friend — you as my friend. Do you know how difficult that is for we women? How hard men make it for us? Were a woman to say to a man, "I want you as a friend," the man would either assume more than a friendly interest or, if he were a man of other instincts, he would decline the offer and seek his pleasure elsewhere. I do not think it is in men to ever have friendships with women. Men only subvert our overtures. They think them either as signs that we want to dominate them — ' her hands fluttered incredulously ' — or as signs of feminine weakness. Either way they smell blood, as if we are some kind of prize in, yes, a — a royal hunt, or a Trojan war.' Anne paused and carefully released her hands and placed them in her lap. She looked down at Peter and he was so open, so vulnerable, that she could have fallen in love with him. His eyes were closed — she had not noticed how long his eyelashes were — and there was such pallor in his face. Underneath his shirt, which she had allowed him to unbutton, his chest was still, as if he was holding his breath. 'If we can be friends, Peter, if we can be equal, I would be the happiest being in the world. And if in time our friendship turned into love, I would know that it would be based on the sweetness that comes between true friends.'

Peter gave a deep groan. He sat up and buried his head in his hands. The sunlight, shining through the apple tree, dappled his body with beauty, and Anne felt moved to reach across the moat of water to touch him. When he looked at her she felt a glimmer of hope and of triumph — were those tears in his eyes?

'You have disarmed me completely,' Peter responded. 'I once thought, when I first met you, that I had swallowed a butterfly — its wings were fanning just here.' He put his hand on his heart. 'But it cannot be a butterfly because I am being stung to death and it hurts. I have never been in love before and so I am impetuous. If love tells me to declare myself, I do so spontaneously. If it says, "Reach out for you," I cannot help myself. And when I want to touch your hair — ' Anne gave a small movement ' — it is because love tells me to.' Peter lapsed into thoughtful silence. 'Dearest Anne,' he said, eventually, 'I think you ask too much of me. You ask too much of yourself. You ask too much of *us*, or what we could be to each other — me to you and you to me. But I — '

A flock of white pigeons suddenly sought the blue vault of sky. Laughter, carolling from far away, interrupted Peter's declaration. He turned from Anne — and the spell of her was broken, and Anne felt him slipping away.

Down on the bridal path a woman in a summer dress was running. Following her was a man who, when he reached the woman, grabbed her in his arms in a tight embrace. The woman gave a small scream and, turning in the man's arms, began to beat him with her small fists. 'They must have left their boat at the point,' Peter said. 'Do you think they can see us?' Anne asked. 'No,' Peter responded, 'not up here in the shade.' Anne bit her lip. 'Perhaps they'll go away. Perhaps the — ' But the woman had seen the garden and, pointing up at it, began to pull the man with her. *No*, Anne thought, *No, No, No, No*, the words banging away in her head like the stamping foot of a vexed and petulant child.

It all happened so quickly then. So shockingly, utterly, quickly. The man saw the statue in the middle of the fountain. He waded across the water to it. *No.* He took off his shirt and mocked the pose of the statue, and his brown masculinity was so overtly sensual against the white marble. He looked so dark that Peter thought he must be a Maori. Dark, so — The woman laughed again, putting one hand over her mouth, trying to suppress her mirth. The man, laughing also, waded back to the woman and took her in his arms again. She squealed at his coldness and wetness. And then he kissed her. Deeply. And he began to unbutton her dress, she helping him, until her own white nakedness was revealed. She fell to the ground. The man stood over her, grinning, and then began to undress himself. He looked victorious, standing like that in the sunlight. The woman pulled him down.

Something gave way inside Anne. She had wanted everything to be so perfect. And she reached for Peter to tell him she wanted to leave *now*, to leave forever. But when she touched him she felt his heat, so strong, and smelt his sweat, that she felt like screaming. It was then that she saw Peter, really saw him. His face had become carnal, his nostrils flaring and his lips widening to show his white teeth. His eyes had narrowed but his pupils were dilated. And it was as if she could see what he was seeing through *his* eyes. And she saw herself, pinned down by Peter. His arms were around her, bending her into impossible shapes, moulding her to his will. Yes, his eyes would be like *this*. His top lip would be beaded, like *this*, with perspiration. His arms, his back would be as red and as hairy as *this*. And —

Anne gave a moan. She backed away and Peter, unmasked by his lust, looked up at her. And he felt a feeling akin to rage because Anne had almost won, almost gelded him. And he thought, *I have you now, my lady, I have you now*. He stood up and over Anne. As he did so, she shivered like a timorous animal and then went very still. Peter nuzzled her neck and deliberately began to stroke her hair. He saw that Anne's eyes were wide, like a deer's.

'There, there, Anne,' Peter said. 'Come along now.' Behind him he heard the sounds of the man with the woman. He turned to watch. Then he turned again to Anne. Oh yes —

'You're perfect, perfect, perfect,' said Peter.

The Halcyon Summer

Once there was a nest, floating on the sea at summer solstice, and happy voices to charm the wind. The nest is gone now, drifting away on the tides. But somewhere, somewhere must surely float scattered straws, even just a single straw, which I may light upon.

It was the year that Sir Apirana Ngata died. That summer the children's parents decided to go to the Empire Games in Auckland. Tama was the eldest — an important eleven-year-old — and had two sisters, Kara and Pari. It was decided that the children would stay with their grand-aunt, Nani Puti, while their parents were away. 'What about the land troubles?' their father asked their mother. 'The kids will be all right,' their mother answered. The children had never been to Nani Puti's — all they knew was that it was way up the Coast somewhere, past Ruatoria. 'I'm coming with *you*,' Tama said to his father. 'No, you have to look after your sisters,' his mother responded. 'Then *you* go with them,' he answered. He tried to pinch her but she only pushed him away and, laughing, said, 'Just as well you're going up there. Nani Puti will sort you out.' But as a bribe — only if they were good children, mind — his mother said she would bring back some toys: a red clockwork train for Tama and a doll each for Kara and Pari. That decided the matter.

One morning, while the children were still asleep, their mother got up and packed a small brown suitcase with the clothes she thought they would need: a few shirts, shorts and a pair of sandals for Tama and some cotton frocks for his sisters. 'You kids won't need much,' she said. 'It's summer and it gets hot at Nani's place. Most of the kids up there run around with no clothes on anyway.' At that remark the children started to kick up a big fuss because they were very shy and didn't relish the idea of showing their bottoms and you-know-what to strangers. 'Oh, don't be silly,' their mother told them. 'You won't have to take your clothes off if you don't want to.' Tama wasn't too sure about that either.

The children had to take a nap that morning — they always took a nap if they were going anywhere, even to the two o'clock pictures at the Majestic. But they couldn't sleep. The thought of being deserted by their parents, and of being taken against their will to a strange relative's place in the strange country, frightened them. When their mother found them still awake she was very cross. 'It's about time you got to know your relations,' she said. 'You kids are growing up proper little Pakehas. And your Nani is always asking me if she's ever going to see you before she dies. Don't you want to see your Nani?' Tama was not feeling very respectful and would have answered, 'No,' if he'd been able to get away with it. This Nani sounded alarming — she was very old for one thing, being sixty, and had white hair and tattoos on her chin. How she ever managed to get married to Karani Pani and have twelve children was beyond his comprehension. Not only that, but the whole family had names longer than Tama's mother, which was Turitumanareti something-or-other, and they spoke only Maori. How would he be able to talk to them? Thank goodness he had been to Scouts, and Kara had learned some sign language from Janet, the Pakeha girl next door, who was a Brownie. But Tama still didn't like the idea of going — it was all Maoris up the Coast, no Pakehas, and he and his sister were used to Pakehas. Furthermore, Maoris wore only grass skirts and probably never even wore pyjamas to bed, and he knew that was rude. 'You kids are going and that's it,' their mother said. 'Nani Puti is expecting you.' At that, the children knew their fate was sealed, because it was impolite not to go to someone's place when they were expecting you; just like the time when Allan had invited Tama to his birthday party and his mother got cross when he hadn't turned up.

So after their nap the children's father put their suitcase in the car and yelled out to them to hurry up as he didn't have all day — both he and their mother acted as if they couldn't wait to get rid of the children. Pari started to cry and was given a lolly. Tama and Kara told their mother not to forget the toys. Then the children all hopped in the front with their father and waved 'Goodbye, Mummy,' hoping that she would change her mind and take them up to Auckland too — but she didn't. Instead she fluttered her hand, cried out to Tama, 'Look after your sisters,' and went into the house. The children wondered if they would ever see her again.

The children slept most of the way to Nani's place. The heat from the Ford always made them sleepy. But most of all they hoped that when they woke up they'd find that going to Nani's place had just been a bad dream. It wasn't a dream though, because every now and then Tama would make a small crack in his eyes and look out and watch as Gisborne went past, then Wainui, and then Whangara. At Tolaga Bay their father stopped to refill the car with petrol. He bought some orange penny suckers for Tama and Kara because they had pointed out that Pari had been given one. At the shop Tama saw a newspaper billboard: *Trouble Deepens On Coast: Arson Suspected*. For a while after that they sat quietly licking their suckers and watching the hills ahead. Then Tama realised that Pari had been given another sucker at Tolaga Bay and that wasn't fair either because it meant that she had had two and he and Kara had only had one. But their father wouldn't stop the car again. He said it was a long way to Nani's place and he was in a hurry.

Sometimes the children sang songs because their father liked them singing as he was driving. He said it helped keep him awake. Shortly afterwards the children stopped singing, but their father remained wide awake. It seemed as if years went past before they reached Tokomaru Bay. That was the furthest away from Gisborne they had ever been. They watched silently as the township slid past and they fell off the edge of the world.

The children must have been asleep for a long time — Tama was having his usual dream about being chased by a giant green caterpillar — because when the car gave a big bump it was night. 'Where are we, Daddy?' Tama asked. 'Almost at Nani's place,' he answered. 'Hop out and open the gate.' Tama peered out and saw the gate like a big white X. The gate didn't have a latch, just a piece of wire wound round and round a batten, but he managed to get it untangled and the gate swung open. When he returned to the car Kara and Pari were awake, and they all sat clutching each other and watching the headlights bobbing along the rough muddy track like a drunken man. Then all of a sudden Pari screamed. The track had disappeared and the car was at the edge of a cliff. Far below the sea thundered against the rocks, white-tipped and angry — hiss, roar, crash, *boom* — and on a small spit of sand shone the lights of Nani's place. 'Here we are,' their father said. Pari started to cry again. Kara said, 'Ooh, don't leave us here, Daddy.'

'Bob! Is that you?' a voice yelled, using their father's European name. Their father yelled back. 'Hang on a minute,' the voice said. The children looked down to the house and saw a man putting on his gumboots in the light of the doorway. He shouted in a strange language and a smaller shadow appeared from inside with a Tilley lamp. The man took the lamp, and the children watched, mesmerised, as it glided along the beach and started to climb the cliff. They heard the man huffing and puffing and swearing when he slipped, and they clutched each other even tighter because he sounded just like the fee fi fo fum man. Then he was there and although he didn't look like a giant, you could never tell. With him were some other children wearing pyjamas tucked into shoes — and one of the boys must have had two left feet.

'Tena koe, Bob,' the man said. He shook their father's hand and, when Tama gravely extended his, shook that too. 'Here, give that suitcase to Albert,' he said. But Tama shook his head — he didn't want to give their clothes away, just in case — the clothes might get thrown away and, with only one set of clothes left, what would they wear on washing day? The man laughed and said, 'Okay, boy. Well, let's all go down to the whare. Your Nani's been waiting for you all day.' The children followed the man down the cliff, just like little billygoats trying to get over the bridge before the troll got them. The man looked at them and he and their father laughed. So did the other children — and Tama knew that they thought he and his sisters were sissies. Tama wanted to box them all.

Then they reached the whare. Tama bent down to take off his shoes. 'E tama!' the man said, 'Leave them on!' But Tama shook his head vigorously — he knew that Maoris were like people from Japan and taking your shoes off was a sacred custom. Suddenly the light seemed to go out and a big mountain was standing there. 'Tena koutou, mokopuna,' Nani Puti said. She couldn't have seen Tama's outstretched hand because she grabbed him tight and squashed him against her and kissed him all funny because she hadn't put her teeth in. Then she held him away, so as to get a good look, and mumbled something in Maori and English. 'You kids look just like June,' she said, referring to their mother's European name. She pressed noses with their father — which Tama knew was the way Maoris kissed, just like the Eskimos — and then began to growl because they had arrived so late. 'Only ghosts arrive at night,' she said. Ghosts? But she must have forgiven their father because she was soon speaking flat out in Maori and giving him playful smacks.

Tama observed Nani Puti carefully. She wasn't exactly the oldest woman he had ever seen but she must have come close. Her hair was certainly as white as he had expected. As for the moko, it was rather pretty really once you realised that it was supposed to be there and not to be rubbed off every night. Nani Puti must have known Tama was staring, because suddenly she stared right back, crossed her eyes and did a pukana. Kara got alarmed — even more so when Nani Puti mumbled something like 'You kids are too skinny' and 'Doesn't June feed these kids, Bob?' and 'We'll soon put the beef on them.' Kara stared at the big black pot on the open fire — she had visions of herself sitting in it with an apple in her mouth just to sweeten her up. But then one of the girls went to the pot, opened the lid, and the pot was already full of stew.

Nani Puti gave a blessing on the food, and the children sat with their father eating the stew. They hadn't realised how hungry they were and ate everything — potatoes, mutton chops and some funny stuff which was seaweed. 'May I have a knife and fork, please?' Tama had asked. The other children had laughed out loud at his accent and, when he started to eat, copied his movements — they were mocking him, and Tama didn't like that. What embarrassed him most, though, was that his father forgot his manners and started eating with his fingers. Tama well knew that that could lead to the end of civilisation. Every now and then the other children would giggle and put their hands over their faces, look at Tama and his sisters, and giggle again. Tama decided to ignore them and to listen to what the adults were saying. The only trouble was that his father, Nani Puti and Karani Pani were talking mainly in Maori, and only a few sentences made any sense to Tama. 'It's good to know you've got support,' his father said. 'We may have lost the case in court,' Nani Puti answered, 'but no one's going to move us off.' And Karani Pani laughed and Tama thought he saw him motion with his head to a corner of the room where there was a rifle.

By that time Tama had been able to put names to his cousins' faces, so that when, after tea, Nani Puti called to Grace, Sally and Lizzie to do the dishes he knew who they were. Grace was the eldest girl — she must have been eighteen — and when she moved she did so knowing how good she looked. Sally had short hair and was growing her chest. Lizzie was around Tama's own age and looked like a boy. Dutifully, Tama and his sisters asked if they could help — and the boy cousins fell about themselves at the thought of Tama doing the dishes. Tamihana was the big brother — he must have been twenty and surely weighed ten tons. George came next, then Albert, Hone, Sid and Kopua, phew. Two other brothers had already left home and were working on a local farm. Baby Emere was crawling on the floor. All these names to remember — but even more confusing was that the cousins with the European names also had Maori names and vice versa. Just as well, Tama felt, he had got good marks at school for memorising words in spelling.

Then, 'Well, I better start heading back,' their father said. Pari had fallen asleep and had been taken to bed. Kara was crying and Tama felt like crying as well. He didn't like the idea of staying here at all. He and Kara walked with their father to the car. Their father kissed them. 'Be good,' he said. 'You will come back to get us, won't you?' Kara cried. 'Of course,' he answered. 'When!' Kara wailed. 'Soon,' he replied. He stepped in the Ford, started the motor, swung the car around — and the children were left there, standing with Nani Puti. Insects buzzed and flitted in the lamplight.

That night Tama was very weepy. Nani Puti had said, 'Why don't you bunk in with the boys?' but he said 'No.' Tama had never slept with anybody else before. The trouble was that this got him off to a bad start with the boys, who then had to sleep in two beds while he slept in the third by himself — and that only made him feel lonelier than ever. Then, after all the lamps had been turned down, Tama heard the saddest sound in the whole world. His sister Pari had woken up and was calling, 'Mummy? Mummmeee.' Tama got up and went to her. 'We just have to be brave about it,' he said. 'We have to be brave little Indians.' He kissed her and went back to his own bed. Just as he lay down he saw Nani Puti — she had heard Pari too. Nani Puti had a candle in her hand and it floated into Pari's room and floated out again — this time Pari was in Nani's arms. 'Shhhh, shhh,' Nani said to Pari. She began to sing a Maori lullaby. The song was so comforting, sounding like something floating on the sea. Then it began to drift out beyond the point where Tama could follow it, and he fell asleep.

The next morning Tama was woken by angry voices outside the bedroom window. He looked out and saw that a policeman was standing there, leaning over Nani Puti. The policeman's face was swollen and red. 'You tell Pani,' he seemed to be saying, and, 'The next warning will be the last,' but Tama couldn't read lips very well at this distance. The policeman strode back to his car.

Tama jumped out of bed and hurriedly got dressed. He called through the wall, 'Kara, are you there?' There was no answer so Tama crept slowly into the room to take a look. Kara was gone, but there was Pari, playing by the fire. Tama ran to give her a hug and that was when Nani Puti returned. 'Morena, Sleepyhead!' Nani said. 'You must have had good dreams, ay?' Tama nodded, 'Yes, thank you.' Nani laughed and, 'My moko,' she said kindly. 'You're June's kid all right. You hungry for some breakfast? Grace! Come and get some kai for this kid.' Tama felt a little ashamed about that, and when Grace appeared he said, 'I'm sorry, Grace.' He just didn't like the idea of her always being in the kitchen like Cinderella. Then Tama asked, 'What did the policeman want, Nani?' A flicker crossed Nani Puti's face. 'What policeman!' she laughed. 'No policeman has been here.'

While he was eating his breakfast Tama looked around the room. In the daytime everything looked smaller — how ever did Nani and Karani manage to live with all their children in such a small house! It was even smaller than the one the Old Lady in the Shoe lived in, gosh. There were just the three bedrooms and this BIG room for eating and living in. The room was very plain with hardly any furniture except the table, two long forms, a settee in the corner, a few extra chairs, a cupboard for crockery, a wireless set and a small tin food safe. On one wall was a picture of the King. On a second was a colour magazine picture of Tyrone Power in *Blood and Sand* — Grace's boyfriend was supposed to look like that but handsomer. Just above the table was a photo of the whole family. Tama couldn't see Emere though, and when he pointed this out to Nani she laughed and said, 'Emere's there!' But Tama still couldn't see her so Nani pointed at her stomach — and Tama thought she was rude. Streamers from last Christmas were strung among the rafters. Hanging from the middle was a long sticky flypaper spattered with dead flies. On the mantelpiece above the fire was a piece of newspaper which had been cut into jaggedy patterns. Every now and then the wind would go *whoosh* in the chimney. Outside was the constant swish, swish, swish of the sea.

Nani Puti went out the back door, and Tama saw Kara playing with Sally and Lizzie. Tama felt she had forsaken him — and Pari too — and Kara made it worse by running in and laughing. 'So you're up at last.' When she went to sit by him Tama pinched her hard. Her eyes brimmed with tears and she ran out again. Tama didn't know what to do. He had finished his breakfast but he couldn't really go out and skip over a rope with *girls*. Not only that, but Grace was wanting to clear up. 'You should go outside,' Grace said. 'The boys are somewhere out there.'

Tama stepped out into the light. He had to shade his eyes from the sun. He saw Hone, Sid and Kopua just beyond the back fence. He walked over to them. 'Hullo,' he said. They pretended to ignore him and then Sid answered, 'Why, *hullo*,' in a put-on hoity-toity manner. Kopua jabbed Sid with an elbow and, looking up at Tama, said, 'You must have had a good sleep, cousin.' But before Tama could reply, Sid interrupted, 'Yeah, especially since he didn't have to sleep with any of his stink — ' and Sid pinched his nostrils sarcastically ' — cousins.' Kopua again came to the rescue, saying, 'Easy, Sid. He's just a townie — ' and he turned to Tama ' — aren't you, Tama.' But Sid didn't want to let it go. He stood up and shoved Tama so hard that Tama fell to the ground. 'Think you're better than us, ay? Just because you live in the town. Just because you speak all la-di-da — ' And Tama felt the heat of humiliation on his face and he rushed at Sid, arms up and ready and fists bunched — he'd had a few boxing lessons at school and was rather proud of his prowess. 'Hey — ' Sid said, pushing Tama away. But Tama's blood was up and he got a few lucky hits in. However, any betting man would have placed money on Sid, who was not only taller and heavier but more experienced. With a great sense of shock and pain, Tama found himself floored with a bloody nose. 'You — you — rotter!' Tama cried. And he launched himself at Sid again. This time there was no option for Sid but to knock his cousin down for the full count.

When Tama came around he found himself next to the outside pump by the horse trough. Kopua had wet a rag and was cleaning the blood from Tama's nose. He looked at Tama's left eye and whistled, 'That's going to come up a real beauty.' Tama was still so humiliated that he pushed Kopua away. 'Hey,' Kopua yelled. 'What's up with *you* then! If you want to fight the lot of us, that's fine. But it will be better for *you* if we're friends. Okay?' Tama shrugged his shoulders. 'Gee,' Kopua sighed, 'you're a hard fulla all right. Come on.' And he jerked his head to Tama. 'I said *come on*, willya! You don't want to stick around here so that your sisters see you got beat, do you?'

Kopua started to walk away and then, like a jackrabbit, he charged up a tall hill. 'Yahoooo!' By the time Tama caught up with him, Kopua was already sitting at the top, chewing on a piece of grass. Tama had cooled down a lot by then, the humiliation receding — and then he forgot all about that when he saw Nani Puti's house below. 'Your house!' Tama gasped. The sea appeared to be ready to snatch it with blue fingers. 'It's almost in the sea!' Kopua laughed and, 'You *are* a townie!' he said. 'Can't you tell a high tide when you see one? You want to come here in the winter time — we turn into a boat then!' Tama felt awed — there seemed such grand *insolence* in the sight of that small tin shack — for it really was just rusting corrugated iron — sitting there for all the world like King Canute daring the waves to come any further. 'Don't you get afraid?' Tama asked. 'What of?' Kopua asked. 'The sea of course!' Kopua was surprised. 'Why should we?' he asked. 'It's only sometimes that our little toes get wet.' The twinkle in his eyes was a dead giveaway that he was teasing. Then Kopua stood up and pointed out to sea. 'Look over there, Tama!' he said. Tama shaded his eyes and saw a small rowboat bobbing like a broken straw on the glistening ocean. 'Is that Karani and Tamihana?' Tama asked. Kopua nodded and, 'They're getting us some crayfish for tonight.' Tama looked again, puzzled. 'But they haven't got fishing rods,' he said. And Kopua laughed again. 'Gee, don't you learn anything at that townie school of yours?'

Suddenly Tama saw a *flash* from the house. Nani Puti was there and she had a mirror in her hand. 'Huh,' Kopua said. There was an answering *flash* from the rowboat. 'Mum must want Dad to come in early,' Kopua continued. 'Something must be up.' The boys were silent a while and then, 'How long have you lived here?' Tama asked. 'All our lives,' Kopua said. 'Do you think you'll ever move?' Tama asked. 'What for?' Kopua replied. 'You don't understand, ay cuz. Didn't your mother ever tell you that she's from here? And that her mother was from here? In the old days there was a big Maori pa, right where our house is. It used to guard the whole Coast. It's famous,' and Kopua puffed the words up with pride. 'And all the land — ' Kopua described a large generous circle ' — that you can see once belonged to us. Now, only this — ' Kopua pointed down at the beach — 'is left. The pa is gone, the land is gone, but our house and we are still here. And Mum's the big chief here. She'll never leave. Even if people are trying to get us out.'

Tama wanted to know more but Kopua appeared to want to go. 'Come on,' Kopua said. 'No, I don't want to go back to your house yet,' Tama answered. 'That shiner's still gonna shine even at night,' Kopua said, then, 'Okay, there's still lots to show you.' Together the two boys walked along the cliff, with Kopua pointing out all the landmarks — where the canoes used to be launched from, where the kumara pits once were, the palisades, the urupa — and Tama began to hear ancient voices calling from the land and to feel an absurd sense of exhilaration, of belonging, of *this* history being *his* legacy, of *this* place being *his* place. He felt cross that his mother had not told him all this herself. 'She probably did,' Kopua said in his mother's defence. 'You probably didn't listen!' Which might have been true, because Tama had always been more interested in the Celts and the Romans. But come to think of it, Nani Puti *could* have been a Maori Boadicea, yes, *and* Mummy too.

By that time it was mid-afternoon and, 'I have to milk the cows,' Kopua said. The two boys returned to the house. Kopua went to bring in the cows and Tama helped him bail them up. 'What do you do at school?' Kopua asked from between the depths of Blackie's udder. 'I'm in form one,' Tama answered. 'So am I,' said Kopua. Squirt, squirt, went the milk in the bucket. 'Oh,' Tama responded, because Kopua was at least thirteen to his eleven. 'And what are you going to do when you grow up?' Kopua asked. Tama didn't want to answer, because if he opened his mouth the smell of the cow bail would get in and it was *atrocious*. 'A teacher,' he said quickly. How come Kopua didn't expire from the odour? 'You have to have a lot of brains to be that,' Kopua said. 'I think I'll be a racing-car driver. Brrmmm, brrrmmm' — and he began to fantasize on the cow's udder and Blackie glared at him as if to say, *Well if you drive your car like you pull my teats the only trophy you'll ever win is* — and she presented him with a cowpat.

For the rest of the afternoon Tama tried to hide his damaged nose and his black eye. But Pari had screamed and Kara had always wanted to be a nurse — and had asked Nani Puti if she could have some bandages and chloroform. 'Your Karani will have something to say about this,' Nani said at dinner, 'when he gets home.' Sid shifted uneasily on the form. But any displeasure of Karani's was nothing compared to Tama's discomfort and, in the end, he just *had* to ask, 'Nani, may I use your toilet?' Nani smiled and said, 'It's outside,' which was exactly what he had been dreading, and 'Hone will show you, otherwise you might fall in,' which was even worse.

Tama put on his shoes and followed Hone to a tin shed at the end of a long track. Hone shone the torch inside and, 'I'll wait here,' he said. 'Oh no,' Tama answered, 'I'll be quite all right.' Hone said, 'Oh yeah?' and shone the torch to the top of the shed where a big black spider was. 'All right then,' Tama conceded. He dropped his trousers and just managed to sit down in time before Hone shone the torch accidentally on purpose in the direction of his you-know-what. 'Oops,' Hone said. But he did it again. Tama wished the shed had a door on it. He felt so shy sitting there in full view of his cousin, the house and the whole *world*. 'Pass me a comic,' Hone said. Tama reached down to the wooden boards and threw him a tattered Western. 'Do you read comics?' Hone asked. 'Our mother doesn't let us,' Tama said. 'Gee,' Hone responded in a hushed voice, as if a world without comics was too awful to contemplate. 'What do you read then?' he asked. 'Oh, classics,' Tama said, trying to brush it all off, 'like Rudyard Kipling and H. Rider Haggard. Have you read *She*? And — ' Hone rustled his comic and, 'Phew,' he said. 'No *wonder*.' For a while there was silence. Then, 'I've finished now,' Tama said, dressing quickly. 'Just in time,' Hone answered and he shone the torch on the black spider. There it was, dangling right over Tama's head. Pari won't like *that*, Tama thought.

When Tama and Hone returned to the house they found that Karani Pani had arrived back from town. 'Sid's for it now,' Kopua whispered as Tama walked in — and, sure enough, there was Sid, looking as if it was high noon and the hangman had come to Dodge City. But Karani was mean and waited until the girls were in bed and there were just himself, Nani Puti and the boys in the big room. Then, 'Come here,' he said to Tama. Karani inspected the black eye. 'Who did it?' he asked. Tama gulped and, 'It was Blackie,' he said, and *Please forgive me Blackie, you can kick me HARD tomorrow morning.* Karani snorted and turned to Nani Puti, who was trying very hard not to laugh. 'Listen to the boy,' Karani said to her. 'Did you know that Blackie could kick as high as Ginger Rogers?' Tama went on earnestly, 'Oh, it's true, Karani, honest Indian.' Then Karani frowned and said, 'Bring the Bible, Puti.' And next minute, there it was, the Word of the Lord, right in front of him. 'Now, SWEAR,' Karani said. And Tama thought, *Our Father Which Art In Heaven, I Can't Tell On My Cousin, You Won't Send Me To Hell Will You?* And he closed his eyes, took a deep breath and — Karani Pani took the Bible away. 'Nothing is worth telling a lie for, boy,' Karani said. He looked keenly at Tama, but all that Tama could hear was the Hallelujah Chorus because he had been saved. 'Yes, Karani,' Tama said meekly. Then Karani turned to the boys and said, 'All right, Kopua, go outside and get the biggest branch you can find. I know it was you.' By this time Nani Puti was red with mirth — just as well she had taken out her teeth. And it was then that Sid stepped forward. 'I'll go,' he said. 'Well, make it a dirty big branch,' Karani told him. 'You should know better than to pick on a boy younger than you.'

Later that night Sid told Tama that Tama was *okay* for not squealing on him. 'We'll be mates, ay?' Sid said, and they shook on it. When they were getting ready for bed Tama asked if they could bunk together. But before getting into bed Tama walked into the girls' bedroom to check on Kara and Pari — they were both fast asleep. On his way back he saw the light still on in Nani's bedroom. 'So how long have we got?' he heard Nani say. 'Maori Affairs is appealing the decision for us,' Karani said. 'I was born here,' Nani replied, 'and I am not going to die anywhere but right *here*.' Her voice was as eternal and as strong as the sea. Pari didn't cry that night.

The next morning Tama was horrified to find his cousin Kopua hauling him up from sleep at five o'clock. 'The cows,' Kopua said. 'Do you get up this early every morning?' Tama asked. Kopua nodded, and Tama shuddered and was glad that in the town milk got delivered by the milkman. On their return from milking, Tama saw that Grace and Sally were also up preparing breakfast. Grace was very beautiful — all dishevelled and untidy, but somehow attractive. Tamihana was awake too and dressed. Sounds of morning prayers came from Nani's and Karani's room. The rest of the household was still asleep. Then Nani came in and, 'Morena, moko,' she said. 'Kei te pehea to moe? Kei te pai?' Tama looked at her curiously and he saw a shadow cross her face. 'You don't know, ay?' she asked. 'I beg your pardon, Nani?' Tama responded. 'You don't know your Nani's language,' Nani said. 'I know some French,' Tama said helpfully. 'Parlez vous français?' Nani smiled at him, a small smile which was only *just* there. Then Karani Pani came in and started ordering everybody around. 'You want to come out with me?' he asked Tama. 'In the rowboat? Oh, yes please,' Tama responded. Nani went to remonstrate, but Karani just said to her, 'Oh, we'll just go to the Point and back. Not far. Just for the morning.' And Nani nodded that was all right then. 'I want to take the mokos to the reef later,' she said.

Tama went with Karani Pani and Tamihana to the boat. The sea was like glass that had just been shined by the sun and polished by the wind. 'I've never been in a rowboat before,' Tama said. 'No?' Karani asked, amazed. 'Gee, what do you do in the town!' He and Tama sat in the boat — and Tamihana pushed it out on the sea and jumped in with them. Karani Pani took up the oars and rowed with a strong, easy rhythm. Sometimes Tamihana took over. Once Tama offered, but all he could do was to make the rowboat go round and round in circles until, 'Never mind, Tama,' Karani laughed. 'Your Karani's too heavy for you. Boy, you wouldn't have been any good in the old days.' Tama, curious, asked, 'I beg your pardon, Karani?' And Karani replied, 'This was the Maori life, Tama. The men did the fishing and the women cooked the fish.' But Karani Pani was wise enough to see that he had hurt Tama. 'Times change, moko,' he said. 'These days, the person who fishes with the brains is sometimes more successful than the one who fishes with the hands.'

The rowboat reached the first marker where the crayfish pots were waiting to be brought up. Tamihana began to pull up the line and, far down, Tama could see the wire cage coming up. The crayfish pot broke the surface, and Tamihana reached in and grabbed the crayfish. Tama thought he was very brave, because the crayfish were very fierce, waving their legs in the air and going click click *click*. Tamihana threw one at Tama's feet and he yelled, almost upsetting the boat. 'Just as well it wasn't a mouse,' Karani laughed, 'otherwise you would have got on the seat and we would have been *over*.' The seagulls thought it was funny too because they cackled and cawed and chuckled and squealed overhead. For the rest of the morning Karani and Tamihana rowed from one marker to the next, bringing up the crays — and while they were doing so, Karani Pani reminisced about the old days. Up until that time Tama had thought that Karani Pani was just, well, Karani *Pani*. He hadn't realised that Karani had been so handsome, so strong, so sought-after, such a fantastic rider of horses, the best athlete on the Coast, the greatest fullback that Ruatoria had ever seen and such an all-round sportsman. 'If it wasn't for me getting those two tries, drop-kicking that goal from halfway in the last five minutes and then going over again right on the whistle, the Coast would have lost,' he said. Tama's eyes were so wide with amazement that he didn't see Tamihana put his finger up to test the strength of the wind. 'That's why your Nani fell in love with me, Tama, right on the spot. She had to queue up for me though, I wasn't an easy catch, they were all after me, Maori and Pakeha girls alike. But I let her come first because she was the only one who was not after my *money*.' At that, Tamihana let out a snort, 'Gee, Dad, dream on.'

But that enabled Tama to ask, 'Karani, why do we call you Karani, and Nani, Nani?' Karani Pani looked hurt. 'You mean you can't see how old your Nani is and how young and gorgeous-looking I am?' he asked. Tama didn't want to offend his Karani so he didn't answer. 'She was sure lucky getting me,' Karani sighed. 'If I had known she was waiting in the bushes to lead me astray — ' He tsk-tsked to himself and then, 'Tama, watch out for these Coast women,' he said. 'They're dynamite.' Then Karani grew reflective and he looked back at the house, floating there on its spit of sand, and said, 'But if you find a woman like her, Tama, you *grab* her, boy. You grab her and hold her so *tight* she can't get away. She's the one keeps us all together. Keeps the land together. Not just for our family but all our whanau. Your mother and you too. She's the one.' He took off his hat in a salute. Then he looked out to sea and said, 'E hoa, looks like you're out of luck today.' Tama said, 'Why, Karani?' But all Karani Pani did was smile mysteriously and say, 'Perhaps next time.'

By the time the rowboat returned to shore it was filled with seething, clicking crayfish. Karani and Tamihana took most of the catch on the truck to Ruatoria. Kara came running to Tama, dressed in her frilly swimsuit, crying, 'Come on, Tama, Nani's taking us down to the beach!' Behind her, Tama could see Pari jumping up and down — she had a bucket and spade in her hand. Nani and the others were watching their antics as if they were creatures from another planet: they went to the sea just about every *day* and couldn't see what the fuss was about. There they were, all dressed in holey shirts and old black football shorts, and *there* were their city cousins all decked out like Christmas. 'All right, all right,' Nani said to Kara, trying to calm down Kara's boisterous glee. 'But work first and then swim.' Work? 'You want to eat tonight, don't you?' Nani asked. 'Haven't you kids ever — You *do* know what pipis and pupus are? — How about kinas? — *What!* — What the blimmin' heck does your mother feed you, you poor mokos!' With that, Nani yelled instructions to Grace and Sid and then, like Boadicea, she led the way to the reef.

The reef was about a mile away and so isolated that the seagulls were outraged at this invasion of shouting children. 'How dare you, how dare you!' they shrieked from the blue vault of sky. Unheeding, the town children ran on while the country cousins followed with the sugarbags and kits for the shellfish. 'Come on, Nani!' the town children cried. The old woman only nodded her head, hoping that the gods of this place would understand that this was a new generation which knew nothing of the old ways and old traditions — and she said to the gods, 'Be forgiving, e Tangaroa, of the ways of the innocent.' As if to reassure her, a bright blue kingfisher scooped low across the inlet, flashing its reflection across the water. 'Oh *look*, Nani, look!' the children cried. Then they were at the reef and the old woman issued instructions — and the town children thought it was such fun and not like work at all. They had to pair up — Tama with Sid, Kara with Sally, Grace with Pari, Kopua with Hone, and Nani with Lizzie — and with Emere slung on her back, wasn't that just sweet? Then out they went to gather dinner.

Tama was wearing shoes to protect his feet from the sharp reef. Sid gave Tama a sack to hold. He reached into the water, underneath a ledge and *tugged*. 'This is a paua,' he said. In his hand Sid had a big shell and inside was a long black piece of rubber. 'You have to be quick,' Sid said, 'because if the paua knows you're going to grab him he sticks tight to the rock. Then you have to use a knife to get him off. You try.' Tama put his hand under the ledge and his face screwed up — what if there were an electric eel there or a giant clam? 'Oouchh,' Tama yelled. 'There's something prickly down there.' Sid laughed. He grabbed underneath and pulled out a brown spikey ball — it looked like it would be good at puncturing tyres. 'This is a kina,' Sid said. 'We eat this too — ' which was just the thing that Tama was afraid he would say.

Once the first sack was filled, the two boys hauled it back to Nani Puti. 'To Tangaroa goes the first of the catch,' she said — and she took some of the shellfish to a deep pool and returned them to the sea. 'Why did she do that?' Tama asked Sid later. 'It is always done,' Sid responded. 'Tangaroa is the Sea God. He gives us blessings. So this is our way of thanking him.' It didn't take the boys long to fill their second sack. Sid did most of the work. Tama had to use the knife. But that didn't matter to Tama because he was feeling so happy and elated — and he just didn't know why. Perhaps it was the whole excitement of not having to go to a grocery store to get food but actually diving for it yourself. Or maybe it had to do with a growing sense of belonging — and of being accepted — by his cousins. Or perhaps it was because work brought with it a sense of achievement — as if he was doing something worthwhile. Perhaps, perhaps — and as he worked, he became more entranced by the reef and more akin with it. And his Nani, watching from afar knew what was happening and thanked Tangaroa for this *communion*.

'Kua mutu!' Nani Puti said. 'We have enough! Work is over! Now you kids can have a good swim and cool off.' She sat on the beach watching for a while and she felt so glad that June had sent the mokos up to her — that was the only way the whanau would keep together. She heard Kara scream and saw that she had caught a baby octopus — or the other way around. 'Why don't you put it back?' Nani said. Kara's eyes were large. 'Can Grace do it, Nani?' Kara asked. 'The — the mother octopus might be out there.' Then Nani Puti glanced over to Pari, and there she was, building a sandcastle and looking for all the world as if she was on a beach at Brighton. *What future lies in store for you, my moko Pakeha?* Nani Puti asked herself. *What future lies ahead of us all.* And then Tama was there, shaking himself like a little puppy. 'You having a good time?' Nani Puti asked. 'Oh yes, thank you, Nani,' Tama answered. 'Would you like to sit and korero with your Nani?' she asked. Tama nodded his head vigorously, 'Uh huh.' And so Tama sat down with Nani Puti and both of them were looking at the reef and the sea. And the minutes went by but not a word was spoken between them, and yet Tama felt as if they had been talking for *ages*. What about? Why, sea and sky of course, earth and ocean, man and land, sea and land, man and man, kinsman with kinswoman, kin with kin. Then, 'All your bones are here,' Nani Puti said, and Tama felt a great sense of *completeness* in her words, and he was falling through the blue well of the sky. 'No matter where you go in your life this is your home. No matter what you do with your life, these are your people. Whenever you need us, all you have to do is call. And whenever you are needed, you must come. Do you understand?' And Tama nodded. 'Yes, I understand, Nani.' And in that mood of absolute enchantment the kingfisher came again skimming its royal colour across the water.

The next days drifted past like a dream. Tama and his sisters grew strong and brown under Nani Puti's dictum — 'Work first, then you can play later.' It was therefore with a sense of surprise that the children received the postcard from their mother. They had been riding horses — or 'hortheth' as Pari would have lisped — all afternoon and having bareback races with their cousins along the beach. Afar off, Nani Puti had appeared waving her apron. As soon as they saw their mother the cousins did a conjuring trick and disappeared into thin air — how were Tama, Kara and Pari to know that the horses belonged to the Pakeha neighbour, Mr Hewitt? 'Don't you worry,' Nani told Tama. 'I know you kids got left holding the bag.' She handed the postcard over to Tama and set off with a big branch to find their cousins. *Dear Tama, Kara and Pari,* Mum had written, *Daddy and I have just arrived in Auckland. We are missing our babies very much. Tama, I hope you are looking after your sisters. Kara, you do as Nani says. Pari, are you being a good girl? We will be back soon. Love, Mummy. XXXXXX.* 'Have Mummy and Daddy been away a week already?' Kara asked. 'Just about,' Tama said.

The children were a little disconsolate at dinner that evening — and matters were made worse when Karani Pani told Pari she could cook her very own crayfish. Until that time Pari had quite happily eaten everything served up to her including crays. But when she popped a 'Pari-thized baby crayfith' into the boiling pot with her own pudgy hands and heard it *scream* she felt like a murderer. 'Put crayfith back!' she said, pointing at the sea. 'Put back, Karani!' and she drummed her fists against his chest. From then on she refused to eat crayfish, using her well-known complaint that 'my bottomth thtuck' — which was her way of saying she was full or had constipation. However, everybody brightened up when Nani said that she and Karani had business with Maori Affairs — Nani didn't seem to be very happy about it though — and that all the family would be going to Ruatoria the next day. 'Can we go to the pictures?' Sid asked anxiously. 'The two o'clock and the eight o'clock?' Grace chimed in because she wanted to see her boyfriend, and night-time made him more daring. 'You kids are given an inch — ' Nani sighed. 'Oh, all right. But I don't want dirty kids to shame me. So, bath-time!' So while the girls were doing the dishes Tama went with the boys to the wash-house, where they filled the copper and lit the fire beneath it. When the water was boiling they stood in a row and swung buckets down the line from the wash-house to the whare, where the bath was. 'Quick! Let's get in now,' Sid hissed. But Nani saw him and said, 'Hey! You boys let Grace and the girls go first. You make the water too dirty with your patotoi feet.' And Grace yelled, 'Yes, we don't want Kopua's kutus floating in our water.' So the boys had to put on their clothes again and wait until the girls had finished.

There was something in the very idea of a 'bath' that always brought out the lady in Grace. She emerged from her usual place in the kitchen in a long pink robe and towel turban, positively t-rrrr-ipping on her toes to the bath. Following behind her came Sally, Lizzie, Kara and Pari like adoring acolytes holding the scrubbing brush, shampoo and Sunlight soap which Grace would apply to her hair, face and person. This was no longer the Grace who tucked her dress into her pants when playing touch rugby with her brothers, nor the sister who yelled endearments like 'Hoi, kina head' or 'Gedouda-here, tutae face', but some other more divine creation. Anybody looking on and listening in as she slipped into the bath would have thought this was Cleopatra swimming in asses' milk rather than in a rusty tub with a candle on the rim. Surrounded by the smaller girls — all in awe of her voluptuous curves — Grace would sigh, 'Make some more bubbles, dahlings' or 'Mmmm, more shampoo, sweet-nesses' or 'Oooo, just a little softer with the soap, babies.' And as they ministered to her she would let them in on the little secrets of How To Be Seductive or What To Do If He Wants To Go All The Way. And if ever she heard the irritated yells of her brothers, 'Hurry up, Grace,' or the *thump* as a cowpat hit the roof, she simply sighed — there was a big difference between brothers and MEN. And was it all worth it? Oh yes, for to see Grace all transfigured by soap and water, gilded by the moon, queening it across the paddock and around the cowpats was to witness — a vision. Not only that, but one knew that one was only seeing part of the miracle. The full miracle would only be apparent after Grace had carefully plucked her eyebrows all off (and replaced them with black pencil ones), lipsticked her lips pink on the outside and deep red inside (to make them look narrower) and applied hair rollers (to substitute her straight hair with a style that approximated near enough to the latest rage). For now, though, this glimpse of the Serpent of the Nile, Ruatoria-style, preparing to go by barge to meet a hick-town Mark Antony the next day, was sufficient.

Once the girls had finished their toilette the boys emptied the bath and refilled it — Have a bath in girls' water? No fear! They were just about to hop in for the second time when Nani Puti and Karani Pani came out. 'You boys last,' Nani Puti said. Oh, the boys were so angry because had they known that Mum would pinch their water, they wouldn't have filled the bath to the brim. But finally it was their turn after all — and there was Tama, for the first time in his life, taking a bath with other people. Initially he was embarrassed about being in the middle with Sid, Hone and Kopua, especially since they were always dropping the soap. 'Oops,' they would say as they hunted for it and ended up with a handful of you-know-what. They splashed each other too. But very soon Tama forgot about his inhibitions. 'Oops,' he said as he searched for the soap.

The next morning, after breakfast, Tama and the boys were the first to get dressed and to be waiting on the truck. There was a certain unspoken protocol to all this, as if it was expected that the boys should wait the longest. Five minutes later Karani Pani arrived in tie, sports jacket and hat, followed another five minutes after by the smaller girls and Emere. Fifteen minutes passed until Nani Puti appeared and 'Oh' went the little girls on cue at the sight of Nani in coat and hat, stockings and white Minnie Mouse shoes, putting on her gloves and trying not to look too self-conscious in this unaccustomed elegance. Head down and still fussing about her seams, she was handed into the cab — an act reserved for occasions like this — by a gallant and proud Karani Pani. Ten minutes after that one of the little girls was despatched to tell Cleopatra to shake a leg, returning to say, 'She's almost there' — wherever 'there' was. Then, just before everybody's patience exploded, she appeared — Grace, the eldest girl and apple of everybody's eye, wobbling on red high heels and dressed to kill.

Not for our Grace a simple dress and a few accessories. Oh no, this kid knew she wasn't going to get to town for another couple of weeks, so she was making the most of it. Her hair was positively rolling in curls. The dress was lime green and the neckline was as low as Grace thought she would get away with. There must have been at least five petticoats to flounce that dress out as far as it went. Not only that, but the dress was surely five sizes too small — and knew it. And why wear only one bangle and necklace when you have a whole drawer full? 'Come on, Grace,' Nani Puti said. Lost in a vision of her own beauty, jangling like a cowbell and walking as knock-kneed as a pukeko, Grace swayed and dipped and staggered toward the truck. Eyes never glittered as green-shadowed as hers, lips were never as luscious or greasy red, and if there was too much powder, don't forget that it had to last the whole day. Only one problem remained: all she had to do was to make sure that her beauty would not be destroyed by the dust on the way to Ruatoria.

Tama didn't have much time to appreciate Ruatoria because it was almost two o'clock — Nani Puti having stopped at a few relations' places on the way to take shopping lists to town — when they arrived. The movie was a double feature, hooray, with Audie Murphy in the first one and 'Oh,' Grace screamed, 'Guy Madison!' in the second. But while his cousins were jumping up and down, waiting for their picture money, Tama and Kara exchanged puzzled glances — was this IT? This one main street with a few shops, picture theatre and hotel? Where was the REST! 'And here you are, mokos,' Nani said. She gave Tama, Kara and Pari five shillings each and Tama said, 'But Nani, we haven't got any change.' Nani smiled and said, 'No, this is for being good mokos. And don't forget it has to last the whole day.' Tama had never seen so much money but, 'Hurry up!' his cousins were saying, 'otherwise the picture will have started before we get there.'

Before they knew it, Tama, Kara and Pari found themselves being whisked off by their cousins, leaving Nani and Karani standing in the dust. 'Come back to the truck after the pictures,' Nani called. She was biting her lips nervously and ruining her lipstick. By then Grace had got the tickets at the movie house and shooed them in, hissing, 'I don't want to see any of you till afterwards. And if you want to go to the lav, Lizzie, you find it yourself.' With that, and in a flurry of hugging and screaming, Grace joined up with her friends and went into a huddle over The One And Only Subject: BOYS. Grace's boyfriend was already inside — it wasn't done for boyfriends to wait; apart from which, he would have to buy the girl her ticket, and he wasn't that dumb. 'Come on,' Kopua said, rolling his eyes.

Inside, mayhem was in power. The rules of the game were that the little children should go down the front where they could be pelted with peanuts and jellybeans — so off went Kara, Pari and the others. The big boys, who grudgingly allowed younger boys like Tama and Kopua to join them, all sat at the back. The middle territory was for the females of the attached and hoping-to-be-attached variety — there they could be looked over or boasted about by the boys behind. Naturally Grace made a wonderful entrance, cracking gum and wobbling her way down the aisle with her friends. Without looking back, she hissed to one of them, *crack*, 'Where is he!' *crack*. 'On the left side, over there!' her friend, *crack*, responded. The first feature was called *Adventure Island* and Tama fell in love with the red-headed lady in it — Rhonda Fleming. He was amazed how vocal everybody was, cheering, hissing, booing, offering advice like 'He's just behind you' or 'Hurry up and KISS her', cheering again — and throwing peanuts everywhere.

During all this, Grace and her boyfriend sat staring at each other through the gloom — that was her, wasn't it, the one in blue? — but not moving towards each other. That would look too forward. No, this was reserved for intermission. At that stage Grace was supposed to somehow be standing at the doors, her hand dangling somewhere in reach, so that — just before the lights went out — her boyfriend could grab it and haul her inside. Once that was accomplished, it was up to the boyfriend to show the goggle-eyed younger boys like Tama how to woo a girl, and up to Grace to make sure he left at least six cherries on her neck to prove he'd been there. As far as Tama could make out, the main object was to plant your lips on hers to stop her breathing — and when she was faint for lack of air, you started to move your hands downward. If you were lucky, despite her struggles, you got as far as the belt — but no further, buster. (The girls always relied on the brevity of the second feature to save them from a fate worse than you-know-what.) Watching all this, as well as the picture, it was no wonder that Tama was in a state of shock when the lights went back on. As for Grace, she had Triumphed and there she sat in absolute adoration of her beloved. Nor did it matter that her hair, lipstick, eye-shadow, powder and eyebrows had been totally obliterated — she had Prevailed. 'Eeee, Grace!' Kopua said pointing at her neck — it looked like a vampire had attacked it. Grace stared at Kopua as if he was a creature from another planet, and, 'Oh go squeeze yourself,' *crack*, 'Pimple-face,' *crack*, she said.

Afterwards Grace, Tamihana and George went off with boyfriend and girlfriends, and the rest of the children raced to the local shop, where they bought dinner — a pie, softdrink and doughnut each. 'Wasn't it neat when — ' the young boys said to each other, reliving the two movies they had seen ' — Yeah, boy!' As for Tama, he was still trying to recover. Then, remembering that they were to meet Nani and Karani at the truck, they raced back. The truck was there, with baby Emere sleeping in the cab, but Nani and Karani weren't. 'They're in the pub,' Hone said, jerking his head at a large building, which shook with singing, boozing and laughing, 'but they'll be out by six.' The children walked around a while with Kopua introducing Tama and his sisters to the locals. Tama decided that Ruatoria wasn't so bad — it was kind of like Dodge City or a sleepy Mexican town south of the Texas border, with the roughest, toughest, meanest, most colourful coyotes this side of Tombstone, *yup*. People still rode horses into town and swaggered in and out of the local cantina —

Then it was six o'clock and people began to burst out of the hotel, clutching crates of beer and each other. 'Here they come,' Kopua said. Tama couldn't see Nani Puti or Karani Pani, and while he was looking in the crowd somebody grabbed him. A bloated face peered into his and an overpowering smell of beer and stale sweat enveloped him. 'Keeoraa morgor, waz za pitcha kapai? Wherez za kidz — ' Before he could prevent it, the figure lurched toward Kara and Pari, who both screamed. 'Wazza madda, morgors? Iz only meee — ' the face said. Then Karani Pani was there to rescue them and, 'Hey, you haurangi moll,' he said as he grabbed her and pulled her away. Were it not for the Minnie Mouse shoes, Tama would not have recognised Nani Puti at all. She looked like some huge macabre cray which had been scalded in hot boiling water and was still *screaming*. Her eyes were red and bulging and her face was hanging in ugly scarlet folds down her neck. Her hair was straggly and the hairline was thick with foam-like perspiration. 'Yezzz,' Nani Puti said, 'iz only your Nanneee — ' She went to lean on the truck and fell over. 'Fuggen hell,' she swore, 'Blimmen hell — ' and she laughed and laughed in a horrible unfunny way, her lips blubbering and her eyes streaming with tears — just sitting there in the dust with her nice dress and coat. Karani Pani went to pick her up and his voice was angry. 'Hey, *Mum*, snap out of it' — and he swore under his breath. Then, 'Lizzie!' he called. 'LIZZIE! Come and take your damn mother to the lav.' And Lizzie said, 'Oooo,' and wrinkled her nose as she and Karani helped Nani over to the public toilet.

It had all happened so quickly that Tama was still bewildered. He felt that the real Nani Puti had been stolen away and a false Nani Puti had been put in her place. Kara came to him, shivering, saying, 'I don't like Nani Puti like this, Tama,' and Pari was still snivelling with fright. Karani Pani returned and, seeing their fear, said, 'Don't worry, kids. Your Nani will be right as rain.' He bent down to Pari's level and kissed her. Then, standing, he addressed Tama man to man, saying, 'Your Nani was never able to hold her beer, and I couldn't stop her. She just wanted to drink her troubles away.' Troubles? 'We've had some bad news, boy.' Lizzie returned with Nani, who was looking much better. Even so, Karani gathered everybody and told them he was taking Mum home — but he had spoken to Auntie Trixie and she was going to the eight o'clock pictures, so she could bring them home afterward. The cousins were glad about that but, 'I think Kara, Pari and I will come back with you,' Tama said. 'Pari's just about asleep anyway and Mummy wouldn't like it if we didn't look after her.' If all else fails, blame Pari. 'Okay, Tama,' Karani said. 'Well, you kids get in the back then.'

Tama, Kara and Pari waved goodbye to their cousins and as the truck trundled out of Ruatoria they huddled beneath the blankets. Night fell quickly and very soon Karani had to switch on the headlights. Tama wondered whether the family were the only ones alive in the whole wide world. Nani Puti was sick three times, and at every *heave* Karani would say, 'That's it, dear. Get it all out and you'll feel better.' As heavy as Nani must have been, Karani carried Nani from the truck into the whare when they got home. Swish, *swish*, went the sea. 'Help me with your Nani,' Karani asked Tama when he had lit a candle and put Nani on the bed. Tama took off her hat and shoes, and while Karani lifted Nani up he removed her coat and Kara took off her skirt. Nani flopped down in her petticoat. Pari got a flannel and cleaned Nani's face. 'There,' Pari said.

That night Kara and Pari came to sleep with Tama. They were upset because adults were supposed to be strong. Yet Nani kept on crying and crying as if her heart were breaking. Nani must have known the children were still awake, because she called out to them. 'Yes, Nani?' they said as they stood at the doorway. Nani was sitting up in bed having a cup of tea. When she saw them Nani's face screwed up and she said, 'I'm sorry, mokos.' Kara said, 'You don't have to be sorry, Nani, because you're big enough to do exactly what you like!' And Pari added, 'We can't be brave little Indianth all the time.' Nani smiled wanly. She kissed the three children on their foreheads. Just before they all left the room Nani shot Tama a piercing, smouldering glance. 'Never trust the Pakeha, Tama, never,' she said. 'And when you get older, you learn all you can about the Pakeha law so that you can use it against him.' The flame from the candle flickered, almost faltered, casting strange shadows on the walls.

Nani Puti recovered quickly and the next day no mention was made of her drunkenness. Tama's cousins had had a wonderful night. 'You would have loved the movie,' Kopua said. As for Grace, she resumed her usual stance as Cinderella in the kitchen, dreaming of the next time her boyfriend would be able to attack her neck. And so the summer resumed, day after day, as if it was everlasting — a long glorious hot halcyon summer. Tama and his sisters continued to work in the mornings and play with their cousins in those joyous afternoons. Sometimes Tama would go out in the rowboat with his Karani and, recalling an earlier occasion, he asked, 'Karani, what was it you were waiting for that day?' Karani looked toward the horizon, seeking a disturbance in the ocean. 'There used to be a pet shark around here. I haven't seen it for a while now.' Nothing but sea ever glistening.

More and more, Tama found himself wanting to wander alone around the hills and bays. He would run to the top of the hill overlooking the whare and look across the beach which was so much a part of his cousins' lives. He envied them their living here, in this seeming timeless place, and would close his eyes hoping to imprint it all on his retina. To see Nani Puti sitting on her doorstep in the sun made him grin with happiness. To watch Karani and Tamihana bobbing in the ocean made him want to be a fisherman like they were. And the cup of his contentment would begin to bubble over, and he would run back down the hill to be with his sisters and cousins.

At the same time, despite the kingfisher days of forever sun, Tama began to notice that little things were going wrong — like, for instance, the long absence of the pet shark. Out of the corner of his eye he would see a cliff face crumbling, or a stone falling into the sea, or a dead fish floating on the surface of the sea. The rowboat sprang a leak one day, and later Hone made a small gash in his leg with a fishhook.

Nani Puti herself was cut by a broken bottle in the sand. Just little things — but both Nani and Karani saw them also and seemed power-less to stop them happening. Something was out there, something, somewhere, some *thing*. Then the policeman arrived a second time, bearing a government letter and — was it Tama's imagination or had Karani Pani picked up his rifle and ordered the policeman away? After that, Nani and Karani seemed to grow older and darker before Tama's eyes, and he realised how vulnerable and how unprotected they were against the ills of the world.

In this mood of disquiet, with the edges of the world crumbling away, Tama found himself returning again and again to the sanctuary of the reef. He wanted to *know*, but know what? — and just as he tried to memorise the landscape he did the same with the reef. In his own helpless schoolboyish way he would measure out the distances between one prominent feature to the next — six paces to the pool with the seahorse, five strokes across to the next with the baby octopus — as if it were all going to disappear. He would watch the ocean and wish the pet shark to appear, as if such a supernatural event would STOP what was happening or make it all right again. He read desperation in the normally routine prayers that Nani and Karani intoned morning and evening. When they started to leave the children for long periods, travelling from marae to marae throughout the Coast, Tama wanted to know why. And then, when Maori kinsmen began to gather with greater frequency at the whare, debating and shouting through the stomach of the night, he wanted to join them. But, 'Don't you worry, moko,' his Karani would say. 'This is for your Nani and me to sort out.'

Just little things — perhaps simply his imagination — like the morning, just before dawn, when he felt the compulsion to visit the reef. He was running along the beach and there was so much earth and so much sky that he could have fallen into it all. Suddenly he heard a sound, a seagull calling. He looked out to sea. He had to shade his eyes because the sun was rising. There, framed in that golden aureole of light, bobbing on that blood-red sea, Tama thought he saw the rowboat. Nani Puti and Karani Pani were in it. Nani was standing in the boat, dressed in black, and she was singing a Maori lament. It sounded like a farewell song to someone, as sad as Snow White's dying. The next day more people arrived. From then on, the kinsmen began to stay.

Then solstice came to an end. One morning when the sea was sparkling, a car appeared on the cliff. Waving to Tama, Kara and Pari from far away were their parents. The children were overjoyed to see their parents, who looked bronzed and happy and — like gods really. When Kara told their mother about all the adventures they had been on, 'I told you you'd like it at Nani's place,' she laughed. Tama watched his parents with growing discomfort because they seemed unaware of what was happening, really *happening*. His parents had brought gifts for Nani and Karani, who accepted them politely, and for the cousins — Grace gave a scream of delight at the new H-line dress that their mother had brought back from Auckland. And the thought came to Tama that his parents and his family were foolish people because they were so privileged that they could never see beyond themselves. 'We'd better go,' Tama's mother said. 'Nani and Karani look like they're having a meeting.' Only then did their father understand. He talked to their mother and she stared around her — and her eyes brimmed with tears. She went up to Nani Puti and, 'How *dare* you,' their mother said. 'How *dare* you even think that we would come and go just like that. We — I — my children — have as much say as you about this place. And *you* were going to let me walk in and out without telling me? Don't you *dare* do this to me. Ever again.' And Nani Puti and their mother began to cry on each other's shoulders, and Nani Puti was firm. 'You would only get in the way, June,' Nani Puti said. 'When do you expect them to come?' their mother cried. Nani paused and said, 'Friday — ' which was two days hence ' — but *ssshh*, we don't want to upset the mokos.' Their father appeared to be arranging something with Karani Pani, about returning with their mother as soon as was possible. Karani Pani showed their father how well oiled the rifle was. Their father looked grim and almost afraid.

'Okay, children,' their mother said. 'Time for us to go. Say goodbye to your Nani and your cousins.' And suddenly Tama didn't want to go at all. He felt a sense of panic, as if the caterpillar train of his nightmares was catching up on him. Something was happening at the edge of childhood. It was just around the corner and, whatever it was, it would forever change all their lives. 'Nani? Karani!' Tama cried. But his Nani and Karani and cousins were gently shepherding him, his sisters and parents along, away from the house and past the tent encampments of kinsmen. Before Tama knew it, they were all standing beside the car. 'Goodbye, my cousins,' Tama cried. 'Goodbye, Karani. Nani, goodbye — ' Nani gave a sudden hoarse cry, as if she were in deep pain. The ocean flowed from her as she grabbed Tama again and again. 'Never forget, my moko,' she said, 'never ever forget.' Tama threw his arms around her. 'No, Nani, I'll never *never* forget. Honest Indian, Nani, honest.' And Tama, Kara and Pari crowded the back window waving and waving and waving. And, when there was

The Washerwoman's Children

Mrs Justice Fairfax-Lawson, sitting in the morning-room of her home at Calverley Park, Tunbridge Wells, received the morning post. Lying on the salver was a brown manila envelope from New Zealand bearing a crest that she had not seen for some fifty years. Despite her usual habit of opening the post before pouring her tea, this letter sat until Penny had cleared. Only then, with a self-directed criticism of 'Elspeth, you are being ridiculous,' did she lift her letter knife and open the envelope. Inside was a form letter, with blank spaces that had been filled in by hand, as follows:

45 Jackson Crescent
Wellington
New Zealand

Dear *Elspeth*,

Your name has been referred to the Karori Primary School Anniversary Committee by *your sister, Lilian Bates.*

The Committee, which has been actively working towards the centennial celebrations of the School, would like to extend to you a warm invitation to attend an Anniversary Dinner in the school hall on 10 August this year, at 7.30 p.m. Roll Call, by year, will be taken at 5 p.m. A photographer will record the happy event. The Committee hopes you will be able to come along.

Yours sincerely
(Mrs) Lena Holmes

The letter was perforated with a tear-off portion bearing the address of the committee and, 'I will be able/unable to attend: I attended Karori Primary School from .... to .... My registration fee of $20 is/is not enclosed.'

Mrs Justice Fairfax-Lawson was somewhat nonplussed. The use of her Christian name by a person whom she did not know, called Lena Holmes, irritated her. But most of all the letter brought memories of school days which she hoped had faded forever. Bearing in mind the time difference between England and New Zealand, she telephoned her sister in Wellington. 'Lilian, dear? *What* is going on?'

181

Given her initial reaction to the invitation, Mrs Justice Fairfax-Lawson was amused to find herself, three months later, sitting in the third row of the Business Class section of an Air New Zealand flight from Gatwick to Los Angeles en route for Auckland. Not only that, but no sooner had she seated herself than the purser, on the advice of the ground staff who had recognised her, invited her to take a seat in First Class. Her sense of gratification was only undercut by the fact that the passenger seated next to her, when told that she 'was in the judiciary', assumed she was a typist or else the wife of a judge (she was not the sort to be mistaken for a mistress); silly pompous little man. Luckily there was a window seat vacant three rows ahead and Mrs Justice Fairfax-Lawson firmly invited her neighbour to take it. Once that was achieved she took up her Dorothy Sayers, but only briefly before setting it to one side and watching England sinking beneath her.

If anybody had been looking at Mrs Justice Fairfax-Lawson, they would have seen a slim and elegant woman of pleasant good looks and a fresh English rose complexion. They would certainly not have guessed from her appearance, or even any intonation of voice or physical mannerism, that she had actually been born and raised in New Zealand. There was not a shred of the Antipodean about her, nor any of the hallmarks of the Antipodean Woman Abroad — the tightly curled perm, twinset and pearls and bright magpie look which characterised all New Zealanders south of Balmoral. Instead, what any other passenger would have seen was exactly what Mrs Justice Fairfax-Lawson had become — a romantic Englishwoman, in her prime, knowing exactly where she is because she can remember quite clearly exactly how far she has travelled — and Mrs Justice Fairfax-Lawson had travelled a very long way indeed. Home Counties style had always meant so much to her that being taken for English was quite a compliment and logical enough. All the same, there was a sense of fairness in Mrs Justice Fairfax-Lawson which allowed her to accept that her country of birth would want to claim her — as it was prone to do, given her successes — as one of its very own. As a judge, Mrs Justice Fairfax-Lawson well knew that all *known* facts must be taken into account when any case came before the bench and, if she was trying herself for identification, she would have to weigh against the fact that although she was British by virtue of her marriage to the late Hon. Rupert Fairfax-Lawson, she had nevertheless maintained dual citizenship with the country of her birth. Much as she disliked the idea of balancing on both sides of the scales, Mrs Justice Fairfax-Lawson had to admit that giving up *anything* at all had always been difficult for her. Add to this that all her side of the family obstinately remained in New Zealand and that they were her *only* family (she and the Hon. Rupert Fairfax-Lawson being childless and not at all pleased with the Hon. Rupert Fairfax-Lawson's scurrilous nephews), and one realised the depth of her dilemma. She was as much a New Zealander because her family made her one. She could not escape them — and nor would she want to — because she loved them; yes, *loved* was not too strong a word. And she did so with familial pride and devotion, particularly her elder sister Lilian, who had become a grandmother again. So it was a *fait accompli* really, with the gavel confirming the decision and dismissing the court.

Mrs Justice Fairfax-Lawson was about to resume her Dorothy Sayers, but by that time champagne and caviar were being served. Not long after that, dinner — either roast duck or lamb — was offered. Bearing in mind the long journey ahead, Mrs Justice Fairfax-Lawson therefore decided to nap rather than to read. Eight hours later, after more champagne and more roast duck, her flight landed at Los Angeles. Shortly thereafter she was on her way again, with fourteen hours of flying time ahead and the vast expanse of the South Pacific below, bound for Auckland and thence Wellington, New Zealand.

Lilian Bates was waiting with her husband George at the Domestic Terminal. There was, at close inspection, a family resemblance to her younger sister Elspeth, but no one would ever have taken Lilian for anything but a New Zealander — at a pinch, an Australian perhaps — and that was where the likeness ended. Lilian's cheeks were ruddy, whereas her sister's were pallid, and Lilian's spontaneity expressed itself in its overeagerness and anxiousness, whereas Elspeth's was under control, *quite*. Apart from that, years of healthy living and appetite had turned Lilian's figure to pear-shaped, whereas Elspeth was still, as ever, a wishbone. Somewhere far back in their lives there had been a parting of the ways. In Elspeth's case it had been the winning of a major scholarship to Cambridge when she was nineteen. As for Lilian, her fate had been forever sealed when George Bates, then garage mechanic and now proprietor of Bates Towaway Trucks, admiring her lines, cast an eye over her, ran her round the block a couple of times, found her bodywork in good condition and pronounced, 'She'll do.'

'Now, George, don't forget,' Lilian told him. 'She likes to be called Elspeth. Not Elsie. Or Ellie. Or Else. Or anything but Elspeth.' She picked at his tie. 'The way you go on,' George replied, 'you'd think she was the bloody Queen of England.' Lilian grimaced as if she had never heard such words from his lips before. 'And keep your bloodys to your trucks, George — or save them up for when it's just us.' George rolled his eyes and Lilian tried to hug him around. 'Oh please, George, *do* behave. You know I haven't seen Elspeth for six years now. That's such a long time. She's my only sister after all and — Oh, there she is! Oh, George' — Lilian broke away from him and began to run toward the woman who had just come through the gate. George had always known that his wife was a real softie, but her abrupt emotional departure surprised him. *Why, they're as different as chalk to cheese*, he thought. He watched as Lilian flung her arms around her sister and wept on her shoulder — he hadn't realised that Lilian would be so affected. He felt a lump in his throat at the sight of these two middle-aged women embracing like this — Lilian, as always, so open with her emotions, and *Elspeth* as gracious as ever — you'd think she was waving from a bloody Rolls. He walked over to them. Elspeth said, 'Why, George!' in that cultured voice of hers and proffered a cheek for him to kiss. And Lilian stepped aside, saying, 'It's really her, George, she's really here,' as if he couldn't see that for himself.

Mrs Justice Fairfax-Lawson had planned to stay in New Zealand for three weeks but had not expected that her sister would want to make the most of it. She should have realised when they arrived at the house and were greeted by Lilian's two daughters and their three children — plus the new baby — that she would be kept busy. And it was understandable, she supposed, that Lilian would want to have dinner on the first evening for 'Just us and the family' — but when confronted with the cheery barbecue that evening and guests including the local mayor, she knew that life was not going to be that simple. Over that first week Lilian would alternate between expressions of 'Oh, you must still be jet-lagged, Elspeth. Why don't you go up to the bedroom and rest?' and frequent trips to answer the front doorbell with, 'Why, hello!' to yet more neighbours bearing yet more platefuls of lamingtons, pikelets or scones. Nor could the visits possibly be accidental, despite protestations that 'We just dropped by' — Oh no. these ladies in their cardies and pearls had just been to the local hairdressing salon, and once ensconced in Lilian's sitting-room with a cuppa, were there to *stay*. Even the innocent 'I'm just popping down to the shop, Elspeth. Why not come for a ride?' would turn into a virtual royal procession throughout the land. And at each house the hostess would be ready and waiting with 'Why, Lilian, do come in! And this is your sister, isn't it! Elspeth? Lilian has told us so much about you. You're just in time for a cuppa tea — ' before opening the door wider and turning to others gathered inside ' —isn't she, ladies!' These ladies knew that New Zealand hospitality was the best in the world, and they weren't going to let the side down — especially with such a famous person in their midst. And so the polite conversation would begin, with everybody minding their p's and q's and trying not to be too colonial — clinking the teacups ever so softly and not dropping one crumb of the lamingtons — until, with a little squeak of a cough, the hostess would turn to Mrs Justice Fairfax-Lawson and ask, 'So you live in England, do you?' Whereupon all tea-drinking would be suspended as Mrs Justice Fairfax-Lawson, as custom required, told them about life as it was lived by those whose Title and Reputation enabled an English Existence spread between an apartment in Westminster and a country home in Tunbridge Wells. On her part, Mrs Justice Fairfax-Lawson knew that *she*, too, couldn't let the side down — her side being her sister — and she rose to every occasion. For despite her caustic tongue, Mrs Justice Fairfax-Lawson would not have hurt her sister for anything in the world. And success was measured by the indrawn gasps of 'You don't *say*!', 'Listen to *that*, Millie!', 'How *interesting*!' and 'Do go on.' And if, near the end of the socialising, the hostess sighed, 'Oh, it sounds so different from life here,' then Mrs Justice Fairfax-Lawson knew also that form required her to offer generalities like 'But you are so lucky, New Zealand is such a paradise, it is so green, and your food is so delicious' — even if she didn't really mean it herself. Then Lilian would drive her sister home, and Mrs Justice Fairfax-Lawson would go up to her bedroom and have a lie-down and listen to Lilian's happy voice downstairs as she responded to telephone calls from the friends just visited — 'Oh yes, I'll tell her! Yes, we are all very proud of her! No, *really*, do you really think we are that alike?' Such things had always been important to Lilian.

However, when, at the beginning of the second week, Mrs Justice Fairfax-Lawson came across her photograph on page seven of the *Dominion* and read the accompanying article she became most displeased. It wasn't really the photograph, which was at the very *least* twenty years old — and while Mrs Justice Fairfax-Lawson was as vain as the next person, a photograph of that vintage could only draw unhappy comparisons with one's current estate — nor was it the article itself, which was succinct and to the point:

Mrs Justice Elspeth Fairfax-Lawson, M.B.E., (pictured right) returned last week for a private visit to New Zealand, her first in six years. Mrs Fairfax-Lawson recently retired from the U.K. judiciary following the death of her husband, the late Hon. Rupert Fairfax-Lawson, M.P. Born in Wellington in 1910, Mrs Fairfax-Lawson will be well known to New Zealanders as the founder and first chairperson of the Wellington Women's Co-operative. Educated at Cambridge, England, Mrs Fairfax-Lawson served in British

Intelligence during the Second World War, where she met her husband. Following the war she began a private legal practice in London, Fairfax and Madden, and was invited to join the U.K. judiciary in 1962. Her M.B.E. was awarded by H.R.H. Queen Elizabeth II in 1970.

The displeasure stemmed from the headline and last sentence of the text, to wit: FAMOUS NZER RETURNS FOR SCHOOL REUNION and 'Mrs Justice Fairfax-Lawson is a guest speaker at next week's Anniversary Dinner of the Karori Primary School, which she attended from 1915 to 1923.'

Mrs Justice Fairfax-Lawson was therefore *very* cross when she went down to breakfast that morning and, seeing this, Lilian said to George, 'You'd best leave us a minute, George dear.' To do her justice, Lilian was looking very contrite. She poured Elspeth a hot cuppa and, 'The photo's nice,' she said. But Elspeth could not be pacified so easily. 'How could you *do* this, Lilian. You *know* that my main reason for coming was to see you, and that I have only agreed to attend the school reunion because *you* want to go. I am going under sufferance, Lilian. You know how much I *hated* that school. The way the parents treated Mother and vilified Father was so unspeakable. Just because she had to take in washing and because father was a bankrupt.' Lilian bit her lip and, 'Yes, Elspeth,' she said. 'Can't you remember anything at all?' Elspeth continued. 'It wasn't Mother's fault that she had to send us to school in dresses made from bits given her by other people — other people's cast-offs and curtain material — but did the other children understand? No, they *didn't*.' Whenever Lilian was embarrassed, her face took on a silly shamefaced smile, and, 'You're quite right, Elspeth,' she said, her heart aching from the pain of the reprimand. *And a vivid picture flashed into her mind of Lena Logan sliding, gliding, dragging one foot, giggling behind her hand, shrilling, 'Is it true you're going to be a servant when you grow up, Lil Kelvey?' And taunting her again with 'Yah, yer father's in prison!' before running away giggling with the other girls.* 'We were *always* on the outside,' Elspeth said. 'They never invited us to play in any of their games, because we weren't good enough for them. And *now* I read in the newspaper that I am to be guest speaker — ' Lilian folded her hands in her lap and looked down and, 'They only want you to say a few words,' she said. 'A few words?' Elspeth cried. 'That's more than they deserve. There was only one girl, just *one*, who ever showed us a kindness and — '

Lilian couldn't take any more. Her silly smile opened too wide and let the tears through. She tried to say something to Elspeth, gulped and instead patted Elspeth on the hand and kissed her right cheek.

Then she stood up and left the table. Elspeth, still furious, sat there in the grip of her own recollections and how, it seemed, she had only managed to survive by holding on with a piece of Lil's skirt screwed up in her hand, holding on all day, *every* day, holding on so tight, so *tight*. And not saying a word to anybody but wanting to scream, just *scream*, with the loneliness and pain and awfulness of it all. Then Elspeth heard George and looked up into his disapproving face. 'You were too hard on her, Elspeth,' he said. 'Lilian may be the elder of the two of you but she's the one who suffers more. You should have a care for your sister. She thinks the bloody world of you.' And that only made Elspeth feel worse — about her petulance and, oh, at Lilian too for being such a *martyr* and running off like that! You'd think they were still children the way Lilian behaved — going off so bravely to sulk like that and make her feel so *mean*. Elspeth looked at George and sighed. He indicated the direction in which Lilian had gone.

'Lilian? Lilian,' Elspeth called. She heard Lilian reply, 'In here, dear,' and found her at a small card table in the lounge. Lilian had put on her reading glasses and was cutting the article about Elspeth out of the newspaper. 'What *are* you doing?' Elspeth asked. She came up behind Lilian and looked over Lilian's shoulder. On the card table was a large scrapbook. Elspeth recognised it instantly — it was the book their mother had begun when her daughters had both started school and filled year by year with school reports, handwritten memories, school magazine photographs, newspaper clippings: ELSPETH KELVEY IS DUX OF SCHOOL; LOCAL GIRL WINS CAMBRIDGE SCHOLARSHIP; MORE HONOURS FOR KELVEY; OUR ELSPETH TOPS CLASS AT CAMBRIDGE; ENGAGEMENT OF ELSPETH KELVEY TO SON OF LORD FAIRFAX-LAWSON — and other memorabilia. Elspeth gave a small cry and reached over to leaf through the pages: LOCAL PERSONALITY AWARDED M.B.E.; FAIRFAX-LAWSON RETIRES FROM U.K. JUDICIARY. 'It's mostly all about you,' Lillian said softly. 'I never did much myself except marry George and have my two girls. But oh, Mother was so proud of you, Else, love. You wouldn't believe the times she would go through this scrapbook. "Look at our Else," she used to say. "All those brains, where'd they come from!" ' The mood sweetened between the two sisters, and Elspeth reached over and put her hand in Lilian's. 'Anyway,' Lilian said, 'when Mother died I kept the scrapbook going. I don't know why really. It would have been a shame to just let it go, don't you think?' And suddenly Lilian started to weep again, saying, 'I'm so sorry, Else, I just didn't realise — ' And Elspeth replied, 'Come, come, Lilian. Oh, Lilian, *do* stop ' — because she had begun to recall how difficult it had all been for Mother and Lilian to keep her at school. 'Oh, *Lilian!*' she said, furious, because tears were so unseemly at their age.

Afterwards Elspeth told Lilian that she had better check with the Karori Centenary Committee how many words a 'few' constituted. They had a cuppa tea and laughed about the absurdity of two grown women losing control like that. 'There was never a jealous bone in your body, was there?' Elspeth asked her sister. 'A couple of times,' Lilian admitted. Elspeth smiled and turned away, intending to go up to her bedroom. Just as she went through the door, Lilian called to her. 'Oh, Elspeth,' she said. Elspeth turned and, 'Yes?' she asked. Lilian's attitude was resolute and firm. 'Although we may have been a washerwoman's children,' she said, 'we were never too proud' — which was just the sort of infuriating commonplace thing Lilian always liked to say.

And after all that, not to mention the effort that Elspeth had put into preparing a ten-minute address, Lilian came down with a bad flu on the very night of the dinner. 'You will get up this instant,' Elspeth ordered. 'Put on your pearls and come with me.' Her tone was similar to that she used when addressing felons from the Bench. Lilian nodded and tried but, 'Oh, Elsbed, I don'd thig I cad,' she said. 'You bedder go wib Geord. Geord? You go wib Elsbed to the didder.' Lilian reached for a handkerchief. George, taken by surprise, said, 'Go back to school? Not on your bloody life.' Then Elspeth interrupted him, saying, 'Lilian Kelvey, it is already after five. You are as strong as a horse and *never* get the flu. Get up at once.' But it was obvious that no command would work. 'Oh, by dose,' Lilian said, blowing on it. 'By hed,' she said, holding it. 'Elsbed, you should rig the cobbidee and ask theb to ged sobody to pig you ub.' And that was that — which explains how Mrs Justice Fairfax-Lawson was delivered, an hour late, by a nice but obviously awestruck Maori committee member called Mrs Maraki.

No sooner had Mrs Justice Fairfax-Lawson walked through the door of the crowded Assembly Hall than she saw a woman gasp and whisper behind her hand to her companion, and then *sliding, gliding, dragging one foot and shrilling* she came, calling, 'Elspeth! Yoo hoo, Elspeth!' And Mrs Justice Fairfax-Lawson reeled backward as if she had been hit, and reached out for Lil's hand and to hold a piece of Lil's skirt. 'Elspeth?' the woman laughed. 'You *must* remember me! I'm Lena Holmes! See?' She pointed rather superfluously at a small tag on her dress with her name and CHAIRMAN ANNIVERSARY COMMITTEE written on it. 'I used to be Lena Logan. Remember? Lil and I were in the same class. But you were much younger of course. Come along with me.' Proudly, Lena Holmes took Mrs Justice Fairfax-Lawson's arm and began to steer her possessively in the direction of other committee members. *Yah, yer father's in prison.* 'Cora? May I introduce Elspeth to you? But you know her of course. Weren't you in Mrs Fredericks' class together? Oh, you will have some stories to tell! And this is Peggy, Elspeth. Peggy used to be the horrid little girl who did ballet — oh, we hated her, didn't we! And you can remember Annabelle? Her aunt was the postmistress. Oh, you *must* remember Miss Leckey and that terrible hat she used to wear! *Oh yes, I remember. When Miss Leckey had no further use for it, she gave it to Mother. Lilian used to wear it.* 'We are so sorry, Elspeth, to hear that Lilian won't be able to come. What a shame. Never mind, you are in good hands now. We'll look after you, won't we ladies!' *Yes, you'll all run after me and make fun of me and sneer and laugh and wrinkle your noses as I pass and —*

'Are you all right, Elspeth?' The voice sounded so loud in her ear that Mrs Justice Fairfax-Lawson was startled. Lena Holmes was looking at her, concernedly. 'Oh. Yes,' Mrs Justice Fairfax-Lawson said. 'The trip. The strain.' Lena Holmes nodded. 'I do hope you aren't catching your sister's flu. There's a lot of it going around,' she said.'But come along, we must get you tagged!' She laughed as she took Mrs Justice Fairfax-Lawson's hand. *Yah, yah, your mother washes clothes and your father's a jailbird.* 'There!' Lena Holmes cried as she branded Mrs Justice Fairfax-Lawson with a label, ELSIE KELVEY, so that everybody — *everybody* — could remember that awful little girl with cropped hair, remember ladies? That's her, over *there.*

Suddenly a hand bell began to ring. A middle-aged man who could *never* have been young was standing in the centre of the hall, swinging the bell to and fro. His face was red with mirth as the bell clanged and boomed and shattered the conversation. Lena Holmes put her hands to her ears and said, 'Oh, that Johnny Johnston! Isn't he a one?' One of the other men ran out to wrestle with 'Johnny' and the crowd watched and grinned with amusement — Wasn't this fun? That Johnny, he *never* changed, good old Johnny. And all of a sudden Johnny was running between people, trying to escape his friend, and the women gave little screams and the men pretended to scrimmage and then he was heading for Mrs Justice Fairfax-Lawson and the shock of recognition spread over his face as, pointing at her, he said, 'I know you! You're you're — ' *Yes. My name is Elsie. My sister is Lil. My mother washes your mother's clothes. You are a horrid boy.* But before he could say anything more he was tackled and down he went. And Lena Holmes, pretending to be a little girl, went over to the two men lying on the floor, wagged a little finger and said in a squeaky voice, 'Bad boys. Bad *boys*. I'm going to tell Mrs Fredericks on you!' What a laugh that caused — that Lena Logan, the same as ever. Then Lena Holmes laughed herself and clapped her hands, clap, clap, CLAP. 'Roll call, everybody! Roll call! Everybodeeee,' and she led the way to the English Room, where the group photograph was to be taken.

Mrs Justice Fairfax-Lawson closed her eyes and took a deep breath. *Pull yourself together,* she said to herself. The shock, the crowd, the smell of chalk, the bonhomie, all these people acting like children, pretending that school had been such fun and they were all friends. Whereas she had only had one friendly gesture made toward her. *Stop it, Elspeth.* For who was she to make such assumptions? *STOP IT.* Feeling better, Mrs Justice Fairfax-Lawson joined the others. She smiled at everybody and was as charming as they expected her to be. She laughed just like everybody else at the photographer's frantic attempts to arrange the 'children' according to height, and when she had to say CHEEEESE she did so as long as the rest did until the flash-bulb popped. But deep inside her the little girl she once was still cringed and sought for a piece of dress to hold on to.

The bell rang again, far away, to announce that dinner would soon be served. Well-wishers approached Mrs Justice Fairfax-Lawson to say, 'We are so looking forward to hearing you speak,' or, 'We are so delighted that you will be speaking on our behalf as fellow pupils of the school,' and she was so surprised, absolutely *overwhelmed*, by the warmth of it all. And she realised that the address she *was* going to give would be too pompous and too serious, for these returned pupils wished only for companionship and good memories and wonderful tributes to friends and school. And she heard Lilian's voice in her mind saying, *We were never too proud, Elspeth, never too proud.*

So that when, following the dinner in the hall, it was time for Mrs Justice Fairfax-Lawson to rise and speak, she had to pause and recon-sider her words. The hall looked so gay and colourful, with streamers hanging from the ceiling and flowers arranged on the trestles and food — jellies, pavlovas, salads, lamingtons — sparkling on the tables. And there were all those ridiculous elderly people, sitting on forms, faces gazing up at hers in expectation. And it came to her just what she should say. 'Ladies and gentlemen,' she began. 'Boys and girls,' and everybody laughed. 'Like you all, I attended this school with my sister. There was once a little girl and her sisters who came to school one day and told us all about a wonderful gift — a doll's house.' To one side Elspeth heard Lena Holmes gasp with pleasure. 'Inside was a little lamp.' Mrs Justice Fairfax-Lawson paused at the memory. *You can come and see our doll's house if you want to, said Kezia. Come on. Nobody's looking.* 'I think that girl died some years ago but what she did stands as a shining symbol to all of us. Certainly it became a symbol for me.' The silence was such that a dropped pin could have been heard. 'Although my sister and I were the children of a washer-woman' — *There, it was out* — 'that girl showed us the little lamp. I have never forgotten that lamp, ever. Its flame has been a constant inspiration to me to always reach out — like that girl did — to others. To extend myself, become a better person and perhaps make the world a better place to live in. Were it not for that kindness, or similar kindnesses which I'm sure you all remember being done to you at this school, none of us would have become the people we are today. I would not have become the person I have.'

Mrs Justice Fairfax-Lawson had to pause again. *I seen the little lamp, she said softly.* She went to resume but somebody had begun to clap and very soon that person was followed by another and another, until the whole hall was on its feet and clapping at the memory of a school-friend, now gone, who had been so important in all their lives. And as they did so, Mrs Justice Fairfax-Lawson smiled a rare smile and thought to herself that what she had said was just the silly common-place sort of thing that Lilian would have liked.